Dry Heat

Books by Jon Talton

The David Mapstone Mysteries
Concrete Desert
Camelback Falls
Dry Heat
Arizona Dreams
Cactus Heart

Other Novels
The Pain Nurse

Dry Heat

Jon Talton

Poisoned Pen Press

Poisoned Pen Press

Poisoned Pen Press
6962 E. First Ave., Ste. 103
Scottsdale, AZ 85251
www.poisonedpenpress.com
info@poisonedpenpress.com

Printed in the United States of America

For Susan

Chapter One

Maryvale! Fortunate home of the American dream. A single-family detached house in the suburbs: three bedrooms, living room, den, all-electric kitchen and carport, laid out in a neat rectangle of a one-story ranch, house. We've got thousands of 'em, ready to sell, on safe winding streets in brand-new Phoenix. New as a hula hoop. New as a teal '58 Chevy. New as this morning's hope. Leave behind those snow shovels and below-zero winters. Leave behind the old dingy cities of the East and Midwest with their crime and racial trouble. Time for a fresh start, thanks to a VA mortgage and the FHA. You've earned it: a backyard lifestyle with a new swimming pool. Here in Phoenix, it's eighty degrees in January, and in summer, we've got air-conditioning. Green lawns, blond children, pink sunsets. All in Maryvale.

Until you go out one fine day and find a body facedown in the green water of what was once the swimming pool.

⟨⟩⟨⟩⟨⟩

I didn't want to know how hot it was. It was the first of April, way too early to be soaking in sweat. Too early to be breathing superheated air and ducking for cover from sunlight so intense I might as well have been on planet Mercury.

Planet Maryvale felt bad enough. I turned off Fifty-first Avenue, into an opening of the seven-foot gray cinder block walls that separated backyards from the six-lane highway. Then I was in the curvilinear maze of half-century-old suburbia, aging badly. Most of the lawns were long gone, replaced by lifeless dirt and occasional sun-bleached weeds. A pile of old car parts sat in one front yard, a rusted hood sticking out of the ground like a gravestone. A few soaring trees attested to the age of the place, but it was a wonder they were still alive. Identical ranch houses were distinguished by their degree of decay or the severity of the burglar bars on the windows. Around some houses, walls and gates with nasty looking spikes had been added in recent years. The occasional well-kept yard and newly painted house only made the overall sense of abandonment more apparent. Lampposts, stop signs, and walls were adorned with the tribal glyphs of graffiti.

Around a wide corner, the street was jammed with city property: six Phoenix police cruisers, two crime lab vans, and several of the uncomfortable alternative-fuel Chevy Cavaliers that had been forced on the city detectives. They were parked closest to a cream brown cinder block ranch with a stripe of faded orange paint along the roofline. Behind the bars, one window was partly covered with cardboard. A pale blue city recycling hopper sat at a jaunty angle in the middle of the "lawn," its jaw open as if to receive offerings. The hopper was empty. Across the street, groups of neighbors were standing on the sidewalk, talking quietly in Spanish. Women, babies, old men. Brown faces followed me as I locked the car and walked toward the clot of blue uniforms at the side gate. I slipped my gold star over my belt.

"Christ! What's he doing here?"

That was a woman's voice, unpleasantly familiar, coming from behind a splintery wood fence. My stomach kicked up some bile. "Hey, professor!" said another voice, friendlier. "May I help you, sir?" came from the young uniform facing me. I could smell dead body over his shoulder.

"You guys called me," I said, imagining other things I'd rather be doing, especially getting reacquainted with Lindsey. It had been only two weeks, too damn long. I felt an achy longing for her, something I'd never grown out of and never wanted to. I sure didn't want to be here. Just that morning I was in a cool place, in another time zone. I was still technically on vacation, not that it was much of a vacation, not that it mattered to Peralta. The cop studied my badge, my ID. He said "sheriff's office" as if he had never heard the words in his life, and then looked back over his shoulder uncertainly.

"That's Mapstone," came a man's voice. "Let him back here."

The man was a detective captain I'd worked with before, named Markowitz. He was tall, florid, and straw-haired. He wouldn't have looked out of place as a coach of a small-town high school basketball team. But I only saw him when murder was involved. This day he was wearing a bilious green golf shirt, chinos, and a film of sweat.

"Goddamned hundred degrees outside," he said.

"I don't want to know."

The sun beat upon us. In two months, an even hundred degrees would be balmy weather for my hometown. But I was trying to avoid the annual dread that built up in Phoenicians as the pleasant winter months wind down and summer hell looms ahead. I looked in vain for nearby shade.

"It's never this hot so early," he said, starting to wipe his brow. He realized he had on latex gloves and thought better of it.

"Pave over the Sonoran Desert and this is what you get," I said, doing a look around the crime scene.

"This heat," he said. "You know what this must be like?"

I shrugged and tried to blow the sweat off my sunglasses.

"This must be what it'd be like, the second after they set off an H-bomb. You haven't been vaporized yet by the blast wave. But you can feel the heat, like somebody ignited the sun right in front of your face."

Mr. Cheerful.

The backyard consisted of dirt, lots of dirt, plus beer cans, full trash bags, and tiny archipelagos of unruly grass that had flourished in the brief spring and now were being burned to death. In the middle was a small, rectangular swimming pool. The ladder had rusted brown. Bobbing strangely above the surface were two heads, young women in ponytails, and they didn't appear to be swimming.

As I got closer, I realized it had been a long time since the gash in the ground had borne any resemblance to a swimming pool, and the heads were attached to evidence technicians in blue jumpsuits. One was using a video camera. I peered over the edge, looked into thick greenish soup that filled maybe two feet of the deep end. The technicians stepped through it in yellow wading boots. A bald tire held one corner of the lagoon. A broken piece of plywood floated nearby. I pushed aside the nauseating temptation to imagine what was in the water.

"What am I looking at?" I asked.

"The final resting place for that gentleman," Markowitz said, nodding toward a body bag lying on the patio, surrounded by more uniforms and detectives. All I could see sticking out of the black bag were a few tufts of gray hair.

"He live here?"

"Nope, somebody found him and called us. By the time we got here, whatever huddled masses were living here hightailed it."

So the house was a "coyote" hideout, a place where smugglers brought their human cargo to disperse to the kitchens, lawn services, and sweatshops of the nation's fifth largest city, or for points beyond. Phoenix was a major transit point in the people-smuggling trade. If an illegal immigrant made it across the border and through some of the most inhospitable desert on earth, he rested in Phoenix before heading off to find work in the slaughterhouses of Nebraska or the chicken processing plants of North Carolina. That is, if he didn't wind up in a shoot-out between rival smugglers. It was a hell of a way to get to a low-wage job.

I kept my thoughts to myself as the cop editorialized. "I grew up out here," Markowitz said. "Right here in Maryvale. We lived maybe a mile from this spot. It was nice. Now it's all Mexicans, living ten to a room. Gangs. Turned to shit."

He watched me, and the line down his forehead deepened like a river channel in a reddish landscape of skin. "I'm not a racist, Mapstone. I just don't understand why they don't stay in their own country."

I said, "Following the American dream, I guess."

Markowitz spat into the yard and the moisture disappeared in the dust just beyond my shadow. It was the shadow of a tall, broad-shouldered man, all six-feet-two of me there as a target for the sun. My hair was wavy and dark, better to absorb the goddamned heat. I was a few months away from forty-five years of age and feeling too old to be broiling in a backyard with the stench of a stranger's corpse. I knew I was in a mood, and tried to keep a lid on.

I asked, "Anybody know who he is?"

"Homeless guy, looks like. An Anglo, I'd bet. But he's got no ID that we could find. Looks like his wallet was taken, if he had one."

"Homicide?"

Markowitz shrugged. "Hard to tell. He'd been down in that water a few days."

It didn't seem like my kind of trouble. That is, trouble with a past. I'm a failed history professor, or maybe a failed lawman. In any event, I make my living doing a little of both, working for the Maricopa County Sheriff, my old friend Mike Peralta. Now they call me a cold case consultant, researching unsolved crimes that can be as old as the city. But I also carry a badge as a sworn deputy, and sometimes a gun.

I could have written a fascinating paper on the evolution of the American automobile suburb in Phoenix, how the places like Maryvale that once seemed so full of promise had evolved into postmodern slums. How abandonment of place in the West is as old as the Hohokam, the ancient Indians who first settled in the river valley that became Phoenix, and then disappeared. It would be fascinating to me, at least. But I didn't see any need for that skill in what looked like one more dreary west-side killing—the "curse of the Avenues," as my wife Lindsey called it, referring to Phoenix's grid of numbered avenues on the west of Central, numbered streets on the east.

I said, "So why do you need me?"

"That's exactly what I was wondering, Mapstone." Kate Vare emerged from the patio and marched toward us, her jaw set to confront me as an intruder. Sgt. Kate Vare of the Phoenix Police cold case unit and, "Christ, what's he doing here?" She was a businesslike blonde with short boyish-cut hair and brown eyebrows. As usual, she wore a pants suit with shoulder pads, exaggerating her natural angularity, making her look like an androgynous toy soldier.

"We don't need any history lessons," she said. "And this is a city case."

"Give it a break, Kate," Markowitz said. "Mapstone is here at the request of Chief Wilson, Sheriff Peralta, and the feds."

As if on cue, a group emerged from the house, better dressed than your average city detectives. The leader came out and shook my hand.

"Mapstone, I'm Eric Pham," the man said. He had a strong grip but a face of fine-boned details. "I'm special agent in charge of the Phoenix FBI. I'm a big admirer of your work."

"Thanks," I said. "But why do you need me or the sheriff's office? Detective Vare is as good a cold case expert as you'll find." I fantasized about pushing her into the pool. "Not that I see an obvious cold case."

Vare glared at me.

Eric Pham said, "Our John Doe there was found with this sewn in his jacket. And this has been missing since 1948."

Pham held up an evidence bag containing a single metal object. I took the bag and studied what was inside. It was tarnished and battered, but unmistakable.

"Is this real?" I asked Pham. He nodded, his lips pursing together until the color drained out.

It never ceased to surprise me—how small an FBI badge is.

Chapter Two

The rubber bag held a misshapen fat man. But the bones of his face, with their narrow planes and prominent juts, seemed to go with a man of average, even lean, build. The sun had done its relentless job bloating, burning, breaking down the remains. Even a few days in this heat were enough to do it. I searched the sore-ridden face, darkened by the pooling of blood. It was an old face with wrinkles around the mouth. He had spiky yellow-white whiskers, like the weeds in the yard, maybe a week's growth of beard that would grow no more. The pupils were blown out black, the tear ducts large. Parts of his face had a hint of fair skin. A mole was still distinct on the crease running below his right cheek. The smell was god-awful, rotting human flesh. I fought my gag reflex and breathed through my mouth.

Pham handed me a pair of gloves, but I didn't put them on. What I knew about forensics I had mostly learned as a young deputy on the street years ago. When I got my Ph.D. in history, emphasis on America from 1900 to 1940, I thought it was my ticket away from dead bodies. Funny how things turned out.

I asked, "How do we know he's homeless?"

Markowitz pointed to a raggedy backpack and two white plastic shopping bags on the ground nearby. An evidence technician was starting to separate and inventory their contents. Another technician used a digital camera to record each piece of evidence.

"We found those near the edge of the pool. Old clothes inside. No wallet or ID. No logos on the clothes. But there's a meal voucher for Shelter Services."

"Name?"

He shook his head.

"But the badge was sewn inside his jacket?"

Pham nodded. "He was wearing the jacket, too."

Just the thought of it made me instantly hotter. I edged toward the dust-caked wall of the house, trying to at least catch as much shade as the small roof overhang would allow. The sliding glass door stood open and hot air drifted out. I thought, Turn on the damned air-conditioning and let's go inside.

I said, "How do we know he's not some undocumented alien who fell in the pool and drowned, or he died here and the coyotes threw him in the pool?"

Pham said, "Next-door neighbor, a Mrs. Morales, said this old homeless Anglo had been out in the alley a couple of days ago. She'd never seen him before. She didn't talk to him. But she says he had some plastic shopping bags, and white whiskers."

The sky had lost all color. It was bleached white. The air felt under pressure. I looked around the yard. It was a hell of a place to die. Sun-blasted dirt. Back fence faded and broken. The house looking like it had been abandoned years ago. I tried to imagine the happy suburban memories, tried and failed.

"So what do you guys think?" Pham asked, his hands on his hips.

Kate Vare had been silent through all this. She suddenly said, "We just don't know enough to know yet. I don't work with guesses. Let's trace the badge number." She looked at me like a small dog that had intimidated a cat. Then they all looked at me expectantly.

"I don't know much," I said. "There was one FBI agent killed in the line of duty in Arizona. It happened in 1948, and the case was never solved. The agent's name was John Pilgrim."

"Go on," Pham said.

"That's all I know," I said. "So is that Pilgrim's badge?"

"Yeah," Pham said. "The badge was never found in 1948. That fact was withheld from the public report. I'm just learning all this in the past half hour." He studied me. "We hoped you could be a help."

"Well, that's what I know," I said, starting for the street. "If you don't mind, I just got back from a trip, and I'd really like to go home and change."

Markowitz put a gentle, heavy hand on my shoulder. Pham said, "I can understand, Dr. Mapstone. But we asked Sheriff Peralta for you to be assigned to this case. You have some skills we might need. So don't leave us quite yet." He turned to Kate Vare. "You don't mind a team that includes Dr. Mapstone, do you, Sergeant Vare?"

She was all smiles for the head fed, a talent called "managing up" that I had never mastered. She said, "We're always happy to have David."

That was when the air force arrived. A yellow helicopter swept in over the trees and did a pivot maybe a thousand feet above the backyard, swinging around to view us. It had the markings of a TV network. The heat seemed to push the engine sound downward until it was as prevalent as the smell of the body.

"Goddamned TV stations," Markowitz said over the din. "Must be a slow news day, if they come out for a stinker in a Maryvale pool."

The first chopper took up station to the northeast, and in a few seconds another one appeared. Kate tried to hold her hair in place from the wind blast, but soon this craft moved off a bit and hovered to the southwest. When I was able to see past the glare to make out the network logo on the second chopper's door, I saw two more helicopters. We were bracketed for the evening news, looking like idiots staring up into the sky. The whap-whap roar of the rotors assaulted our ears. Then I noticed a commotion over toward the side gate. The uniforms parted, the helicopters seemed to shimmy downward, and a giant in a tan suit and white Stetson strode into the backyard. Mike Peralta.

His physical presence washed into the space like a concussion wave. In my mind's eye, for just a moment, it was 1977 and academy instructor Peralta was stepping onto a gym mat to show me how to dominate and control a resisting suspect. I was eighteen, with an idealistic urge to be a cop, and my ears rang for a week after he slammed me onto the inch-thick fiber that separated my head from a full-blown concussion. "Dominate and control" were his words, classic cop speak. But his tree-trunk frame, impassive dark gaze, and confident wide-legged stance made any threat a promise. With his record of combat in Vietnam and heroics on the streets of Phoenix, he scared the hell out of the cadets.

He could still intimidate. But in the years he climbed the cop bureaucracy, years I was gone from law enforcement and from Phoenix, he had learned some polish and politics. He'd learned to smile. The media, hungry for charisma, had taken to him. People I respected said he'd be governor someday. I still wasn't sure he was comfortable with any of it. I knew him in the way ex-partners know each other, but I couldn't tell you where the old Peralta ended and the new one began. He was a complicated man who denied it.

Pham shook his hand. Markowitz and Kate Vare got nods. He ignored me.

Pham said. "Sheriff, I was just telling Dr. Mapstone how much we need his expertise on this case."

"I'm sure he's grateful for the opportunity," Peralta said, doffing his Stetson. "So is this connected to the John Pilgrim murder?"

I stared at Peralta. "It looks that way," Pham said.

We trailed Peralta and Pham on another once-over. I wondered how the victim got into the pool. Nothing was obvious, such as bloodstains on the concrete. Peralta walked over to the body, handed me his hat, slipped on some gloves, and felt around the man's face. Then the corpse's hands were in his giant paws, being minutely examined.

"A prior suicide attempt...," Peralta said. "See the scars on his wrists." Everybody nodded, but it was the first time they noticed the small, whitish rivulets under the skin. "But they're damned small."

"Maybe a small suicide attempt?" Markowitz said.

"Long time ago," Peralta said, unsmiling, sliding the arms back into the body bag.

Peralta studied the FBI badge intently, holding it up to the sun. I retold the story of John Pilgrim, the only FBI agent to be murdered in Arizona, an unsolved crime. Markowitz offered a briefing on what little the neighbors could tell. Peralta was complimentary. Peralta was grateful. Jurisdictional niceties must be observed. He slipped off the latex gloves and took back his Stetson.

He put a meaty hand on Pham's shoulder. "So tell us what you have in mind, Eric?"

"A cross-jurisdictional, multidisciplinary task force," he said, "Dr. Mapstone, Sgt. Vare, some of our people, of course. They say alliances are the way to get things done in the New Economy."

This was not the G-man talk I expected. Peralta said, "And you can push some of the costs onto us local peace officers." He smiled.

Pham smiled. "Well, Sheriff, it's no secret that we're stretched with the war on terrorism. I know you folks are, too. That's why I thought we could be more effective together. This may be connected to the murder of an FBI agent, so we're definitely serious players. But we need your help."

Peralta's handsome features changed subtly. "I've got my problems, too. The state fiscal crisis keeps running downhill to the county. We're humping it just to keep shifts covered. Got a major war between the Hell's Angels and the Mongols. My jail system is over capacity..."

"Of course, of course."

"But," Peralta sighed, "we're always happy to help. Mapstone will be assigned to this for as long as it takes." He shook hands again and swept out, this time with his arm around me. Past the gate, he said, "He's the nicest damned fed I've ever met."

I said, "How the hell do you know about John Pilgrim?"

"I know history and stuff, Mapstone. You keep teaching me, remember."

"Despite your best efforts," I said. We walked past TV cameras and TV questions, which Peralta ignored. He motioned to a uniform, who corralled a handful of TV reporters in the side yard. Peralta was already striding to the street.

"Sheriff Peralta with his media coterie," I said, making a gesture to take in the reporters, the helicopters, the world.

"What the hell is a coterie? You sound like my wife the Famous Shrink."

"Wait." I caught him at the curb. "What the hell good am I supposed to do in an investigation that should be the feds' business?"

"Why are you in such a foul mood?" he asked mildly. "You got to get out of this place for a few days. I thought you liked Portland."

I was about to say something I'd probably regret, but he was talking to the neighbors in a patois of Spanish and English. They crowded around him as if he were a star. An ice cream vendor pushed his cart up the street, and the children abandoned Peralta for the sweet stuff.

In a few moments, he took my arm again and led me down the sidewalk, but not far enough to find shade. A huge river of sweat was running down my back. He looked as cool as a November morning.

"You look miserable, Mapstone," he said.

"How the hell do you stay so cool? It's a hundred degrees on the first of April."

"It's a dry heat," he said.

I said, "Hell is a dry heat."

Peralta glanced back toward the house. "All those reporters are going to be disappointed. To them, it will just be a story about a homeless man who died in a green pool."

"The badge?"

Peralta shook his head. "Pham doesn't want to release that information yet."

"But," I said, "a homeless man doesn't fall in a pool without the Maricopa County sheriff noticing."

A carload of young men drove slowly up the street, slowing more as they passed us. It was a Cadillac Escalade, big as a starship, and emitting enormous pulses of sound. It made my heart beat funny. The noise almost concealed a few hissed profanities concerning our parentage and relationship to swine. Peralta ignored it, except for a subtle gesture—he slid his hand around his waist, pulling back his suit coat just enough that they could see the large .40-caliber Glock semiautomatic in a shoulder rig. They couldn't have been more than twenty years old. Tough young stupid guys with nearly shaved heads. Just past us, they kicked in the hydraulics and the Escalade hopped along, slowly thrusting itself into the asphalt and coming back up. We could hear the sonic thuds long after the car made a languid turn and exited the neighborhood.

"Aren't you curious about how an FBI badge missing for more than a half century turned up on a homeless guy in a swimming pool in Maryvale?" he demanded, his voice freed of the constraints of public attention.

"Sure, but 'cross-jurisdictional' is another word for cluster fuck."

One side of his mouth started to smile. He said, "Not always. Look at Lindsey's big score."

"So I heard," I said, missing her even more.

"One of the biggest credit card fraud operations, taken down by her work with a federal task force."

"I read about it on the plane. The *New York Times* carried the story."

Peralta's large black eyes fluttered. I could see his publicity meter running. That was the most obvious reason to get me involved in this case: good press meant more resources from the citizens of Maricopa County. "Anyway," he said, "the feds are in trouble since 9/11. They've had to shift over to preventing terrorism. They really could use our help."

"When did you get generous?"

"Be a good soldier, Mapstone. Your bride cut the nuts off the most profitable worldwide operation of the Russian mafia. You should be proud. It should motivate you to outdo her."

"We're not in competition. She's a lot smarter than me."

"Don't play games, Mapstone. No fucking April Fool's." I could sense his mood withdrawing into a darker basement. "This is a serious investigation. The feds need an independent third party to investigate this. And I want the sheriff's office to come out looking good."

"Sure," I said, gratefully feeling a hot breeze interrupt the blazing stagnant atmosphere. "And everything will be dandy and collegial with Kate Vare."

"You just have to know how to handle her."

"She can't be 'handled,'" I said sarcastically. "Why the hell does she hate me?"

Peralta paused. We'd reached an intersection maybe two hundred yards from the drama at the orange-striped ranch house. The street was completely empty. "Because," he said, "you're the enemy."

I started to speak but a wall of dust slapped me in the face, stinging my eyes.

"Hope they get that scene secured," Peralta said, rubbing his heavy jaw. "We're gonna get a helluva storm."

Chapter Three

The dust storm rolled in from the west. I drove east, home to central Phoenix, trying to outrun it. Behind me hulked the dust cloud: rising ten thousand feet and stretching across the horizon, looking like diluted chocolate. The White Tank and Estrella mountains were swallowed up and disappeared. Flags at car dealers and distribution warehouses stood straight out. Bits of the desert slapped against the windshield. Even though it was four in the afternoon, streetlights were coming on. Any small clue left in the yard in Maryvale was now in the atmospheres, traveling east in the hot, particle-drunk wind.

I was driving a 1968 Olds 442 convertible, "borrowed" from the impound lot by Peralta and lent to me after a previous case involved the destruction of my beloved BMW. A drug dealer had been good enough to restore the car, painting it a discreet bright yellow, and the big engine wasn't as sweet as the big air conditioner. "You'll like driving a piece of history," said Peralta, who enjoyed making me uncomfortable. So I was encased in what seemed like a football field of General Motors steel, the dearest dream of any kid being shipped off to Vietnam in the summer of Sgt. Pepper and the assassinations of Martin Luther King and Bobby Kennedy. Now it was in the new millennium, an ancient machine surging across the hot concrete. I was socialized enough by my years as a college professor to be almost ashamed to like a car that was so big, so wasteful, so laden with the baggage of American excess. Lindsey approved, however, reminding me of the difference between a porcupine and a BMW—"With a BMW, the pricks are on the inside."

After I got to the Papago Freeway it was a straight shot home, the ragtop flapping violently in the wind. But by the time I crested the Stack, the big freeway interchange on the northwest side of downtown, the skyscrapers and mountains that should have been ahead of me had vanished. The horizon closed in, turning from milky to brown. Slowing below sixty, putting some space between me and the sea of red taillights ahead, I felt the big car getting strafed by brush and garbage blown into the freeway. I slowed just in time to avoid an SUV that crossed two lanes and plunged into the tunnel under Hance Park doing maybe ninety. When I took the exit to Seventh Avenue, my hands relaxed enough to make me realize how tightly I had been gripping the wheel. Seventh took me the half a mile to Cypress Street, to the 1924 Monterey Revival house in the Willo Historic District, where the lights blazed welcome through the dusty murk of the street.

We left a trail of clothes from the front door to the bedroom. Not a long distance: up a step, through an arch, down the hallway. Our bedroom faced the street on the first floor, and you could look out the window and see the front door. We made love face-to-face while, on the CD player, Charlie Parker enchanted the saxophone and the wind jangled the Soleri bell outside. Then, after I made Bombay Sapphire martinis and she slipped on one of my starched white dress shirts, we lay on the big rumpled bed, legs entangled, and we talked.

"I'm sorry you had to go alone," she said, running her hand light and slow across my chest. Lindsey draped a fine, long leg across my thigh, her five-foot-eight-inch length neatly fitting my six-two. The twilight made her fair skin seem to glow. Her dark hair was, as always, worn in a simple cut parted in the middle and falling to brush the tops of her shoulders. Her eyes were their familiar incandescent dark blue.

I had gone alone to Portland, to say good-bye to a dying friend. His name was Dan Milton—my mind was still getting used to the past tense in referring to him. Once upon a time, he had been one of my professors. He was the one who made me think I could make a mark in the world as a historian. Now he was dead, and up to the moment I was in Lindsey's arms I had been besieged by all manner of devils bearing regret, guilt, and mortal fears. I said, "I wish I could have been here for you." I sipped the martini, feeling the cold liquid turn hot as it went down my throat. "I worry."

"I worry about you, Dave. Mine was just work."

I stroked her hair. "But did you get Mr. Big?"

Lindsey's full lips opened into a smile. "Meester Beeg!" She shot off a string of Russian sentences, her face animated and lovely.

"Come again?"

"In time, Dave." She ran a hand up my thigh. "I said, 'Mr. Big's name is Yuri, and nobody has ever seen him. We don't even have a photo. He's very mysterious.' Unfortunately we got everybody but Yuri. Maybe I just said 'surface-to-air missile' instead of 'mysterious.' That's what happens when you learn Russian in the Air Force."

"Yes, one of your adventures. Sgt. Lindsey Faith Adams, USAF."

"My adventures pale beside yours, my worldly lover," she said. "Besides, it's Lindsey Faith Mapstone now. Detective Sgt. Lindsey Faith Mapstone."

It was indeed, but it was a strange, exhilarating sound: Lindsey Faith Mapstone. We were still newlyweds. So I allowed myself the husband's prerogative of listening to his wife's dulcet alto, a voice that so soothed me. She talked about her big case. Most of the technology went over my head, the extensible markup language, secret sharers, buried code, and identity masking software that the good guys used to get the bad guys. I just want a computer to do what I want. Lindsey is way ahead of me. That's why she was picked for the task force that spent a year tracking some super-stars of international crime. They had hacked into every major credit card network, stealing identities, draining cash, reselling stolen credit card numbers. They had even discovered a way to steal information off smart cards. Tracks led to Russia, Malaysia, and Gilbert, Arizona, a quiet suburb outside Phoenix.

"The mistake we were making was to think these guys were in a place, using a computer," she said. "They were, of course, but the real crime was happening on the networks, out in cyberspace. They could operate from a phone booth, from a moving car. So we fought fire with fire."

"I bet that was your idea," I said.

"I helped," she said, sipping her martini, then replacing it on the bedside table. "I infiltrated their network. I mean, I found them out there, in the Visa system, and I followed them home, so to speak. Not only was I able to get into their computers, but I set up a dummy network around them. Every time they logged on, wherever they were, I could hack their computers. Pretty soon, they thought they were stealing real credit card numbers, but they were really in this dummy network." The big smile, the amazing mouth. "Yeah, I guess I did good. And I got lucky—they got careless, just like street scumbags get careless."

"So how'd you get them?"

"You won't even believe it, Dave. Once we got into their computers, we could get into every file. So it wasn't hard to figure out the real identities. One guy, we got him when he logged onto AOL to check his personal e-mail. So two days ago, police in three countries carried out simultaneous raids. A dozen were arrested. I felt like sending a virus that would pop up on their screens just before the cops kicked the door in, and it would say, 'You're busted!' I didn't, sad to say. Anyway, all that came to a head while you were in Portland, love. And I never had to leave the study in there"—she nodded toward the other end of the house—"except to sit through excruciating meetings with the FBI."

"Did you meet a guy named Pham?"

"Eric Pham? No, he's the SAC." Special agent in charge. "I just dealt with his minions. Minions in search of Meester Beeg." She had a nice laugh. I told her about my encounter with Pham, the homeless man in the swimming pool, and the long-missing FBI badge.

"I think El Jefe is a prick for making you work the minute you get back, especially after what you've been through. He lost his father last year. He ought to have a little more emotional intelligence."

It was true. Judge Peralta's death had barely registered on him, on the outside at least. It was just the way he was.

"I always loved the judge," Lindsey said. "So courtly, so old school. You'd think Mike would be more of a sensitive guy considering his wife is such a big time psychologist."

"I knew them when he was just a deputy, and she was just a scared housewife."

"You are an old guy, Dave." She tickled me, and I nearly upset what was left of my drink.

"Yeah, kid, I remember you on my very first case back at the sheriff's office. Seems like only yesterday. I said, 'Who is this babe in the miniskirt and the nose stud.'"

"I saved your ass, Dave."

"True enough."

She snuggled against me. "You saved me back," she said.

"Anyway," Lindsey said conspiratorially. "Dr. Sharon living in San Francisco, what does that mean for the sheriff's marriage?"

I shrugged. "They have their own thing, and it's survived for thirty years or so. I think her radio syndicator wanted her in San Francisco. And the daughters live in the Bay Area. I still can't imagine Mike and Sharon as grandparents. But Sharon says she's just commuting there during the week." I listened to the wind, stroked her soft hair. "Do you regret we didn't go to San Francisco?"

She said, "Sometimes." Before the dot-com bubble blew up, Lindsey had what seemed like a stack of offers from companies in the Bay Area.

"I would have gone with you," I said.

"Damn right you would have," she said. "But I wanted to do something that mattered. It's never been about money. And this is your home, Dave. I know how much that means to you."

"Sometimes I wish it weren't," I said, thinking about the premature hundred-degree day on April first. Suddenly, I lost the high that Lindsey and sex and Bombay Sapphire had conjured in me.

Dan Milton disdained Phoenix as a barbarous place, all subdivisions and automobiles. It was one of the reasons why I disliked him when we first met. I had barely been away from Arizona when I went to the Midwest for my Ph.D. work. A protégé of Arthur Link, Milton had been an enfant terrible in the 1960s, engaging in violent intellectual jousts with Arthur Schlesinger Jr., and legendary party binges with Robert Conquest. By the time I came to study with him, he was one of the most distinguished scholars of Woodrow Wilson and the Progressive era, widely published, cherished, and still controversial.

He was hard on his students. To study with Dan Milton was to live in the library—this was before personal computers—learning what he called "real research methods…not the candy-ass lazy shit you learned scamming your master's degrees at state colleges." He was a native Texan and reveled in being a profane scholar. He had a weakness for guns and fine Kentucky bourbons. He affected to be uninterested in my youthful detour to become a deputy sheriff. To him, scholarship, done right, meaning Dan Milton's way, was heroic.

Out in the house, I heard Billy Bragg's "California Stars" on the stereo. I let the guitars and wanderlust harmonica stoke my melancholy. I was now approaching the age that Milton was when I arrived on his doorstep as a twentysomething Ph.D. candidate. It made me feel strange, caught in time's riptide and unable to see the shore.

He was hard on his students because the ones who made it were his great legacy. They went on to become noted professors, cutting-edge scholars, influential authors, in-demand advisers to secretaries of state, and national security aides—and me, I came back home to Phoenix and took a job at the sheriff's office again.

I read to Dan Milton as he lay dying from stomach cancer. He had long ago moved to Portland, a wonderfully civilized city for a man who prized civilization. Writing a pair of bestsellers—one book won the Parkman Prize—had supplemented his family money, so the high cost of living was no object. His condo overlooked downtown and the river, Mount Hood in the far distance. Its rooms were occupied by books, modernist paintings, and a young woman with honey-colored hair named Kathleen. Milton always had a Kathleen or a Heather or a Pamela, intellectual young women who ran through his life, each for a few years, and amused him. He favored Smith graduates. He was as much auteur as scholar.

Finally, a hospital bed was added. And a part-time nurse. He dismissed the entreaties of his grown children to go to a nursing home.

I visited almost every day, and read to him from Robert Caro's Lyndon Johnson biography, *Master of the Senate*. Milton was often groggy and sometimes in terrible pain, but he had lost nothing of his incisive mind. He made me see the book in new ways, made me see Caro's shortcomings as well as triumph, even as I watched my professor slide into darkness.

"He never forgave me for leaving teaching, for not making something of myself as a scholar," I said aloud. "He never said so, but I know…"

Lindsey laid her head on my chest, letting her dark hair sweep against my skin. I went on, "Milton wants me to take a lecturer job at Portland State." I corrected myself, "Wanted me. He talked to the dean and recommended me. It's a two-year appointment, in American history. It's some kind of interdisciplinary deal with the criminal justice program. Milton said it was tailor-made for me, and the class load is light enough to do research and writing, too."

"Do you want to do that?" Lindsey asked, not facing me.

"I don't know," I said, looking into the murk of the ceiling, listening to the wind. "All the politics and political correctness drove me nuts before. But I didn't have you before. Oh, it's probably silly to even consider it. You wouldn't like the rain…"

"Oh, History Shamus," Lindsey stroked my head. "You're tired. You're grieving." She held me close, and her body heat was a wonderful force field against a cold world.

Finally, she said, "You can do anything you want, Dave. Even as an old guy."

She smiled at me, and sipped the last of her drink. "I know what will cheer you up. I got takeout at the Fry Bread House. Let's eat Indian tacos, drink cerveza, and screw all night." She sat astride me, and my body quickly responded.

"I'll make some history with you, Professor."

Chapter Four

"Can you help me out? Some change to get something to eat?"

I shook my head like a heartless bastard and walked into Starbucks. The man lingered for a moment, staring at the big Oldsmobile. Then he walked toward Safeway, slipping into a forlorn limp as he approached a woman getting out of her car. She hurried into the store and he resumed a normal walk, wandering across McDowell Road into the park.

It was Friday morning, a day after the body was found in the Maryvale pool. The storm's aftermath was a yard littered with downed palm fronds, and the neighbors anxiously cleaning their pools, but the day dawned clear and mild. My apocalyptic environmental visions of the previous day were replaced by fond, familiar appreciation for my hometown. At the foot of the broad streets, mountains glowed vivid purple and brown. The ascending morning sun turned wispy clouds from pink to alabaster. Even the last remnants of citrus blossoms were lingering in the seventy-degree air. So I put the top down on the Olds, slid in an Ellington CD, and got to work.

The first twenty-four hours are critical in a homicide investigation. But in my line, the first fifty-six years are critical, at least for a body carrying an FBI badge that disappeared in 1948. From the quiet of my office in the old county courthouse, under high ceilings, big windows, and the gaze of Sheriff Carl Hayden from his 1901 photograph, I imagined my battle plan. Its basics had evolved as I had learned the job, invented it really, over the past several years since Peralta had taken pity on my untenured, unemployed state and given me an old case to research. I would need a timeline, a gallery of the major players in the case, lists of key evidence, plus all the case records and newspaper clippings. My job was to find connections as a historian and researcher, bringing something to an investigation that the regular detectives might miss, or so I told myself.

But as I sipped a mocha, my legs went up to the desktop and laziness set in. I didn't look forward to falling all over the feds, and I sure as hell didn't want to deal with Kate Vare. I picked up the phone, eager for a shortcut.

As it happened, my friend Lorie Pope was in the newsroom over at the *Republic*. She was yelling even before I finished the first sentence.

"John Pilgrim!" she exclaimed. "Do I know about John Pilgrim? Jesus Christ, David, this case has been driving me crazy for my whole career!"

She had a big voice, one that had gotten raspy with years and too many cigarettes since the first day I met her, back in the '70s when she was a cub reporter and I was a rookie deputy. I moved the receiver closer to my ear again and continued.

"Why driving you crazy?" I asked.

"Because the whole thing is…Wait a minute, David. Why? Why do you want to know?"

"I'm just naturally curious." I could already imagine the explosion from Peralta if the story of the found badge appeared on the front page of the local newspaper.

"Bullshit," she said, glee in her voice. "David, you were a lousy liar when you were my boyfriend…"

"Was I your boyfriend? I recall there were several of us."

"What can I say," she said. "I'm loveable. But I guess you're happier now with Leslie."

"Lindsey," I said.

"Don't try to change the subject. You've got something new on Pilgrim."

Now it was my turn to be obstinate. "'Bye, Lorie."

I held the phone out just enough to hear her hollering. "Stop! Don't hang up!"

I said, "So give me the short version of why this case matters to you, and I'll try to help you, too."

"Bastard," she said, not without affection. "OK, it's the only unsolved murder of an FBI agent in Arizona history. John Pilgrim was found floating in an irrigation canal on November 10th, 1948. He had a single gunshot to his heart. The locals and the FBI interviewed more than a thousand people, and they never made an arrest in the case."

I asked her why.

"That's what always drove me nuts. I was assigned to do a story on the Pilgrim case years ago, just a historical feature on famous local cases that had never been solved. I'd never even heard of the case before. But I didn't get anywhere with the FBI. Even some of my good sources wouldn't talk. And I'm like, what's the deal? This is a case that happened decades ago. Why do they give a shit? Well, let me tell you, David, they do. I came back five years ago and filed a FOIA, Freedom of Information Act request, for the Pilgrim files. Guess what? They blocked it."

I sipped the mocha, trying to square Lorie's information with Eric Pham's willingness to share the case with the local cops.

"What about the county files?"

"The assholes tried to block that, too. The paper took them to court. I got this very redacted version. Lots of reports were missing. This was all before you came back to Phoenix, David."

"So why do they care so much?" I asked.

"I'd like to tell you it's the great Phoenix murder mystery, that's it's got sex, betrayal, a dead body and somehow ties the FBI into the Kennedy assassination. But my theory is that Pilgrim killed himself, and that would have been an embarrassment to the FBI. But who the hell knows. Not everybody would agree."

"Who is not everybody?" I asked.

"There was someone I spent some time with who was one of these amateur crime buffs. A.C. Hardin—how could I ever forget. A.C. was convinced that Pilgrim was killed by gangsters."

"Where can I find Hardin?"

"Used to live down in Tubac. Hang on..." I heard her banging through drawers, and then she came back on with a phone number. I thanked her.

"Yeah, well, A.C.'s a nut," she said. "So now it's your turn, Deputy-Professor-Ex-Boyfriend. Talk."

I saw a shadow at the pebbled glass of my door. "Later," I said, and hung up. I could hear her cursing as the phone sank to its cradle.

Kate Vare opened the door without knocking. "We've got to canvass the shelters, find out who this guy was," she muttered.

"Can't the detectives do that?" I asked.

"We are the detectives, Mapstone," she said. "Didn't you see TV this morning? A fourteen-year-old girl kidnapped at gunpoint from her parents' house. Everybody in my shop is busy on that. Not that we didn't have enough to do already."

She looked around my office. "How do you rate so much room? And this furniture?"

"This was just a storeroom when I cleaned it up," I said. "Actually, it was the sheriff's personal office when the courthouse was built in 1929, but it had been forgotten all these years..."

I wasn't even going to get into how I found the 1930s hardwood chairs and bench, and the leather sofa, in county storage. Her eyes were blurry with boredom.

"I didn't hear about the kidnapping," I said. I was just making conversation. My stomach hurt, the ache of unpleasant people. My stomach said, Be somewhere else.

"Oh, that's right," she said, giving me a small, sad smile. "You read books."

"Or the newspaper."

"Who has time."

She fished in her tote and held out two handfuls. "We have some photos of the guy, and his jacket in a bag. Maybe someone will remember dealing with him."

I stayed at my desk. "Kate, I have a wonderful idea. You check out the homeless guy, and I'll work things from the Pilgrim angle. That way we'll stay out of each other's way."

"No way," she barked, and squared her shoulders against me. "I'm not taking the shitwork while you play professor."

"This isn't—"

"I've dealt with sexism my whole career, Mapstone. So don't think you can pat me on the head, tell me I have pretty legs, and send me on my way."

"I—"

She drilled an index finger my way. "If you want to be part of this case, you have to step up and do the real work, just like me."

She stalked off toward the elevator, pausing to toss her head at the door into the great sexist's office. She said, "Coming?"

Chapter Five

I followed her down the curving, Spanish tile staircase, feeling more amused than annoyed. Amused in a lethargic way. I was still wrung out from my time in Portland, and this case just didn't make me feel territorial about who would discover the connection between a homeless man and a missing FBI badge. Maybe it was diminishing testosterone—I sure didn't feel that in other ways. Maybe I was growing a little bored playing cop, as Dan Milton had wondered about me before he died.

My task with Kate that morning seemed like a fool's errand, but that was why I had never made it in the law enforcement bureaucracy. I didn't understand the importance of process. Of appearing to do something. Maybe I would get credit as a good team player, "handling" Kate Vare, as Peralta put it. I would try it for a while, at least. But it seemed like a lousy way to make progress. We didn't have a good photo of the dead man—the morgue shots definitely didn't make him look "so lifelike, so at peace." A bloated corpse face stared out at us. As for the jacket, it was standard-issue Levi's, very faded and authentically "distressed." Even beneath the heavy clear plastic of the evidence bag, the jacket felt vermin-infested.

"We can take my car," Vare said.

"My legs won't fold into those Cavaliers," I said. "Let's take mine."

Across the front seat of the big Oldsmobile, Kate was halfway into the next county. So there was no need to force small talk as we made the rounds of the beleaguered shelters and social service agencies that clustered in unwanted, homely buildings on the fringes of downtown. A plan to build a multimillion-dollar campus for the homeless had been discussed for years but nothing ever seemed to happen. Pearl Buck wrote that the test of a civilization was the way it cared for its most helpless members. Phoenix didn't read Pearl Buck.

The social workers either got along with cops or they didn't. The cynical and jaded ones did. But cops were part of their daily landscape. There to stop a fight. There to find a suspect. We were just two more cops wanting something. The whitewashed walls, government-issue furniture, and unpleasant smells took me back to the few years in the '70s when I worked as a patrol deputy. Not much seemed to have changed. We were all just factory workers in the giant human meat grinder where society's front line intersected with a big city's underclass.

"Do you know how many people come through here every day?" demanded a male social worker with a ponytail and a pharaoh beard. "We've been over capacity for something like twenty years. Nobody gives a shit."

Nobody seemed to recognize the person in the Polaroid. "This guy looks dead," one shelter staffer observed. Because I read the newspaper, I knew the city's hardcore homeless numbered 3,000, and some estimates were much higher. So identifying our corpse wasn't going to be easy. But then we caught what might be a break. At a food bank on Third Avenue, someone remembered a middle-aged Anglo guy who always wore a Levi's jacket, even on the hottest day. He was one of the local alcoholic indigents they called "the home guard." Maybe the guy's name was Weed.

"That's worse than nothing," Kate said. "Just a nickname. All these transients have nicknames and aliases."

"Maybe it's proper name," I said.

"That's ridiculous." she said.

"Didn't Patty Hearst date a guy named Weed when the SLA kidnapped—?"

"Don't change the subject," she said. I noticed that, in dealing with me at least, she was speaking even before I finished my first sentence. I felt a fresh surge of annoyance, and was tempted to tell her about Thurlow Weed, the abolitionist political boss in New York in the mid nineteenth century.

More silence took us to lunch. We stopped at a little taqueria on Jefferson and Seventh Avenue for burritos. We were only a block from police headquarters, but the little shack that promised "burritos y hamburgers" was a gathering spot for the woebegone neighborhood between downtown and the state capitol. We ate with the top down, and every time somebody hit us up for money, we showed the photo and asked them about a guy named Weed. Pretty soon word got around we were cops, and foot traffic dried up. Kate looked distinctly uncomfortable, and I took way too much pleasure in that.

Then there was nothing left to do but cruise and ask questions. I drove across the Seventh Avenue overpass, made a right on Grant Street, and then turned back north on Ninth. Up through the 1970s, this had been the industrial heart of a much smaller city. The Southern Pacific and Santa Fe railroads sliced through on their way to Union Station. The railroads also served scores of produce warehouses and other agricultural terminals. Old Phoenix was a farm town, where irrigated fields and groves yielded oranges, grapefruits, lemons, lettuce, and cotton for markets back east. Mile-long trains of refrigerator cars were made up here, sending fresh Arizona citrus to the tables of families in Chicago and Dayton and Minneapolis. Now those families seem to have moved to Arizona, and the old produce district had been long abandoned.

Could the man from the pool, the dead man without a name, maybe nicknamed Weed, have walked these streets? It was a long shot. Only a meal card told us he could.

We were in sight of the nicest new investments downtown, the Dodge Theater, Bank One Ballpark, and America West Arena.

But these streets held blocks of bleak single-story warehouses, some close to falling down. The produce businesses were gone. Almost everything was gone. One building held the Interfaith Cooperative Ministries. Another said it was the Joe Diaz Top-Level Boxing Gym ("There is no substitute for experience"). Concertina wire flashed menacingly off fences and rooftops. Vacant lots glistened with broken glass. A few early bungalows sat incongruously beside the industrial buildings—if you could have moved one to one of the historic districts and fixed it up, you could have sold it for half a million bucks.

The streets were covered with the memory of pavement. Curbs and sidewalks were cracked, broken, or nonexistent. Long unused railroad tracks ran down the center of the cross streets, Jackson, Harrison, Madison, heading nowhere. As we drove slowly up Ninth Avenue, they appeared. Singles, pairs, and clusters of people. They stood or walked aimlessly up and down. Most were black, but there were also plenty of Anglos, a few Indians. On one corner a man huddled by an open water faucet, rinsing his face. An ancient-looking Anglo hobbled across railroad tracks using stainless steel crutches. Across the street, a black woman pulled what looked like a new wheeled suitcase and two small children.

"Jesus Christ," Kate Vare said quietly.

"Don't you remember the Deuce?" I asked. The old skid row in Phoenix had been centered around Second Street, hence its name.

"No," she said. "I moved out from Wisconsin in 1989."

"When the city proposed tearing the Deuce down to build Civic Plaza, a few people asked where the transients would go. Here's where they went, as well as to every neighborhood park in the center city, behind big billboards, at camps down at the riverbed…"

"Mapstone," she said, "Spare me your history lessons."

"Sorry. It's just interesting."

"Maybe to you," she said. "You know, I am so unimpressed with the great Dr. David Mapstone."

"That makes two of us."

"Oh, please. Spare me the false humility, too. The famous David Mapstone is the genius who solved the disappearance of Rebecca Stokes from the 1950s, who discovered the bodies of the Yarnell twins who were kidnapped in the Depression. What else? Oh, yes, the David Mapstone who uncovered the scandal in the sheriff's office from the 1970s and helped free an innocent man."

"He was killed," I said quietly, stopping so a man in pink pants and a long yellow prospector's beard could pull his two shopping carts laboriously across the potholed street.

"You're famous, Mapstone. I read about you in the newspaper. I see you on TV, even if you don't watch. I'm just a police officer who plays by the rules and works as a professional. I work on real cold cases—crimes from 1982, say, or 1990, where real people are waiting for some word of what happened to a loved one. I can't just deliver some bullshit scam graduate history seminar. Like I really have time to waste on this wild goose chase."

She went on, growing more animated. "I worked to get where I am. I didn't go off for fifteen years to teach college and then come back so my buddy the sheriff could get me a job."

"Good for you, Kate," I wished I could get out of the car. The top being down helped relieve the oppressiveness of the talk, but the sun was starting to broil us. We bumped across the Southern Pacific tracks. Off on one corner, as far from the technology economy as I could imagine, sat unattended stacks of shrink-wrapped computer screens. Maybe for recycling? Maybe "fell off the truck"?

She said, "The point is, I'm working with you because I have to, not because I want to." She readjusted her sunglasses and stared straight ahead. "And I hate this old car."

I pushed against the seat to ease my stress-made backache. "Gosh, Kate, I'm crushed. You're so charming, even flirty, if I may say, that all this comes as a surprise to me."

"Fuck you."

I tried to ignore her. A good night's sleep had helped me set aside the sadness of the past two weeks. Good night's sleep, my ass—I got laid. The universal antidote to heartbreak, loss, anxiety, frustration, second thoughts, and fears of mortality. Anyway, Kate was right: I had a good gig. I had come home to Phoenix and found a sweet little niche for someone burdened by something as useless as a Ph.D. in history. In fact, my life was rich with blessings: Lindsey, a good marriage, a nice house in the Willo Historic District far from lookalike subdivisions, good health—I was still in good shape, even if I was undeniably in middle age. Lots of people would think my life was a fantasy come true. Looking around at all the suffering souls on these streets was reminder enough of that.

I slid the big car slowly up to a group of men wearing layers of filthy old clothes. I showed them the photo and they asked for money. I showed them my badge and they went away. Another man, his face frozen in a desperate contortion and baked red-brown by the sun, swore he remembered a guy named Weed, an old guy who claimed he had come from a rich family in New York. No, he didn't know his full name. A prostitute walked up in a short, dusty dress and asked us if we wanted a partner for a threesome. A patrol car gave us the once-over and drove away. We crossed the railroad main line a dozen times, going back and forth. So it went for an hour. Most police work was even more boring than this.

"Pull in there," Kate said, pointing to a shady area under the overpass, "if you won't put the damned top up. I need to check my messages." She pulled a cell phone out. "Jesus, I can't even see the phone display in this glare."

I was sweating, too, so I drove slowly toward the shade, north from Lincoln, right onto what looked like an access road beside the overpass. It was really old South Seventh Avenue, which once crossed the railroad at grade, and was frequently blocked by trains. After the overpass was built, it was blocked off at the tracks, making a street that went nowhere. We hadn't checked back here for a lead on Weed or whatever the hell his name was.

The area under the overpass was still seedy with industrial castoffs. I pulled back as far as the road went, letting my eyes adjust and feeling the temperature drop instantly when the sun went away. I slipped the car into park and looked at the lovely old mission-style building of Union Station, a hundred yards to the east and across the tracks. My grandmother had taken me there as a boy to see passenger trains like the Sunset Limited, the Imperial, and the Golden State. Now they were all history. The tracks were empty, torn out or sprouting weeds. It made me sad.

My eyes adjusted to the dark and I realized we had landed in a little colony of some kind. Groups of men watched us from a distance, men whose clothes and skin had all been turned the same color of brown-black by the sun. I counted a dozen I could see. We had landed in their world, cut off from the street grid, shaded from the sun. I couldn't believe we were welcome.

Just outside my peripheral vision, I saw movement. I turned to see three men walking toward us from a squat building under the concrete pilings. They were younger, moving without the beaten down arthritic shuffle of the transients a block over. They weren't walking past. They were walking toward us. Something in their expressions...

"What are you doing?" Kate closed her phone.

"I was a Boy Scout," I said, pulling my Colt Python .357 magnum revolver from the locked console compartment and concealing it between my legs. "'Be Prepared.'"

"You got the time?" asked a muscular black man in a white sleeveless T-shirt coming to my side of the car. I told him the time. He said, "Nice car." I agreed it was. His buddies surrounded us. I couldn't see each of them at once. I felt my heart rate take off.

"So what you want down here?" he asked. I kept my hands in my lap, covering the butt of the Python. He went on, "Score some crack? Never seen you before."

His buddy said, "Lots of white folks come in from the suburbs to buy crack from the brothers, but we never seen you here before."

Another voice, high-pitched, said, "Maybe they just lost."

"Lost, my ass!" came a call from the gloomy periphery of the street.

The leader, Muscle Man, thought about that, looking at us intently. "You lost, we give you directions. But you got to pay the toll."

The high-pitched voice behind me said, "Pay the toll to the troll." Everybody laughed except Muscle Man. Even I laughed.

Kate flashed her badge. "Get lost, asshole. We're busy."

"Sure, Officer," Muscle Man said. He walked in a small circle, breathing in and out deeply. He came to face us again. "You heard her, let's get lost."

"Maybe I don't want to get lost." This from the Tenor. I turned my head enough to take him in. He was the biggest of the bunch, a giant with walnut-colored skin, wearing a very long lime green T-shirt and long-short pants. He also sported a sideways green ball cap atop what looked to my unhip eyes like a skullcap. His sneakers were smaller than destroyers. In other words, he looked like every suburban kid at the mall. He walked over to Kate's side of the car.

I let my eyes again take in our surroundings. The street around us was really not much more than an alley. Old warehouses rose up on either side of us. Traffic rolled over us on the overpass. In the distance I could hear jets taking off from Sky Harbor. A train whistle came from the west. We might as well have been a hundred miles from any help.

"You hear?" said Muscle Man. "We don't want to get lost."

"Maybe we'll take this car, understand what I'm sayin'," said the thin man.

It was a curious expression, "understand what I'm sayin'." Was it born of unempowered people desperate to be heard, accustomed to the powerful classes failing to "understand"? That would be a fine politically correct paper to present at the Modern Language Association—my amused subconscious was actually thinking this. My conscious felt the heavy butt of the handgun against my concealing hands as the thin man walked up beside my door and leaned a dirty arm on it. He had large black freckles on his face, large, expressive eyes. His hands were scarred and sinewy.

"Maybe we'll take her badge," said the Tenor. "Badge like that bring some good money on the street. Shit, maybe we'll take her." He slouched against Kate's side of the car, giggling "Pay the toll to the troll."

Someone from the shadows repeated, "Pay the toll to the trolls."

Another voice from the gloom: "Kill him and rape the bitch!"

This is how it was going to go down: the Muscle Man was on my side of the car, joined by the thin guy with freckles. On Kate's side, the giant Tenor, his hat cockeyed. The chorus surrounded us at a distance, the monochrome street people watching the little drama, maybe ready to join in if we appeared weak enough.

I was watching the hands of the three surrounding the car. Nobody seemed armed, but I couldn't really tell. I kept my hands in my lap, feeling a huge lump of panic in my middle.

A little bit of long-ago training bubbled up. I turned the ignition and put my hand on the gearshift. "'Bye, trolls," I said.

But in that instant, Muscle Man dove at me. I wasn't fast enough. Strong, rough fingers closed around my throat. I almost blacked out right there, but turned my head a little sideways, sucked in some air, and drove my arms up viciously to break his grip. He fell back. I heard an ugly murmur from the shadows, and before I could get out of the damned seat Freckles came at me. I slammed the heel of my hand into his nose and he snapped back, falling on his ass. But Muscle Man dove over the door, grabbing for the gun. He had all the leverage of a strong, standing man fighting a man who was pinned down in a car seat. I could feel myself losing the fight. Didn't want to imagine the consequences. Couldn't.

But I fought dirty. When he reached for the pistol, I grabbed one of his fingers with both my hands and torqued it in a direction nature didn't intend. I felt the finger snap, heard the bone and cartilage separate. He screamed, lurched back, and fell out of the car, landing on his back. I rose right up after him, leaped out of the car-without even opening the door. I had a foot on his chest and the big Python in his face. Freckles was also in my field of fire, raised up on his elbows staring at me, blood streaming out of his nose.

Kate was being pulled from the car by the big guy. She had received a nasty blow to one eye, and I could see him reaching for her holster, with her desperately trying to keep his hands away. High-voltage panic shot up my spine.

There was no time for negotiation. I kicked Muscle Man in the nose to stun him, took a chance on Freckles staying down, and ran to the other side of the car for a clear shot. I got within five feet, dropped into a combat stance and leveled the Colt Python at the chest of the big Tenor. I did some quick arithmetic: six .357 hollow-point bullets, three targets, shaky hands, and my Speedloader reloading magazines were in the glovebox. And all that assumed nobody from the shadows decided to get a piece of us.

I was not articulate: "Die, asshole."

He stared at me, stared at the gun. A large drop of sweat materialized on his forehead and ran to his eye.

He sighed. "Fuck."

He let go, and Kate used her suddenly free arm to deliver a nasty haymaker. He sprawled on the asphalt, holding his face. I noticed Freckles was on his feet, thinking about intervening. When I moved my gunsights to his chest, he took off to the south toward Lincoln. I could see Kate tense, ready to give chase.

"Let him go," I said. "We can find him through his buddies here."

The Tenor looked at me mournfully. Kate had a wild look and had retrieved her semiautomatic and handcuffs.

"Face down on the ground," I ordered, keeping my finger on the Colt's finely machined trigger.

I looked around: the street was empty. Everyone was gone. I said merrily, "Toll booth is closed."

But Kate mouthed something silently, looking at me. If I had been a lip reader, I would say she called me a bastard. And she said, "You'll pay."

Chapter Six

"Dave, I continue to be amazed…" Lindsey paused to watch Luis Gonzalez slam a single past the second baseman. She cheered like a banshee, took a sip of beer, and continued. "I am continually amazed that a bookworm like you gets into such trouble."

It was Saturday night and we had our usual nosebleed seats at Chase Field, our way to take in the Diamondbacks—unless Peralta was treating and we could enjoy his season tickets two rows above the home dugout. One of the surprises about getting to know Lindsey was to see her evolution into a rabid baseball fan. This night the D-Backs were six runs ahead of the Braves headed into the eighth inning, a margin comfortable enough even for a fatalistic fan like me.

"You haven't been a street cop since you were in your early twenties." Lindsey continued, a carefully kept scorecard on her lap. "So how come you get in a confrontation with some drug dealers and you know how to save your bacon?"

"Luck," I said. "And truck knowledge."

Lindsey said, "Truck what?"

"Truck knowledge," I said. "It's the stuff you know so deep that you can get hit by a truck and still remember. Like good training at the Sheriff's Academy. You learn moves that kick in even if you're tempted to panic. That's truck knowledge."

"I like that."

"It was a phrase I learned from Dr. Milton."

"He must have been a character," she said. "I wish I could have had a chance to meet him." She put a hand on my leg. "But your scrapes with the wild side of Phoenix scare the hell out of me. You need to stick to the library; History Shamus."

I could still feel a stranger's rough fingers digging into my neck. Rolling my head from side to side only exaggerated the soreness. Lindsey was right, of course. We had been lucky as hell. The confrontation beneath the overpass could have turned out very differently, very unhappily. Somehow I had a gene in me that let me remember my training, and fight back when I was scared— even though most people living comfortable, middle-class lives would have been terrified into paralysis. And I had been lucky.

I sat back high above home plate, surrounded by 30,000 friendly strangers, and felt glad to be alive. Phoenix had come a long way from the dusty little farm town that my great-grandparents discovered when they came to Arizona before statehood. In good ways, with big-city amenities like the beautiful downtown ballpark, with its retractable roof, air-conditioning, and right-field swimming pool. And bad: with the rough characters like the kind Kate Vare and I encountered the day before.

They were in Peralta's jail now, wearing stripes and eating green baloney. But a fleeting hope that they might somehow be connected to the old FBI badge—what with the one scumbag's comment about taking and selling Kate's badge—had led to nothing. They were ordinary drug dealers and low-life generalists seeking whatever criminal opportunity presented itself. So we were still nowhere on the investigation. The medical examiner was behind on autopsies and cranky, so we didn't even know if the old guy in the pool was a homicide. My request to see the FBI file on John Pilgrim's death was somewhere in the outer rings of bureaucratic perdition. There was nothing to do but turn off our pagers and cell phones and go to a baseball game.

When the game ended in triumph, we spilled out with the crowd, down the big escalators, past the murals with scenes of Arizona, past the dedication to the People of Maricopa County. That was when two burly uniformed deputies intercepted us.

"You David and Lindsey Mapstone?"

I asked what the problem was.

"Sheriff Peralta needs you in Scottsdale immediately."

I started to protest, but they were already hustling us into a service elevator. "We'll drive you," one said.

"We couldn't reach you on pager, sir," his partner said.

"Can't I just call Peralta on the phone?" I asked.

"No, sir. He was very specific. He wants us to bring you."

"What's in Scottsdale?"

"I don't know, sir. We were just told to bring you."

I tried to imagine what was on Peralta's mind. The sheriff's personal security detail cost the taxpayers of Maricopa County more than a quarter of a million dollars a year. So much for the *High Noon* sheriff making a lonely stand. So I could see him going to extravagant lengths to lasso me, if I had given fresh cause for annoyance. But I had duly updated him on the nowhere status of the Pilgrim case, and endured his amusement and critique of the fight with the drug dealers beneath the overpass. This errand was surpassing strange.

As we drove east on the Red Mountain Freeway using emergency lights, I knew this was no Peralta highjinks. Lindsey knew before me. She had fallen into a watchful silence that was so Lindsey. We sat on the slick vinyl of the backseat, closed in behind the prisoner screen, behind two silent deputies. She held my hand tightly. The city slipped by, the lights of three million people. The lights of airliners taking off and landing from Sky Harbor. The lights of the squad car reflecting off the freeway underpasses. City of lights. In the hot and smoggy ugly seasons, when we were short of spectacular sunsets and clear mountain views, nighttime favored Phoenix. Exit signs to the Piestewa Freeway north, the Chinese Cultural Center, Papago Park, and downtown Tempe. The Papago Buttes looming in the twilight. We rejoined the street grid at Rural Road, kicked in the siren, and headed north into Scottsdale.

"Dave, I have a bad feeling," Lindsey said.

Her premonition hardened as we came up Scottsdale Road and turned east on Fifth Avenue, winding around the Galleria. A ribbon of flashing red, orange, and blue lights waited at the end of the street. The deputies cut out the siren and coasted past the bland single-story buildings that contained, among other establishments, a bar called the Martini Ranch.

Lindsey said quietly, "Oh, no." She checked her ankle holster, which discreetly held her baby Glock semiautomatic. Her blue eyes seemed to have turned an intense black. I felt a deep dread in my middle. Peralta's face loomed in the window.

"Where the fuck have you been?" he demanded. He was wearing black jeans and a long Guayabera shirt, supernaturally white.

"We went to the D-Backs," I said as we emerged from the backseat. "I didn't know I had to clear my movements with you." The night was warm and dry. Crime scene tape was festooned along the street. Peralta lasered me with his expression.

"I got two cops dead here, smart-ass," he said. "From here on, your movements belong to me."

We followed him past a row of parked cars and SUVs, through a cordon of khaki-clad Scottsdale cops. Bright TV lights flooded us from across the street.

I heard Lindsey's voice catch in her throat. Beyond the car bumpers, a couple of tarps barely concealed two bodies and a lot of blood, congealed on the hot sidewalk. One of the bodies was wearing cowboy boots, the other sneakers. The feet of the dead were splayed at strange, sudden angles. Lindsey bent down and examined both bodies. They were men in their thirties. One had a flamboyant red beard. The other was clean-cut, bald-headed, and boyish. Both were marred with multiple wounds and blood. Lindsey gave me a stricken look. I was not the cop. I was the husband. I came up behind her, put my hands on her shoulders, and pulled her back to me.

"What...?" she began.

She lunged toward Peralta. "Why aren't the paramedics here!" she demanded, her hands outstretched. "Why aren't you doing CPR?"

He shook his head. She looked over the bodies again and then sagged against me. I walked her a little ways down the sidewalk. Peralta followed us.

"Talk to me, Lindsey," he said.

She stared out at the night, the streetlights gleaming in her tears. "The guy with the beard is named Jim Britton. He's with Treasury. The other one is Gary Reece, Department of Justice." She looked at me. "They worked with me on the credit card case. They were part of the task force."

"What were they doing here?" Peralta demanded, his big head leaning in to face her.

"They were celebrating," she said. "They invited me to have a drink tonight. I turned them down because Dave and I had tickets…"

Peralta muttered profanities and walked to his black Ford Crown Victoria. He popped the trunk, dug around inside, and walked back with something in his hand. He held out a flak vest to Lindsey.

"Put this on," he said.

She hesitated. "You think it's a hit?" she asked.

Peralta was silent. Lindsey stared at him. She said, "You think this is the Russian mafia?"

Peralta stared at the sidewalk. "I don't know what I think. But I don't want to take chances. Scottsdale cops have some witnesses inside. They said the victims were at a table inside when another dude comes in and joins them. The conversation gets a little loud. Britton and Reece pay and get up to go. Next thing anybody remembers there's gunfire like this is a war zone. When somebody gets up the nerve to look outside, these two are dead on the sidewalk and whoever did it is gone."

"Do we have a description on the third man?" she asked. Peralta shook his head.

She slipped the vest over her T-shirt and fastened the Velcro. I glanced uneasily around Scottsdale's little downtown office district. A crowd of yuppies and beautiful people was being kept at a distance by SPD. They couldn't see the bodies lying this side of the parked cars.

I could see bullet holes gouged into the white paint of one Chevy Suburban, the shattered glass of a Toyota parked beside it, and more bullet holes chipped into the wall of the bar. A lot of bullet holes. I had counted to thirty holes when I heard Peralta's voice again.

"Where the hell is your firearm?" he growled.

"I don't take it to baseball games. Sorry.'

He just worked his heavy jaw and shook his head slowly. "Mapstone, do you have any idea how much…"

"Shit!" Lindsey yelled. "What about Rachel?!"

Peralta just stared at her.

"Rachel Pearson!" Lindsey said. "Deputy Rachel Pearson. She works for you in Cybercrimes. She was invited tonight. Has anybody seen her?"

Peralta shrugged. "I guess she didn't come tonight, like you."

"She said she was going to come."

Alarm flickered briefly across Peralta's face. He stabbed a thick finger into my chest. "Stay here." He disappeared into the bar.

Lindsey looked at me, and we followed him inside. The room was dark and comforting, with an old Bonnie Raitt song on the sound system. "'Push comes to shove'," Bonnie sang. In this old watering hole I had salved a hundred bad days, lubricated a hundred entertaining evenings. But I had no appetite for a drink. We stood on the threshold. Nearby, Peralta conferred with a Scottsdale police captain, then turned to a pair of civilians, clad in the expensive Euro-trash outfits of Scottsdale's trendy needy wealthy. The conversation grew more animated. Two young Scottsdale cops ran past us out the door. Peralta noticed us, and walked heavily to the top of the stairs.

"It's a new scenario," he said grimly. "The female officer may be missing. Those witnesses remember a woman who went out to the street with the men. Nobody's seen her since the shots were fired."

Chapter Seven

"We need to talk."

Peralta turned to face us. We were sitting in the backseat of Chief Deputy Kimbrough's ford Expedition. Kimbrough was driving and Peralta was talking. It was a lot of departmental brass to be shoved into one SUV.

Peralta said again, "We need to talk. Lindsey, did you hear of any threats, anything at all?"

"No," she said. "Where are we going?"

"Around," Peralta said.

"He doesn't want to have to deal with Scottsdale PD and the feds," Kimbrough said, gently grinning, making a half turn to look at us. The chief deputy was wearing a khaki summer suit already, a bad omen for a gentle spring. But, as usual, he carried it off beautifully. The suit was set off with a starched white shirt and abstract pattern blue bow tie that somehow all complemented the rich dark chocolate color of his skin. We were driving north on Scottsdale Road doing the speed limit. Cars and trucks howled impatiently past us.

"I don't want to be screwing around in public if somebody's trying to kill Lindsey," Peralta said. "Better to be mobile."

"You think that's what this is?" I asked, a worry pain stabbing me at the bottom of my breastbone.

"How the hell would I know, Mapstone? It's a damned strange coincidence if this wasn't a hit. We shut down the Russian mob's big profit engine. So they retaliate. Why else would somebody take out two feds, working for two separate agencies?"

"And," Kimbrough said, "do it with that kind of firepower. I thought we won the Cold War? How the hell did the Russian mafia get to Phoenix?"

"It's a global economy,' I said. "More people on the move around the world than anytime in history. It's all because we won the Cold War."

"Thank you, professor," Peralta grumbled. "But you'd think these Reds would stand out like a sore thumb here. I can even spot the people who just rolled in from Iowa."

"You guys should get out more," I said. "I hear Russian spoken by customers at Safeway."

"That's 'cause you live in the 'hood," Kimbrough said, grinning broadly. "I'm sorry, the historic districts."

"You're just jealous," Lindsey said.

To break the tension, I decided to needle Peralta a little. "To continue the lesson," I said. He let out a groan. "There are some school districts in Phoenix where more than one hundred languages are spoken."

"I can't even get most deputies to learn Español," Peralta sighed.

"And," I added, "the Russians have been in the Salt River Valley a long time. I think the first big group came around 1911, to work in the sugar beet fields in Glendale."

"What about Rachel?" Lindsey said, drumming her long, slender fingers on the tops of her thighs. Kimbrough said officers had checked Rachel's apartment in Chandler, called her mother in Prescott, tracked down her boyfriend, who was on a business trip to Las Vegas. Scottsdale PD had done a search on foot over a ten-square-block area around the Martini Ranch. Nobody knew where she was.

"They've got her…" Lindsey said, her voice flat.

Peralta faced front and everyone fell into silence. Resorts and restaurants flashed past, the pleasure provinces of movie stars, corporate titans and the anonymous extremely wealthy.

The lights of mountainside mansions twinkled at us from a safe distance. The police radio kept up a steady conversation about mayhem around the county. I half listened to it, and remembered the only time I met Rachel Pearson.

It was an after-work party at Portland's restaurant, and Lindsey brought some of her colleagues from the Sheriff's Office Cybercrimes Bureau. One was a young woman with a pleasant smile, golden brown hair, and a long hippie-retro dress. Rachel talked about her favorite restaurants in Cincinnati, where her family lived and she was raised. I would have imagined her as a schoolteacher or social worker, not a cop. Rachel said Phoenix had no soul.

Like Lindsey, Rachel was a sworn deputy who specialized in computer crime—in Rachel's case, she had an aptitude for spotting the security weaknesses of large, corporate and governmental computer systems. So if Yuri's mobsters had kidnapped her, they had a valuable asset. Here was a woman who could tell them how the task force had defeated their credit card scheme. She could tell them how the joint task force worked, maybe allow them into law enforcement computer systems. I didn't imagine they would ask her politely. And that was only the start of the horrors one could imagine. Car lights flashed across the dark streets. She was out there somewhere. And we were blind and powerless to help her.

"We should have anticipated this," Peralta said. He swung sideways in his seat, facing Kimbrough and then turning his big head in our direction to make the point. "I've talked to the FBI and other agencies. There were thirty members of the task force around the country, including the four in Phoenix. The others are safe. We're going to arrange for protective custody.'

I looked at Lindsey. She said, "I don't look good in pink jail jumpsuits, Sheriff."

He didn't smile.

"We have safe houses," Kimbrough said. "We're arranging for one now."

Something on the back of my neck tightened. "Slow down," I said. "We can't just go into hiding. You"—I nodded toward Peralta—"never ran away from anybody who threatened you."

"This is different," Peralta said, staring out at the traffic, shaking his head slowly. His eyes looked like polished black stones. "Can you remember the last time a cop was kidnapped? Kidnapped! Christ! And she's more a technician than a cop, just sitting in front of a computer screen. No offense, Lindsey. I know you've been a real deputy…"

Lindsey faced away, her dark pin-straight hair brushing her collar.

"Bad guys don't play by the rules," Peralta said, his deep voice seeming to make the windows hum with a tuning fork echo. "But when the bad guys start snatching cops out of public places, we've got a new ballgame. The old Sicilian Mafia wouldn't have dared kidnap a cop. Even that dirtball Bobby Hamid wouldn't do this…"

As Peralta spoke, I watched the upscale shopping strips and the gated housing developments slide by the window, all seeming so look-alike safe. But one of the September 11th hijackers had lived briefly in Scottsdale. It was a good place for people with money who wanted to be left alone, who didn't want to know their neighbors or to be known. Hell, Yuri could be right behind that ornate faux-Spanish gate.

Peralta continued, "These Russians are on the offensive. They don't follow any of the old rules. We can't take the chance of Lindsey getting killed. Or captured. Everybody who worked on the task force is being moved to safety right now."

"You guys can't go home," Kimbrough said. "Not even for a change of clothes."

"How long?" Lindsey asked.

"Two weeks, maybe longer," Kimbrough said. "Depends on how quickly we can find Yuri and take him out."

"I have an old cat," she said. Her voice seemed suddenly tired. "He can't be left alone."

"We'll send deputies for him," Kimbrough said.

"My garden," she said quietly.

"Where is this safe house?" I asked.

"We have several," Kimbrough said.

"Do the taxpayers of Maricopa County know this?"

He just smiled.

"One is up on the highway north of Wickenburg," Peralta said. "We've stashed a few witnesses there before. But it's too far away from the cavalry if there's trouble. I have someplace else in mind."

"Well, this FBI badge thing can certainly wait," I said. "Nothing's happening anyway. We don't even know if it's a homicide."

"No," Peralta said, facing me. "You're going to stay on that case. It's important."

"Working from a safe house? OK, you're the boss."

"No," Peralta said again. "You need to get out in the field and find out what the hell happened to that badge and how it ended up with some homeless guy."

The inside of the SUV was instantly claustrophobic. Peralta said, "I can't have you coming and going from the safe house. The Russkies might follow you. If they can find these guys out for a drink in Scottsdale, they can sure as hell track that gigantic Oldsmobile you drive. Kimbrough can give you a voucher for a motel or whatever."

"I'm not leaving Lindsey," I said.

Peralta ignored me and started giving Kimbrough instructions on securing the departmental computer systems. I looked over at my lover, encased in her flak vest. An intense chill ran around my neck.

"Hey," I said, louder. "I'm not leaving Lindsey alone."

Everyone went silent. She held my hand. Her hand was warm and seemed small.

"David," Kimbrough said, "this is just for a couple of weeks."

"This is bullshit. You guys worked on this case for months and you never found Yuri. What are two weeks going to change?

There is no way I am going two weeks or two hours without knowing she's safe."

"Results, Mapstone," Peralta said. "I want results on your case."

"My case has been open for more than half a century!" I argued. "It can wait a few more weeks."

"It's the murder of a federal agent," Peralta said, "in my jurisdiction."

Lindsey said, "I want my husband with me. If they came after me, they might come after him."

Peralta said quietly, "It's an order, Mapstone."

"Then I want to take vacation," I said. "Now."

"You don't get vacation," Peralta said. "You're a consultant."

"I just got back from taking vacation time!"

"Then why do you want another vacation?"

I was getting angrier, rowing into a dangerous estuary with Peralta. It was too late to turn back, and I damned well didn't want to. I said, "I quit."

Kimbrough snorted, then fell silent. I saw his eyes in the rearview mirror, looking intently at me, telegraphing caution.

Finally, Peralta said, "You can't quit."

"What, and miss all this fun?" I said. "Not to mention the big salary and benefits. The generous vacation time. I quit."

"You can't quit, Mapstone," Peralta said. "That's an order, too."

Kimbrough said, "You're a former sheriff, Mapstone. You have to set an example."

"I was acting sheriff for a month," I said. "I'm not leaving Lindsey."

Peralta turned to face me full on. The pores of his face seemed blackened with rage. Then swiveled and faced forward, I imagined the anger rippling the muscles of his thick neck. Kimbrough drove around the landscaped perimeter of the Scottsdale Princess. Inside the hotel, rich people were fucking, drinking, snorting coke, bragging to their mistresses and minions, sweating out the latest SEC investigation. Fifteen miles away, around downtown, the homeless camps were settling down for the night. Inside the black cabin of the Expedition, the radio once again broadcast a BOLO for Rachel Pearson. I was being sensible, I told myself. No way was I going to be away from Lindsey if she was in danger. And I was being bratty—I had already been away from her two weeks, time when my friend was dying and I could only think of being in the shelter of her arms.

"How about this," Kimbrough said suddenly. "David goes to the safe house with Lindsey. But he continues to work the FBI badge case, too. We can get him a second car, and a transfer point. The transfer point is a garage that's secluded, maybe attached to an apartment. So it makes sense for him to be going there. When he leaves the safe house, he makes sure nobody is following him, then drives to the transfer point and gets in his car to drive to the office. When he quits at the end of the day, he drives his car back to the transfer point—again, making sure nobody's on his tail—changes to the second car, and drives back to Lindsey."

It sounded OK to me. Peralta didn't make a sound. The thick roll of flesh at the back of his neck tensed and rippled.

"Xray Two, Xray Two." We all responded to the dispatcher's voice. Xray Two was Kimbrough's call sign.

"Xray Two," Kimbrough said into the microphone.

"Xray Two," said a cool female voice, "Chandler PD is responding to the Price Freeway at Ray Road, southbound lanes. A report of a female subject being thrown from a car or jumping from a car."

Lindsey squeezed my hand until it started to ache.

The dispatcher continued, "Witness on a cell phone says the female subject has MCSO identification. PD and paramedics are en route now."

Chapter Eight

Phoenix is less a city than a 1,500-square-mile collection of real estate ventures connected by city streets that have been widened into highways. When people say Phoenix has no soul, they're really referring to this incoherent sprawlburg. From the mid-1950s until the bubble burst in the great real estate crash of 1990, the developers built skyscrapers along a five-mile length of Central Avenue. All this speculation took place a mile north of the city's old downtown core, so some projects were called "midtown" and others farther north became "uptown." The city finally sought to put a sheen of bureaucratic respectability on the mess and called the entire area the Central Corridor.

Take all the skyscrapers and concentrate them, and Phoenix would have as impressive a skyline as any American city outside New York or Chicago. But Phoenix was built by land speculators, not great city planners. So it ended up with a narrow strand of tall buildings running for miles north to south along Central. After 1990, the real estate boys abandoned the corridor for fresh speculative baubles in North Scottsdale and the East Valley. The result was that the heart of the city, after business hours Monday through Friday, became one of the quietest places in the urban West.

There's a coral-colored, High Modernism condo tower that sits right in the middle of the corridor. Del Webb built it in the mid-1950s, when he was just a small-town Phoenix builder, and for decades it sat quietly as the city grew up around it. The tower flares off in an X-shaped floor plan with balconies and Bauhaus-inspired slab overhangs. It's right at the foot of Cypress Street, not two blocks from our house. And that's where Peralta stashed us, on the eighth floor. The place was expensively furnished, with large colorful abstract paintings on the wall. "A friend of the sheriff lets us use this place when he's in Europe," Kimbrough had said, Must be nice to have such friends. So after a weekend of deputies bringing over some necessities from home, Lindsey and I had done our best to settle into this odd "safe house." Other deputies, officers with training in special weapons and tactics, had replaced the retired gentlemen who acted as concierges at the entrance to the building downstairs.

I felt uncomfortable sleeping in a stranger's bed. Lindsey had bad dreams, She would wake up sure she was hearing the fighter jets that had protected the city in the days after September 11th I couldn't hear them. Lindsey was a walking array of high-charged senses. After I settled her down and felt her breathing become regular with sleep, I would swing out of bed and pad over to the huge windows I would watch the sparse traffic on Central, the little blocks of lights in the skyscrapers as the cleaning crews worked. Police choppers darted through the metropolitan sky like large fireflies. On clear nights, I could see the jagged black outline of the Sierra Estrella, for the bedroom faced southwest. For days, a hot wind came up in the late afternoon and forced the smog out.

Rachel Pearson had died beside a suburban freeway, out amid the endless red-tile-roof tract houses and shopping strips of Tuscan-themed fakery. The detectives figured she had come out of a vehicle that was doing at least one hundred miles per hour. By the time we got there, she was covered with a yellow tarp. But I couldn't avoid seeing what looked like skid marks of blood and tissue left as the body hurtled down the oily, ribbed concrete, Smashed wire eyeglasses sat another seventy-five feet south, against a noise wall. Evidence technicians methodically marked everything with small red flags. The shoulder of the free-way was a poppy field of small red flags. Lindsey was convinced that Rachel had jumped. "She fought them," Lindsey had said. "She knew she didn't have a chance if she stayed in the car."

Law officers came from around the state for Rachel's funeral. Lindsey wasn't allowed to leave the condo.

〈〉〈〉〈〉

Peralta demanded that I work. I dreaded leaving Lindsey alone. But she kept her Glock on her belt, and an M-4 carbine, checked out from the sheriff's armory, just inside the front door. So on Monday I began my new routine, one I repeated every morning and evening. I drove a commandeered white Crown Vic from the condo tower's underground parking garage to the new Roosevelt Square apartments near downtown. They had a big parking garage, so I could wind my way to the top floor and swap the Vic for my yellow drug dealer's Oldsmobile. The entire trip was made in curlicues and backtracks on the charming streets and alleys of Willo and the Roosevelt and Story historic districts. No one appeared to be following me.

Peralta had forbidden me to drive by the house on Cypress, but of course I did, first thing Monday morning. The trumpet vines and oleanders were starting to bloom and soon the palm trees would need trimming. There was a contractor's van in the driveway that I knew held several well-armed deputies.

Finally, at my high-ceilinged office on the fourth floor of the old county courthouse, I had set to work on the case of FBI Special Agent John Pilgrim.

My mind was still on Friday night, on the dangers of the here and now. My desktop reinforced it, with an *Arizona Republic* sitting faceup, the lead headline shouting, COPS AMBUSHED, and, on a smaller deck, COMPUTER SLEUTHS TARGETED BY RUSSIAN MOB. The Scottsdale shooting had pushed aside the usual Phoenix menu of hit-and-runs, child drowning, dysfunctional state government, and real estate news.

I had to force my mind back to ancient history, the previous Thursday, when a homeless man had been found in a green pool in Maryvale, and sewn in his jacket had been the FBI badge of dead agent Pilgrim. A case that happily was ignored by the local news media.

I set up some basics that would help me tell the history of John Pilgrim, interpret it, maybe understand it. I wheeled over the large combination bulletin board and chalkboard to stand by my desk. On the bulletin board, I posted an index card for each player in the case—for now, John Pilgrim and the home-less John Doe. One part of my task would be to increase those cards, On the blackboard, I started a timeline with November 10, 1948, the day Pilgrim's body was found. I ended the time-line on April 1, 2004, the day the body was found in the pool. Another task was to fill in the dates between. Maybe they were silly tasks. I needed tasks.

Monday was a records day. From the county's deep-storage archives, I checked out or copied everything I could get my hands on regarding the Pilgrim case, and crime in general in 1948. There was actually a sizable Pilgrim file because the body had been found in what was then county jurisdiction. It was all joyous, tactile paper. Files made decades before databases, web browsers, and personal computers. But I noted numerous blank file spacers where reports should have been, a black-ink stamp saying simply "removed by FBI." Other reports contained pages that had been blacked out, "redacted" in the legal language.

Then I braced myself for a confrontation with Kate Vare and went to Phoenix PD records. Kate was not in her cubicle in the Criminal Investigation Division, so my day got better. The PD records clerk was cooperative and friendly, and my rucksack of records grew.

Back at my office, armed with a Starbucks mocha, I began to read and make notes. By the end of the day, here were some of the things I knew:

John Pilgrim was thirty-eight years old. He had been an FBI agent for twelve years. He hadn't served in the war. A photo of him showed a rather round-faced man with thin lips and dark hair. An earnest, serious face. A delicate long nose. I posted the photo on the bulletin board. Pilgrim had been born in Lexington, Kentucky, and had a law degree from the University of Kentucky. He would have been one of the new breed of professional, degreed agents around which J. Edgar Hoover built the FBI somewhere in the 1930s. Pilgrim was posted to Phoenix in the spring of 1947.

Pilgrim was found floating in an irrigation canal in the late afternoon of Nov. 10, 1948. A farm worker there to let water into some lettuce fields found the body. I posted a city map on the bulletin board and marked where the body was found: near the present-day intersection of Fifty-first Avenue and Thomas. It was half a mile from where the homeless man would fall into the pool half a century later. What the hell did that mean? The landscape had changed from farms to suburbia to the new melting pot. I made a note to find a map of the old canal system.

I read the narrative of the lead county detective, typed on flimsy paper with a cockeyed "T" key. Pilgrim's body was wearing a suit and tie. He artfully declined to mention the badge, or the gun, for that matter. The condition of the body made the investigators believe it had floated quite a distance. Pilgrim was last seen alive two days before, November 8, by his partner, Agent Renzetti. Pilgrim told Renzetti he was going to work late that night, running down a lead. The report didn't mention the nature of the lead.

I paged through the detective's notebooks, handwriting in blue ink, and set them aside for later. The dust from the old files made me sneeze.

The coroner's report, a Photostat with white type blaring out of black background, said Pilgrim had one gunshot wound to the heart. He was dead when his body went into the water. The bullet was a .38 caliber. This report was heavily censored, whole paragraphs wiped out like a landscape in a snowstorm. But they hadn't removed the last page. I held it in my fingers for at least a full minute. I can't tell you if I was breathing or not. For at the bottom of the coroner's report was the signature, Philip Mapstone.

My grandfather.

My grandfather had been a dentist, and he had died in 1977. And as to what his signature was doing on a line that said "coroner," I had not a clue. When I talked to Peralta on Tuesday, he said it probably didn't mean anything. The old coroner system, which predated the science and professionalism of medical examiners, was very informal, and a coroner's jury might be led by a lawyer, an ordinary citizen, a medical doctor, even a dentist. Whatever the reason, the Pilgrim case suddenly grew personal. I didn't like it.

On Tuesday I received a gift. The medical examiner's office reported that the homeless man had died of apparently natural causes. Kate Vare sent me a suspiciously friendly e-mail that morning, saying she was taking herself off the case. I wasn't sure she could just do that. She was a cold case expert and this was not just cold but freezing. But I wasn't going to argue. She was needed on the case of the missing teenage girl. The abduction had several disturbing similarities to cases in the 1980s, and Kate said she would be working on analyzing those links. In the '80s, two girls in their young teens were taken from their parents' houses in well-to-do north Phoenix neighborhoods. They were raped and murdered, and the cases were never solved. Now another girl was missing. The media were going berserk. I overcame my mistrust of Kate's sharp features, and wished her well.

The homeless man had died of natural causes and then some. Although he suffered a massive heart attack before falling into the pool, he was also dying of lung cancer, congestive heart failure, and untreated diabetes. The medical examiner speculated the man had "coded out" on the edge of the pool and tumbled in headfirst. It wasn't a homicide. It was just very damned strange. And whether he was murdered or not, my case was still alive because of the FBI badge sewn into his jacket. When I briefed Peralta and Eric Pham, they agreed I should continue on the case alone. I reminded Pham that the bureau still owed me access to the Pilgrim records, and he said he'd make another call to his bosses to get me clearance.

For now, the Pilgrim case was mine.

Chapter Nine

That evening, I walked on a sidewalk laid down in 1948. I had walked on it a hundred times, going from my office in the old court-house to the county lot where I parked. But this time I noticed the date chiseled into the concrete block I wondered if Special Agent John Pilgrim had walked this sidewalk when it was new. I thought about the world of John Pilgrim in Phoenix in 1948. Men wore suits, ties, and hats, even when not at work. Women were rare in offices and factories, even though the war had added to their numbers. The diversity we take for granted in any American city and town in the early twenty-first century was not found in Pilgrim's Phoenix. It was an overwhelmingly Anglo place, with the blacks and Mexicans "kept in their place." Society was similarly fixed, men worked, women raised children, everyone married, and roles were clear. Authority still meant something, ruling with a combination of respect and fear. For entertainment, people went to movies and listened to radio; only a few well-off families could afford the new televisions. A middle-class family owned one car, not three or four. But the mode of travel preferred by most Americans was still the train, with the new streamliners promising more luxury than ever. And Phoenix—it was little more than a big town, instead of America's fifth largest city. John Pilgrim's world, America a mere half century ago, seemed more foreign than some distant historical epoch.

Those were the musings that took me to the parking lot, to the back of the Oldsmobile.

I sensed movement behind me. Even though I had been carrying the Colt Python in a nylon holster on my belt, I felt nauseatingly vulnerable. I'm sure I visibly jumped.

"I'm not going to hurt you, mister."

"I know," I said, pride quickly replacing terror. The Russian mafia had not fallen on such hard times that they had sent a bag lady to kill the husband of their nemesis, the brilliant Lindsey Faith Mapstone.

The woman must have been concealed by some of the vans and SUVs nearby. I leaned against the car door and took her in: straight, dirty blond hair; broad, sunburned face; a stocky, medium-height body Throw her in a shower, dress her differently, and put her in a minivan in Chandler, and she might be mistaken for a soccer mom. If you didn't look too closely. Someone had knocked one of her teeth out. Her tan was raw and uneven. The collar of her T-shirt was filthy.

I don't have any money," I said, and started to get in the car.

"I don't go hitting up cops," she said. But she didn't move on. She just stood there, watching me.

She said, "You were looking for *Weed*."

I stopped, gently reclosed the door, and faced her.

"They said at the shelter you were looking for Weed," the woman said. "Two cops, a woman and a man. They said the man was tall and looked like a schoolteacher, and he drove this big yellow Olds 442."

David Mapstone, the master of concealment.

"You know Weed?" I asked.

She folded her arms tightly around her breasts, causing them to balloon out beneath the faded purple T-shirt. "I hang out with him sometimes."

"Around here?"

"He liked the deck park," she said. Margaret Hance Park, which sat above the freeway a mile north of us, and was home to festivals, joggers, sunbathers, and drug dealers. "We'd sit there by the library. I like to read books."

"Was Weed a nickname?"

She shook her head. "I don't know. It was just his name. What's your name?"

"David," I said. "David Mapstone."

"I'm Karen," she said. "You're a cop, right?"

"I'm a deputy." I asked her what she could tell me about him.

"He was nice to me. I've been on the streets four years now. He helped me find food, a place to sleep that was safe. He'd share cigarettes. We'd talk."

"Any idea where he was from? How long he'd been living on the streets?"

"He had family in California, I think. Somebody told me he had been in the Navy. He never said much about himself." She kept her arms clasped tightly and tilted slowly from side to side. She asked, "What are you looking for him for?"

I looked behind her into the blue-black of the western sky. We had been deprived of spectacular fiery sunsets for months. Even so, the sky seemed supernaturally large over our heads, the dry air conducting light intensely but with none of the velvety intimacy of the sky back east. Over Karen's shoulder, the downtown towers still glowed from the last of the sun.

"Weed is dead," I said. "He died last week. We're trying to find next of kin, or anybody who knew him."

Her eyes widened for several seconds. "Shit!" she whispered, stamping the gravel. "You got a smoke"

I shook my head.

Her shoulders suddenly sagged. She stared at the ground.

"He never hurt anybody." She licked her chapped lips. "Somebody finally killed him."

"What makes you think somebody killed him?" I asked.

"What, you live on the streets and you expect to die a natural death? I don't think so. Not in this town. I've been in county hospital so many times, beaten up, robbed, raped, anything they think they can do to me. You cops figure I got it coming to me because I'm homeless. People in this town will kill you for five dollars."

I couldn't argue the point. After a moment, I prompted, "Tell me more about Weed."

"Did he have his jacket?" she asked suddenly.

I nodded.

"I always thought he might get robbed and killed for that jacket."

I asked her why.

"He had something sewn inside it," she said, her eyes wide and gray. "I never knew what the hell it was, but he was sure protective, and secretive. He wore that jacket every day, even when it was the hottest day in August. One time, I felt something in there. Something sewn into the lining. When he caught me, he just went crazy. Slapped me down."

"What do you think was in it?" I asked.

"Maybe jewelry," she said. She added, "From his old life maybe."

"Which was?"

She shook her head. "He never said. I never asked." She rubbed her eyes. "Shit," she said. "Poor Weed. I hadn't seen him in days, and when I heard you were looking for him..."

"Did he ever mention the name John Pilgrim?"

She shook her head.

"What's your last name?" I asked.

"I'm Karen. I told you."

"Just Karen."

"Yeah," she said, suddenly sullen. She turned and walked away.

"Karen," I called. "What if we need to talk to you again?"

"You don't need me," she said. "When I came to find you, I thought maybe if I told you about Weed, you might help me, too. Maybe you could talk to the caseworker and let me see my daughter."

"Maybe I can," I said, feeling uncomfortable, like a cop in the middle of a family dispute.

"Bullshit," she said. "Weed is dead. Life is fucked up. I can't get off the streets. You don't care."

I let her go. Whatever had impelled her to seek me out was now evaporated.

I called to her as she walked: "How can I talk to social services if I don't know your last name, or your daughter's name?"

No answer.

I watched her become a shadow against the streetlights. But then I heard her voice.

"The Reverend knew Weed," she called. "You should talk to the Reverend."

"Who is the Reverend?" I yelled. "Where can I find him?" She yelled back an address. It wasn't in the nice part of town.

Chapter Ten

The next day, Wednesday, I locked the car and walked across an empty lot strewn with glass. The angle of the sun made the ground appear covered with diamonds or something precious. The glass crunched softly and dust stirred by my step covered the toes of my shoes. As I got closer to the bleached, one-story block building, I could see less an entrance than a void. In the middle of the white wall was a dark square where double doors might close. But there were no doors. I could only see the darkness of whatever lay beyond the bright sunshine of the outside. I pulled off my sunglasses and stepped inside. Under my feet, the dirt was replaced by concrete.

I stopped maybe five feet inside and let my eyes adjust. The space around me felt large and smelled of dust and sweat. A persistent breeze came from a large fan built into a far wall. The fan went to another room, or to the outside, and provided the only light source, a far moon with fan blades turning slowly. It created a foul-smelling breeze. As my vision extended, I realized the room was very large and people were all around me.

They lined the walls, and sat in clusters out on the floor of what was once some kind of warehouse. My cop side kicked in and I counted: five, ten, at least twenty people I could see, probably more. They stared at me with faces ruined by the sun and streets. Or they paid no attention. The room was very quiet. I spoke to the person nearest to me, an old woman sitting in a muddy wheelchair, her fat encased like sausage in a Phoenix Suns T-shirt.

"I'm looking for the Reverend," I said.

She ignored me.

I looked around for anyone in charge. Any structure to the room. I only felt eyes. On me.

I remembered from my patrol deputy days how to roust someone. I remembered from my professor days how to reach a bored class of students. Neither seemed worth a damn in this place. I walked deeper into the room, asking again. Nobody answered me. They didn't seem to acknowledge I was there. The people were Anglos, Hispanic, Indian, black, mostly older, mostly dressed in dirty thrift store castoffs.

Then I felt a rough bump from behind. When I turned I was facing an anachronism.

Phoenix is a magnet for rough-hewn faces. Misfits, losers, con artists, ex-cons, desperate Okies and Oaxacans, second-chance Johnnies—they all end up here, as if the city is the last fence line catching the unattached debris of a windy world. I often imagine faces from the streets of Phoenix transported into primitive black-and-white photography of the Old West. You couldn't tell the difference. Only the clothes give away their place in time.

The man who stepped out of the gloom was about my height, but he wore a tall, sweat-stained cowboy hat. He had a lean, lined face harnessed in a waxed, black handlebar moustache. To complete the daguerreotype effect, his shirt, jeans, and even skin were all lighter and darker tones of sepia. Turn back the calendar a century and a half and he just stepped out of a cattle drive. The pleasing little historical anomaly was spoiled by his eyes. They were unnaturally blue, unsettlingly bright, wide spaced. The kind of eyes you imagined in nightmares, the last pair of eyes you saw before a violent death, O pioneers. Turn back the calendar and he just stepped out of a gunfight.

"You don't belong here," he intoned in an accentless voice.

My heart started hammering against my ribcage, but I lowered my voice and asked again for the Reverend.

He started to advance on me. I noticed his knuckles were bloody and deformed. Suddenly this errand seemed like a lousy idea. I took a step back and then another. I dropped back into a T position, my left foot pointed toward him, my right foot behind me turned at a right angle, my weight well balanced against any attempt to push me down. I felt the reassuring weight of the Python on my belt, and hoped I wouldn't have to start my day with a shooting.

"That's enough, Bill."

The big man halted and stared at me. I didn't want to take my eyes off him, but I glanced quickly in the direction of this new voice. It was coming from the darkened far end of the room.

"I'm looking for the Reverend," I called in that direction.

"Who the hell are you?" the voice demanded.

"I'm David Mapstone. I was hoping the Reverend could help me."

"Are you a cop?"

"I'm a sheriff's deputy," I said.

The room congealed again into silence. I could barely hear the fan turning. Then the voice told me to come to the back of the room. Bill made sure I found my way. Finally, I was presented before a broad-chested man wearing a white, open-collared shirt. A rough, dark cross hung around his neck with a leather strap. He was sitting at a folding card table lined up with white Styrofoam cups. The man shook a cup at me, put it in my hand.

"Ice," he said. "Ice is important."

His eyes were gigantic, and buttressed with deep sockets and soaring brows, high arched cheeks and strong nose, as if cathedral builders had constructed his face. Above a generous forehead, he combed lead-colored hair straight back. His skin was the color and texture of cordovan leather.

"Bill is right," he said. "You don't belong here. And I wonder if you're telling me the truth. You don't have cop's eyes."

I held out my ID and star, and he squinted at them across the rows of white cups.

"You look like a professor," he said.

"In another life," I said. "I'm looking for someone called the Reverend."

He stuck his large hands in his pockets and regarded me. "I was a pastor in another life," he said. "So for shorthand, they call me the Reverend. You can call me Quanah Card."

"You're Comanche?"

"No," he said. "Tohono O'odham. But my mother, she was a reader. She loved the stories of heroic Indians. And when I came along, she was reading about Quanah Parker."

"I'm looking for somebody, Reverend Card." I pulled out my Polaroid and a computer-generated sketch of the homeless man, perhaps nicknamed Weed. But Card looked at my cup of ice. He picked up another cup and handed it to Bill. Then he took a third cup and held it up to his full lips. He and Bill ate the ice, as if showing a primitive tribesman that it was safe to consume. I sucked on the ice. It felt like everything that room was not: cool, clean, and fresh.

"They would not give Jesus water on the cross, much less ice," Card said, a dreamy look in his eyes. "So you are a very blessed man, Deputy." Then he fixed them on me again. "How did you find this place?"

"A woman on the street," I said. "She said her name was Karen."

"Karen…" the Reverend said. "She's got a crack problem. On top of mental illness. She won't take her medicine."

He finished his ice and handed the cup to Bill, who went away. "It's a goddamned mess, this world." Card said. "What did you profess, Professor?"

"History."

"History," he repeated. "Well, David Mapstone, what do you know about the history of homelessness in America?"

I knew that if I let my natural impatience take over, I would get nowhere with the Rev. Quanah Card. So I said a little about hobos during the Depression, about the deinstitutionalization of the mentally ill in the 1970s, about how urban renewal tore down so much affordable housing. It was nothing brilliant, the kind of stuff I picked up from the Sunday *New York Times*. The homeless were without much of a voice in history, or so the faddish new historians would say. Dan Milton didn't have much use for fads.

"Very good, professor," Card said. "But you make it sound so goddamned nice and academic. Look around you. What do you see? Addicts. The mentally ill. People with HIV. The disabled. The elderly. Young runaways. The ones who live paycheck to paycheck, and then the paycheck is cut off. Weather's nice in Phoenix, so they come here. They hang out downtown, sleep behind billboards, camp down at the riverbed or beside the freeways. The kids go to Mill Avenue. The saddest of all come here."

As he talked, I pulled up a wobbly folding chair and sat at the table. He handed me another cup of ice, and I dutifully ate the crystals.

"I give them ice," he said. "It doesn't make them want to work a nine-to-five job, or take away the years of abuse and neglect, or end the hallucinations. I do what I can.

"They're not really like you and me," he went on. "That's why it's easier for society to abandon them. The homeless problem got worse under Reagan. Then it got worse again under Clinton. Here in Arizona, we refuse to fund social services, and the homeless haven't gone away and gotten jobs. Nobody knows what to do.

"And yet…" He swept his arm to take in the humanity seated and standing around us. "Christ is in them. 'Inasmuch as you have done it unto one of the least of these my brethren, you have done it unto me.'" He let his arm drop. "I don't mean to make you uncomfortable, Professor. Bible quoting is an occupational hazard where I come from."

"So this is your church?" I asked.

He laughed without humor, his huge eyes closing into slits of artificial mirth. "I was a United Methodist minister for thirty years," he said. "For the first five years, I was a street preacher in the Deuce. You know what that was?"

I nodded.

"I didn't feel like I did a damned bit of good. So I ended up pastoring rich, white churches—and they thought it was so god-damned exotic to have an Indian minister. 'Native American.' I could have been a bishop, but I couldn't stand the politics. Every Sunday, I'd try to get them to care about people like this. But I couldn't push too hard. That would have made people uncomfortable. Shit, thirty years. I felt like such a failure.

"So," he continued, "I took my savings and I bought this old warehouse. I open it every year from April through the end of October. It's the worst time of year to be on the street. I lean on some rich old bastards who owe me a favor to give a little money to keep it going."

"No soul saving?" I asked, trying to avoid falling out of the barely serviceable chair.

He narrowed his dark eyes, boring into me. "You believe in an unseen world, Mapstone?"

"Doesn't everybody?"

He snorted. "In my services, everybody prayed, 'Thy will be done.' But nobody wanted that. I want *my* damn will to be done. We don't want God loose in the world…That would scare the shit out of us."

He pulled out a cigarette and lit it, loudly drawing in the smoke. "When I was ordained, I was twenty-five years old and it was the happiest day of my life. I felt called, Mapstone." Card's face was remade with emotion. Canyons cut their way into his cheeks. His eye sockets deepened further. "I would preach the forgiveness of my Savior and Lord to penitent sinners. I would comfort the heartbroken and the dying."

He studied the orange tip of the cigarette and added, "I didn't know how perilous the borderlands would be…"

"Borderlands?"

He gave a sacramental wave of his Marlboro. "It's where we all live, Mapstone."

I cautiously asked about Weed.

"The old man with the Levi's jacket," he said, half to himself. "I haven't seen him in awhile. He used to come by here. Said his teeth hurt too much to take ice."

"Did you know his real name?"

"George was his first name," Card said. "George Weed. Mapstone, you lapsed into the past tense. Has something happened to our brother Weed?"

Chapter Eleven

Now I was armed. Armed with a name. I could do the thing that had allowed me to make a living in the years after I quit being a history professor: bring in new information on the county's most notorious unsolved cases. That history was written in names: Rebecca Stokes, my first big case, the woman who took a train home to Phoenix in 1959 and turned up dead in the desert. The Yarnell twins, the grandsons of a great rancher, kidnapped in the Great Depression and never found. Jonathan Ledger, the famous sex doctor who gave birth to the brave new world and ended up in a nasty drug deal and cop killing. In each case, I saw something the cops had missed, connected the dots in a different way, stumbled onto the fortunate clue. All from names that had found a bad end in Maricopa County.

Now I had a new name: George Weed. And an age, if what he told Card could be trusted: sixty-six. The data went with a man who had been coming to the Reverend's shelter for three summers. Sometimes he would sleep there three or four nights a week. Other times he might camp behind the rocks in the vacant land just outside the boundary of Hance Park. He didn't talk much. He never took off his jacket. One of the few things he told Card had stayed in his memory. "He said he was a native Phoenician," Card had told me. "There are so few of them, you almost never see that."

After I left Quanah Card, I drove to the sheriff's headquarters on Madison Street. I avoided Peralta's office until I had more to report. After the tension the week before in Scottsdale, it seemed better to avoid the sheriff for a while. My errand was to the computers, where I checked the local databases and the NCIC, the National Crime Information Computer. Even though the old vagrancy laws had been overturned in the '60s, someone living the life of George Weed could still have found dozens of ways to become a violator. Public drunkenness, trespassing, sleeping in a park after sundown, soliciting. Shoplifting was a favorite. Any of those and sundry other offenses could land a name in the system, never to be forgotten. A different database gave me county social services clients, whether for food stamps, health care, or the paltry mental health and drug and alcohol rehab programs. But George Weed was not in any of the databases.

Next I walked six blocks in the brilliant April sun to Phoenix Police Headquarters. Unmolested by Kate Vare, I spent two hours picking through other records, especially the field interrogation cards of the patrol officers. Here the information could be more haphazard, the continual budget shortfall cutting into the technology and clerical help necessary to make sense of hundreds of thousands of lower priority records. I found someone named Carlos Wong and a young man known only as Winston. But no George Weed. For someone who had been on the streets of Phoenix, who was carrying a stolen FBI badge, and was headed toward a bad end in an abandoned swimming pool, he had assiduously avoided the law.

Was that possible? I heard Dan Milton's voice in my head, warning against the limitations of governmental records, against the biases of observers. I was hearing his voice a lot. Back in Portland, toward the end, he had been so weak he couldn't hold up his head. Am I reporting the truth or betraying my friend to say he was close to raving the days before he died? The pain was so intense, his sense so keen that time was running out. Outside his window, the Oregon spring was gorgeous, mocking us all. He refused drugs, not wanting to lose time in a haze of pain medication.

I should have been wondering about the pain that brought George Weed to the abandoned pool in Maryvale. But my thoughts were too much still back in Portland. Anyone who expects the old to pass gently into that good night didn't know Dan Milton. He was angry with Plato, furious with Rousseau. His age-old antipathy for Lenin had not abated at all. "Ideas with a body count!" he shouted. Other times his voice would calm and his eyes regain some of their old gleam. "I don't want to go out a madman, like Wilson," he laughed. His head was nearly all skull, covered by a tent of sickly skin and the rough whiskers that wouldn't stop giving his face hope of fresh life. "It's a new dark age," he said at one point. "Nobody reads anymore. People are losing the ability to think. Television has destroyed us. I'm glad I won't live to see the worst of it."

When it hurt the worst, he would whisper through gritted teeth. That last night, I heard him whisper, "Drop by drop upon the heart." He had whispered it twice, from a pain-laced half drowse.

"What is that?" his young amour Kathleen had asked. She was holding his hand, wiping a cool cloth on his bony forehead.

I recalled Aeschylus: "In our sleep, pain that cannot forget falls drop by drop upon the heart, and in our own despair, against our will, comes wisdom to us by the awful grace of God."

His voice was still in my head when I went out to the county's records storage warehouse on Jefferson Street, a few blocks east of the baseball stadium. I avoided decades of property tax assessments, voter records, court documents, and jury rolls. Now I was playing hunches. Digging in cardboard boxes, shockingly un-state-of-the-art manila file folders and paper reports. Getting paper cuts, sneezing at the dust from the space age and the disco era. Exhuming microfiche reels from heavy metal cabinets and praying the old dried-out film wouldn't break in the creaky old reader. Taking chances in bottom drawers, in card files and leather-bound registers. After two more hours, just when I thought the Rev. Quanah Card had played me for a fool, I again picked up the trail of George Weed.

<>‹›‹>

That night I grabbed Thai takeout at Wild Thaiger. I swapped cars and made my circuitous way home, believing I could still smell the last sweet vestige of citrus blossoms in the streets of Willo. Then I slipped down into the underground garage of our hideaway and took the elevator past a watchful deputy to the eighth floor.

Lindsey was in the back bedroom, which had been converted into a home gym. She was in gray spandex, an oval sweat stain darkening the fabric from her breasts down to her belly. Her hair was pulled back in a ponytail, her fair skin was flushed, and she sat cross-legged on the floor. Her old tomcat, Pasternak, watched her from a chair. Liz Phair was coming out of the stereo, "Johnny Feelgood." Lindsey's fine head was lolled back against the wall. She was mouthing the lyrics and smoking, greedily inhaling from a cigarette.

"Sorry, Dave, you caught me."

I bent down and kissed her. Even in her smoking bouts, she had the sweetest breath. I noticed the pack on the floor, Gauloises Blondes. An indulgence she had picked up on our trip to Paris two years ago.

"How'd you get a deputy to find French cigarettes for you?"

"I asked nicely," she said. "Now I'm on the road to hell."

"I found the name of the homeless guy," I said, eager to share my triumph. "George Weed. A preacher knew him. Then I found he had a county hospital card from the 1980s. But he was hardly in the system at all."

"He couldn't escape my History Shamus," she said softly, a small smile.

"It doesn't tell us how an FBI badge ended up sewn into his coat," I said. "But it's a start." After a long silence, I said, "You're working out, at least."

"I'm going nuts, Dave." A long plume of smoke left her lips, on the way to the open window.

I had seen Lindsey smoke twice under pressure. Then she could stop again. It was a neat trick for a vice. I didn't smoke cigarettes, but I knew that wasn't because of moral greatness. It just wasn't one of the itches I couldn't scratch. Otherwise, my vices were my virtues. So I saved my judgments for major historical questions and tastes in different Mexican cuisines. Hell, I didn't know what I was missing—the sensual cigarette after sex, humanity's dance with death captured in a strange looking paper-wrapped consumer product, fire harnessed for our pleasure. We were all going to die—that was reinforced again by the fate of Dan Milton the health nut.

I took her hand, pulled her up, and walked her into the living room for another vice, a fine martini.

"I know you're bored," I said, once we were settled on a long, deep sofa that gave a magnificent view of the city and the Sierra Estrella.

"I'm shit," she said, her voice darkened with anger. "I'm a piece of shit."

"Because you're here?"

"Rachel's dead." She gulped her drink and lit another Gauloise. "I'm the one who told her she should loosen up and come to the party that night."

"It's not your fault," I said, too hastily perhaps. Her eyes drilled into me. I shut up and we watched a muted sunset accumulate over the mountains.

"I keep imagining what she must have been thinking going down that freeway," she continued. "She was a gentle nerd girl, not some hero type. But in a nanosecond, there she is, being dragged into a car by people who are capable of anything."

Lindsey studied the blue smoke drifting away to the window, and said in a low voice, "They were going to rape her. Then they were going to torture her."

"There's no point—" I began.

"You know what happens in the world," she said, a hard edge in her voice. "They were going to rape her. And if they didn't kill her, they'd sell her into slavery. You know that goes on. She'd end up drugged in some…place…in Russia or the Middle East, where an American girl is a prize. Then in a few years, she's worse than dead."

I sipped my drink and stroked her hand. It took me a minute to notice the tears filling her eyes.

"I miss my garden," she sobbed. "I miss seeing you in your library, and us reading to each other in bed. I miss our old life." I put my arm around her and pulled her close, feeling the warmth of her body through the thin fabric of the workout togs. I once favored fair-haired women just this side of voluptuousness. But Lindsey was dark-haired, long-limbed, and undeniably leggy. Her breasts were handful sized and perfectly shaped, which I could feel rubbing pleasantly against me. With my free hand, I took her cigarette and deposited it in an ashtray. She whispered, "Oh, baby, I'm afraid I've gotten us into something really bad."

Lindsey rarely called me "baby." She never called me "honey," much less "hon." Mostly, she called me Dave, as she had since we first met, and sometimes, with affection, she called me History Shamus. I called her Lindsey. My wife was kind and wise, smarter than her husband in most ways. She did not have a college degree, having escaped from her family to the military when she was eighteen and the PC revolution was taking off. I had enough degrees for the whole family.

Lindsey managed her demons with a discipline that made it seem effortless. But I knew her better than most people. She had been born in 1968 to hippie parents, had been forced to raise herself, had seen her mother destruct under schizophrenia. This made her afraid to have children, which was OK with me—I didn't handle noise and chaos well. But she didn't believe me, knowing I was an only child, the last of my line. It was one of our few uncomfortable topics.

We rarely fought, and when we did one or both of us were tired or scared. We had built a good life, our "old life." It revolved around the house my grandparents had built before the Depression, a house Lindsey loved even more than I did. We didn't have the money to keep up with the exquisite restorations going on up and down Cypress Street. But Grandfather's house had good bones and wore well.

Our old life was walks in the neighborhood, on the narrow palm-lined streets with the sunset bursting across the horizon, the enchanted metropolitan twilight of the New West. We might stop by Cheuvront for a glass of wine, or the Thursday night event at the Phoenix Art Museum. I had learned to ride a bike on these streets—spent all my young years there. The ghosts were mostly benign.

Lindsey had taken over Grandmother's gardens and brought them to new glories. I worked intermittently on a history of the great Central Arizona Project, which brought water from the Colorado River to the desert of Phoenix, and I taught a class at Phoenix College every fall. We cooked on the *chiminea* in the backyard and celebrated with cocktails in the courtyard that filtered out the sun on even the worst days of August.

My old friend Lorie Pope, who wrote for the *Republic* and knew me in my restless years, had remarked more than once on the change in me. "I never imagined you living such a domestic life, David," she had said. I didn't take it as a criticism.

I pulled Lindsey close and kissed the top of her head. I said, "You didn't get us into anything. You were just doing your job."

I added, "Peralta can fix this." I wasn't sure if I really believed it. "It might take more than two weeks." That was closer to reality. What we did for a living was inherently dangerous, and all over the world—Colombia, Sicily, Bosnia—cops were killed as a political statement or a business expense. A New Economy of borderless evil. Another manifestation of Dan Milton's new dark age.

I felt an involuntary shudder. The absentminded professor lost in his reveries of archival research jolted back to reality. Lindsey held me closer as the sun slipped behind the mountains.

She said, "I know these people. This will never be over."

Chapter Twelve

Friday, eight days since George Weed's body was found and a week after the shooting in Scottsdale, I was in my office on the fourth floor of the old courthouse. I was leaning back in my chair, feet up on the big wooden desk. Downtown sounds were filtering through the expansive, arched windows—this place had been built to last in 1929. I was thinking about Lindsey. Across the room was the black-and-white photo of Carl Hayden, sheriff of Maricopa County a century before. Sheriff Hayden looked back at me across time from beneath his Stetson. The future senator from Arizona had met his wife at Stanford, I recalled. She had never been threatened by the Russian mafia. When a knock came on the pebbled glass, I called out that the door was open, and the security guard stepped inside and shut the door behind him.

His name was Carl, too, and he had been a highway patrolman for thirty years before retiring. But he had a white pencil-thin mustache and an erect bearing that always made me envision him in the uniform of a British army officer at a remote post. After exchanging pleasantries, I was about to ask him what he knew about the John Pilgrim murder, when he said, "This is my last day, Mapstone."

"You don't want to be bothered protecting the sheriff's office historian anymore?" I beckoned him to sit, and he did.

"It's been fun to know you, Mapstone. But Marcia and I are leaving Phoenix. We've got a little piece of land in southern Arizona, about an hour from Tucson. We've built a house."

Sometimes I get stir crazy, alone with my records and my idle thoughts. I was glad for the company, and made obligatory small talk about Carl's milestone, wishing him well. I'd probably talked to him every day I came into the courthouse over four years, but I never knew he and his wife were thinking of moving.

"It's this damned place, Mapstone," he said. "It's been ruined. Too many people, too many cars. They've paved over the citrus groves and the Japanese flower gardens. The whole damned Midwest moved here, but nobody really wants to be here. Nobody knows anybody else, or wants to." He stared past his hawk nose, through the windows at the hazy shape of the South Mountains. "The heat, the damned smog…"

I wasn't going to try to defend Phoenix. Everything he said was true. It broke my heart. Carl was about to continue when a mountainous shape appeared beyond the office door, and Peralta burst into the room.

"Sheriff," Carl said. About to say more, he noticed the foul storm massed over Peralta's brow and withdrew in silence.

When the door closed, Peralta slapped a cassette on my desk.

"The noon news," he snarled.

"What?" I pulled my feet off the top of county property and sat up.

"Play it," he said. "I want you to have the full experience, just like I did when it came on an hour ago."

I took the cassette, rose warily and slid it into a player attached to a small TV on a nearby bookshelf. TV news logos flashed across the screen.

"What am I watching?"

"Turn it up," he ordered.

It was the top story. "A dramatic break today in a fifty-six-year-old murder case!" the blond anchor chirped. I felt the sub-basement drop out of my stomach. The voice continued, "For details, let's go to Melissa Sanchez, who is at a special briefing at Phoenix Police Headquarters." Peralta appropriated my chair and sat back, his meaty hands folded across his chest, his suit coat and tie bunched beneath.

"...Kate Vare, the department's cold case expert, made the revelations, Megan," the reporter said. "A cold case expert is someone who works on some of the very toughest crimes, the ones that have been unsolved for years." I heard Peralta sigh loudly I didn't want to meet his eyes. I looked at my fine rolling bulletin board, which stood there in all its ridiculousness.

"An FBI badge, missing for fifty-six years, has been recovered by Phoenix Police. Sergeant Vare said this badge was lost when FBI agent John Pilgrim was found shot to death in November of 1948."

"This is bullshit!" I said. Peralta held up a hand for silence.

"Pilgrim's badge was found on the body of a homeless man, who died last week from natural causes..."

I mumbled, "They don't even have the date right." On the screen, Kate Vare stood before a crowded room of reporters, nodding her head officiously, pointing to a diagram that included a photo of Pilgrim and the reproduction of the badge.

I reached over and shut off the TV.

"This is bullshit," I repeated. "Grandstanding. I've actually got the homeless guy's name! I've got a Social Security number, a date of birth, even an address from 1981."

"It's not about the rummy, Mapstone. The rummy died of natural causes. It's about the goddamned FBI badge!" His voice echoed into the far corners of the high ceiling.

Sheriff Hayden looked on but declined to intervene. "Don't you know how the media works, Mapstone? We never announced we found the badge. Nobody knows. So now Kate acts like she's made a breakthrough. And in the mind of the public she has made a breakthrough."

"Jesus!" I yelled back. "Is this about your petty little who-gets-the-credit game?"

"It's been a good game for you," he snapped back. "Why the hell would the sheriff's office need a historian, a deputy with a wooptieshit Ph.D. in history, if it wasn't all just a goddamned media effort!"

I sat down, wounded amidships.

Peralta went for more damage. "I've supposedly got the smartest cold case guy in the country, and he makes us look like morons. He spends his week playing social worker with all these fucking derelicts, and he comes up with dick."

"I'm just a consultant." I said quietly, all the smart ass drained out of me.

"What's the matter with you, David?" He stared hard at me. I gave my head a shake and held open my hands, no answer.

"You're not working this case. It's like you're in dream-land."

'Well, let's see. My wife is targeted for death. My mentor died a terrible death…" I was getting madder and madder, which did no good with Peralta. I knew this. "Not all of us can lose a loved one and just go into the office next day like nothing happened." Like the way you reacted to your father's death, I wanted to add.

"Did you know she was going to do this?" he demanded.

Of course I didn't. I told him about Kate taking herself off the case. He snorted and unleashed a string of profanities, slamming his fist down on my desk as the encore. Then we sat like survivors of a bomb detonation, until the ringing faded and the room was only silence.

In a conversational voice, Peralta said, "There was a laundry mark in the jacket. She traced it to the Salvation Army used clothing program. So the jacket was at least secondhand, and the badge might have been sewn into it for years."

Nausea washed over me. I sat in one of the straight-backed wooden chairs facing my desk.

I asked, "Did Eric Pham agree to release this information, that we had found the badge?"

"How the hell do I know," Peralta said. "Maybe she batted her goddamned eyes at him or something…"

More silence. I could hear the bells at St. Mary's, all the way across downtown, chiming two o'clock. A train whistle blared from the south.

"So," Peralta said finally. "Tell me again what you found."

I went through it again. With the information I had now on George Weed, it could lead me to his family, some sense of where he was all those years before he ended up dead in a pool.

"Why do we care, Mapstone?" Peralta said, his voice calm again.

"These guys are all over. All they want is money. You give 'em the money and they go buy booze and drugs. Some of 'em are as able-bodied as you and me, but do they get work? No."

"I know," I said.

"How often do you hear about a case where some transient is the suspect? Remember that poor little girl a few years ago, when I was still chief deputy? She's walking to school when this fucking pervert grabs her, a 'homeless man,' the news stories said. Homeless, my ass. He was just a predator vagrant scumbag."

"Sheriff," I said. "Weed is all we have. You wanted me to work this case, remember? I wanted to be on the vacation that you told me I am not allowed."

"The badge, Mapstone. Kate Vare doesn't give a rat's ass about your vagrant."

"I can't do anything about the badge without the vagrant," I said. "You heard the TV. The badge is in Washington for extensive testing in the FBI labs. Now, I can go to Washington and wait for a press release, or I can follow the only human thread I have."

"What if the poor bastard was wandering around for years without even knowing he was carrying it?"

I stared down at the floor. "I don't believe that," I said. These guys check the coin return in newspaper racks that haven't been stocked in years. He'd know if something was sewn into his jacket. A jacket he wore even on hot days."

Peralta raised his bulk out of the chair and looked me over from the summit of six feet, six inches.

"I want progress within a week," he said as he stalked out of the room.

〈〉〈〉〈〉

Or what? You'll put my wife in danger, treat me like a twenty-year-old rookie and not even allow me vacation time? Oh, my mind was full of arch and devastating comebacks all the way home that evening. I was nearly talking aloud to myself when the elevator came up from the garage to the lobby, the doors opened, and standing there was Bobby Hamid.

He raised his eyebrows in surprise and lit up his 50,000-watt smile. He was only getting better looking as he got older, the slightest veins of gray working their way into his luxurious wavy black hair. He was wearing one of his tailored-by-God suits, which probably cost half my year's salary. A wine bottle was tucked under his arm.

"Dr. Mapstone!" he said.

I nodded to him. Then I realized I hadn't even stepped out of the garage elevator.

My mind took a quick pop quiz: the godfather of Arizona organized crime was standing in the lobby of the building where Lindsey was secretly stashed. What to do? I stalled with conversation.

"Bobby, I thought Sheriff Peralta had run you out of town."

"You know better than that." His green-brown eyes twinkled.

"And if I were gone, what would happen to the dozens of Valley charities and non-profit organizations that I help?"

I made a half grunt. "From your venture capital profits, right?"

"Of course," he said amiably. It was pretty much the same tone Bobby had used when I watched him put a large-caliber bullet in the kneecap of a man, then repeat the maneuver with the other leg. Unfortunately, or fortunately, that man had been trying to kill me, so Peralta had to once again lose his chance to put Bobby away forever. Yes, our history was long and uncomfortably complicated.

"So," he said, making a point of noticing the badge and holster peeking out from beneath my cream sports coat. "Does business or pleasure bring you here tonight?"

The deputy, sitting behind the lobby desk and pretending to be concierge, made eye contact with me. I signaled nothing. I didn't know what the hell to do. If I made a fuss, Bobby might become suspicious, and where the hell might that lead? I said, "I'm visiting a friend."

"As am I, Dr. Mapstone," he said. He walked over to the elevator that went up to the condos and pushed the button. "Maybe we're visiting the same friend?"

I tried to ignore him. He said, "Isn't this a magnificent building? A bit of Bauhaus, a touch of le Corbusier, right here in central Phoenix. I must say, I don't care for the balconies."

The elevator arrived with a whoosh and I let him step in first.

Then I stepped in and the door closed. I felt my palms sweating.

"Floor?" he prompted, smiling like Torquemada on the verge of uncovering a heretic.

"Seven," I lied. I sure as hell wasn't going to lead him to Lindsey on the eighth floor. How did I know he was visiting a friend? Whatever he was doing, the seventh floor was now his destination, too.

The machine did its work, rising slowly up the shaft.

"I was sorry to hear about that unpleasantness in Scottsdale," he said, arms gracefully crossed, eyes watching the lights mark each floor we passed. "And that poor young deputy who died."

"It's a dangerous world," I mumbled, wondering what were the signs of a person becoming a claustrophobic.

"It is, indeed," he said. A pause, then, "I do hope Miss Lindsey is taking good care."

I stared hard at him. He appraised me with cool predator eyes. "These Russians are very frightening, Dr. Mapstone. They have no respect for any civilized convention."

And you would know this how? I wanted to ask it. My mouth felt like a dry lake bed. Then the elevator slid to a gentle stop and the doors opened. I held out my hand: After you. Bobby bowed and stepped out. I followed him, not knowing what the hell I was going to do. The halls were short affairs, with only four condos on each floor. Bobby stood there looking at me, an amused expression crossing his handsome features.

Inspiration. "Damn," I said, pointing to his wine bottle. "I left my gift down in the car." I turned back to the elevator and hit the call button, too hard.

"Dr. Mapstone," he said, insisting on shaking hands. "Good evening."

As I stepped in the elevator and waited for it to depart, I listened for the sound of Bobby's knock on a door, the door opening with a cheerful greeting, maybe the sound of party laughter beyond. All I heard was the hum of the building's hidden electronic nerve endings.

Chapter Thirteen

Eric Pham looked perturbed. The slightest wrinkle, an under-lined W of skin, pulled at the middle of his smooth forehead.

"You're sure that Kate didn't invite you to the press briefing? She said you were busy and couldn't make it." He waited for a response. I kept quiet. He added, "I'm genuinely sorry if you felt excluded, Dave."

We were all on first-name basis now. It is an aggressively casual age, more obnoxious in its way than the Victorian married couples that called each other "Mr. Smith" and "Mrs. Smith" in public. And you can't really screw someone over without calling him by his first name. Maybe I was being unfair to the head fed. Beneath his regulation gray suit, Pham seemed pleasantly oblivious to how much his press stunt had put me in a mess with the sheriff. Would it be wise to curse out an FBI man, much less the special agent in charge? Probably not. Was it possible to do my job without a knife in the back from Kate Vare? No way. All these thoughts were fighting to get out, but I shut up and picked at my salmon Caesar salad.

We sat by the window at Kincaid's, a medium-fancy expense-account joint on the second floor of the Collier Center down-town. Over Pham's shoulder, I could see the bulk of Bank One Ballpark. It was Monday, and three days had passed since Peralta's "within a week" bullshit ultimatum. I had used the time to put in requests at a dozen federal and state agencies for information on George Weed. The bureaucratic wheels grinned at me: "You want it when?" But I was not without weapons of my own. After Kate's press conference, I leveraged some of my own media events, gathered in my short career as a curiosity, a history professor who carries a badge. Two TV stations interviewed me on the discovery of the old badge and what it might mean. Lorie Pope wrote a story for the *Republic*—after giving me requisite hell for failing to tell her about the badge. But she quoted me prominently and ignored Kate Vare.

If it was just a media contest, I had faltered in the first lap but then pulled ahead. But it wasn't.

I did use the TV segments and the article to ask the public for information about George Weed: Call the Sheriff's Office's tip line at this 800 number. Aside from the usual psychos and conspiracy nuts, the line yielded nothing. But I did get a call from Eric Pham, promising me lunch.

Across from me, Pham ate the turkey and tomato slices from the shell of a club sandwich—"My wife is making us do the Atkins diet," he explained—and I tried to figure out my next move. My life had too many moving parts. It seemed like madness not to gather up Lindsey and flee until the threat to her ended. Two weeks were passing and we still couldn't go home. But what if the threat never went away? And our protector, Peralta, insisted I work on this damned Pilgrim case. Lindsey did, too, sensing I needed something more to do than nervously prowl through the rooms of a stranger's condo. At least she had found new work, helping the feds track down terrorist bank accounts. A Secret Service type had delivered some kind of super-duper laptop computer, making Lindsey sign for it on multiple forms. So now she sat cross-legged on a big sectional sofa and spied on the secrets of banks in Zurich or Bermuda. Meanwhile, Bobby Hamid in the hallway. Coincidence or something sinister? If we told Peralta, he would send us to the middle of nowhere, maybe just send Lindsey. Too many moving parts.

Pham wrapped his voice in the timbre of calm diplomacy. "Dave, I asked you here today to tell you that things have changed. I have to tell you that we won't be needing your help on the case after all."

"I get it," I said, not unkindly. "If you tell the media the case has been solved, then it really has been. Image becomes reality."

"It's not solved," Pham said, his voice dropping an insistent octave. "Look, this whole thing sucks, OK?"

He stared at me. All the win-win consultant lingo fled from his voice. He spoke so softly I could barely hear him.

"When the badge was found, I had no idea what I was getting into," he said. "I acted in good faith bringing you in. I wanted this case solved. I'd never heard of it before. But I absolutely wanted to run it down. I knew you'd help us do that."

He paused and stared at me. I stared back, and after a few beats he continued, his lips barely moving.

"As it turns out, the John Pilgrim case is still a sensitive matter in Washington. My bosses didn't like the press conference any more than you did. And now they want the whole thing to go away."

I thought about what Lorie Pope had told me of sealed records and stone walls, even though the case was more than fifty years old. I said, "There's a chance to solve the murder of an FBI agent, and they just want it to go away?"

Pham nodded slowly.

I asked why.

Pham leaned in as if he were going to share a confidence. It was the kind of body language that makes the listener lean forward, too.

"Phoenix is a strange place, isn't it?"

There were too many lines to read between. I said, "It's an acquired taste, Eric."

"I came here a year ago from Seattle," he said. "The real estate people said the only place to be is North Scottsdale. So I live behind a wall—'gated community,' they call it—and I don't know any of my neighbors. The homeowners association is like the Soviet Union, watching every aspect of how you landscape or roll out the recycling. The whole front of the house is taken up by a garage door—and this isn't a cheap house. It's all strange."

"I live a mile from here," I said, "on a real street, with front porches and neighbors who know each other and look out for each other. That's the side of Phoenix I prefer."

"I know," he said, setting his silverware with military precision on the plate. "You live in the same house where you grew up. Although you haven't been home for two weeks…"

I felt the illogical rush of the paranoid. It must have shown in my face.

"I wanted to check you out, Dave. To know that I could trust you."

I just looked him over. I had always liked Lindsey's use of "Dave"; somehow it foreshadowed greater intimacy to come, something I had greatly desired with her. With others, I had never cared for "Dave." I was not a "Dave." except with Lindsey.

Pham said, "John Pilgrim killed himself."

I shifted my weight in the chair. My eyes wandered to other tables. Jerry Colangelo, the owner of the Diamondbacks, was in a hushed conversation with a very tall, expensively dressed black man. The president of Bank One walked by, followed by her pin-striped assistants. China rattled back in the kitchen.

I said, "If that's true, why did the records indicate this was an open homicide investigation?"

"In J. Edgar Hoover's FBI, the special agent was supposed to be a superman," Pham said. "His integrity, above reproach. His steadiness, unquestioned. In reality, John Pilgrim was a problem. He was a drunk and a disciplinary nightmare who was sent to Phoenix to clean up his act. He had symptoms of what we'd call depression. He'd threatened to kill himself before."

"How do you know this?"

"It's what my bosses told me," he said. "Get it? Pilgrim was bad for the FBI's image. They wanted this case forgotten as quick as possible in 1948, and nothing's changed."

"That's nuts," I said. "That was fifty years ago. The FBI's had a few problems since then that are worse than an agent killing himself. Why is this such a big secret?"

"Because it's a family secret," Pham said. "And you're not family. No offense. But you're not only local law enforcement, you're unorthodox, and an outsider. I find that appealing. But this wasn't my call to make."

"So Pilgrim stands in front of a canal, shoots himself, and falls in?"

Pham shrugged. He had his orders.

"And the badge just floated away," I said. "Somebody picks it up, and it begins this wondrous journey around the pawn shops, junk drawers, and secondhand jackets of Phoenix."

"That could be just what happened," Pham said.

"Don't you think that if the average person found an FBI badge, he would call the police and report it?"

"Maybe he thought it was a toy," Pham said, unconvincingly. "Anyway, Kate says the homeless man might not have even known the badge was in his jacket. Kate says he probably got the jacket second- or thirdhand."

Ah, yes. Kate. Bonnie Kate. I said, "The homeless men I notice are very aware of any fungible wealth they might come into contact with They check every pay phone coin return. And they're not going to feel something sewn into a Levi's jacket? The detectives found it first thing when they examined the body in Maryvale. Maybe George Weed had carried that badge around for years. Maybe Weed somehow came in contact with John Pilgrim. He would have been ten years old when Pilgrim was shot."

"Look." Pham said. "I don't like this any more than you do. That's why I said it sucks."

I let the waiter take my plate away. "Fine," I said. "End of story. Maybe Pilgrim doesn't even have family left, anybody who would care what happened."

"There is still family," Pham said.

"Maybe I can talk to them," I said.

"Impossible."

"What about his partner, Renzetti?"

"No way, Mapstone," Pham said. I had lost first-name status.

"So Renzetti is alive?"

Pham's eyes widened when he was exasperated. "You don't know when to quit," he said quickly.

"Let's just say I have a very demanding boss. He's not going to care that the Bureau has changed its mind about me being on this case. Pilgrim and George Weed were both found dead in Maricopa County. I think he'd say that you don't have a say in my involvement." David Mapstone, doing his part for inter-departmental relations.

"Eric," I said, forcing a slower, easier tone in my voice. "I don't want to cause you trouble. But you won't let me see the FBI files on the case. You don't want me on the case. What harm would be done if you called retired Agent Renzetti and asked if he might speak to me?"

Pham said nothing. He faced his plate and absentmindedly ate the bread from the remains of his club sandwich.

Chapter Fourteen

The carousel at Encanto Park was empty. But, at the command of a maintenance crew, it spun around to calliope music, dispensing old-time joy for a PlayStation and DVD world. This was another part of Phoenix that up-and-comer professionals like Eric Pham never saw: the lovely old city park nestled into the Palmcroft neighborhood about half a mile from my house. What did it say about me that I preferred a habitat from the jazz age rather than the sprawl age?

On Tuesday afternoon, the park was nearly empty. Instead of families picnicking under the stately old trees, lovers lingering on the foot-bridges or kids fishing the lagoon, a few homeless men lounged on the grass. I lingered at the locked gates of Enchanted Island, watching the workmen at the carousel, remembering a ten-year-old's memories in this park. Then, the little train ran every day, the lagoon was stocked with fish, and no one seemed afraid.

My legs and middle were still giggly sore from loving Lindsey two hours before. Somehow all the uncertainties and worries of the past two weeks had made us hornier, and we were in the process of having sex in every room, and on every piece of furniture, of our unknown host's elegant tree house. Pictures of memory kept rerunning deliciously in my head. I came into the living room to find her sitting in a big leather chair. She wore a black summer dress with a quiet flower print and dainty black shoulder straps. I'm sure it was a demure dress, until Lindsey wore it. She was drawn up in the chair reading, a paperback propped on her naked knees, the dress riding up on her thighs, falling just right in the front to show a hint of cleavage. I put down whatever forgotten work I was doing and knelt down in front of her. Then, my hands stroking the soft, warm, taut skin of her leg. Her giggles turning into soft moans. Sliding the fabric slowly up her thigh, kissing her perfect smooth knees, pulling off the black flip-flops, sucking her toes. Gently, slowly, removing one tiny strap from her pale shoulder, then the other. The exquisite construction of her shoulder blades, her collarbones, her breastbone, her slender form. Dark tresses of hair fell into her face as she looked down at me, one renegade black strand trying to get in the side of her sweet mouth. She was wearing very white cotton panties.

"David Mapstone." The voice was tough, metal on metal, familiar. I turned to shake hands with Harrison Wolfe. He was as tall as me, with a long ruddy face and thick white hair combed back from a sun-etched forehead. His unblinking cornflower blue eyes lacked any hint of warmth.

"So what mess have you gotten yourself into?" he asked.

You didn't just call Harrison Wolfe to arrange a meeting. Since he had retired from the Phoenix Police back in the '70s, he had done everything he could to stay away from the cop world. He was just another anonymous old man in a city park, if the man looked twenty years younger than his eighty-some years, and if he moved with a vague sense of coiled menace. You didn't just make a phone call to a legend, the homicide detective who worked every major case in Phoenix from the 1950s to the 1970s. So I had left a message with a guy I knew at the Police Museum, and waited for Wolfe to call me.

We walked to a quiet spot overlooking the lagoon while I laid out the Pilgrim case as I understood it. I started with the body found in Maryvale. Finding the badge. Identifying George Weed. I ended with what I knew about dead FBI agent John Pilgrim. When I was done, Wolfe worked his lean jaw and stared out at the golf course, and across the trees at the Central Corridor sky-line. Lindsey was in one of those buildings. Yuri could be riding the carousel at Encanto Park and the cops wouldn't know it.

"So the Bureau sent Pilgrim here to get him clean." Wolfe said, and snorted without humor. "Fat chance. Phoenix brings out the worst in people."

He turned back to the lagoon, picked up a stone, and skipped it across the water—one, two, three, four skips before it gave up to gravity. "Pilgrim was ancient history when I joined the department in 1955," he said. "Detective bureau didn't consider it an active case."

I asked why.

"You've been dealing with the Fucked-up Bureau of Instigation, so you know the answer to that. Mapstone. They don't want local law enforcement sticking its nose in. Scuttlebutt was that Pilgrim shot himself. Yeah, it was the only unsolved killing of an FBI agent in Arizona history. But that's just inter-esting for civilians. The cops know what really happened, and they move on to the next mayhem. What really happened was that Pilgrim shot himself."

"And nothing in your years in homicide made you doubt that?"

"Never gave it a second thought," he said. His eyes blinked rapidly, uncharacteristically. "But I never knew they hadn't recovered his badge…"

"There's a lot not to know," I said. "Somebody's gone through the local files. They've removed the ballistics report, God knows what else."

"So ask your friends at the Bureau."

I said nothing. Wolfe said, "It's always a one-way street, running to the feds' benefit."

"They didn't take everything," I said. "I found a detective's notebook, a guy named Dan Bird." I watched Wolfe's expression, but he knew he was being watched now and he just bored his eyes into me, waiting. I went on, "Bird's notebook said Pilgrim didn't have any gunpowder residue on his hands. That's not consistent with a suicide. He had a single .38 slug in his heart. He was dead before he hit the water. He floated several miles in the canal."

"Dan Bird was still in homicide when I went to work," Wolfe said. "You could trust his report."

"Another place in the notebook, there's an interview with a farmer out by Seventh Street and the Arizona Canal. He says the night before Pilgrim was found dead, he sees some people up on the canal. One of them looks like Agent Pilgrim. But it's dusk and the farmer has work to do, and he moves on. A few minutes later, he hears a gunshot and sees a car tearing down the canal bank."

"Too bad for you Bird died in 1971, "Wolfe said.

I went on, "Here's another thing: for a washed out loser, John Pilgrim had spent a lot of time on very sensitive cases." Maybe I couldn't get the FBI files, but Bird's notes and the newspapers told me some things. Pilgrim was assigned to counterspy work during the war, and after 1945 he led successful investigations of corrupt state and city governments in New Jersey, Maryland, and Illinois. He held five citations for bravery.

Wolfe watched a foursome in the distance, lugging golf clubs. They were undeterred by the hundred-degree temperature. He said, "I guess I'd trust Dan Bird's notes more than the say-so of some G-man.

What about PPD? Can they help you?"

"Kate Vare is their cold case person. She hates my guts."

"She wants to be chief," he said simply "Don't give me that look. I keep up with the department. Talk about ambitious."

I was surrounded by ambitious men and women. Lean and hungry looks, dressed for success.

"Mapstone," he said quietly. I watched the sun-dug lines on his face deepen. "How much do you know about old Phoenix?"

It sounded like a trick question. I started cautiously, as if I were defending a paper before a panel of hostile—and jealous—professors. "The city had fewer than one hundred thousand people then. The industries were the Five 'C's—copper, cattle, citrus, cotton, and climate. In 1948, Phoenix hoped to surpass El Paso as the leading business city of the Southwest. But it was still an upstart."

"Very good, professor," Wolfe said. "Now, look deeper. Phoenix has always been a corrupt city."

My chamber-of-commerce native pride made me protest. The mob had been in Vegas and Tucson, after all.

"Jesus, you're naïve for an educated man," he said, his voice giving off no more edge than usual. "In the mid 1950s, when I came here from the LAPD, the feds had identified five hundred known mobsters in Phoenix. That was more per capita than in New York City."

I didn't say anything. My mind just processed this new information.

Wolfe just shook his head as if he was instructing a child. "Remember Gus Greenbaum?"

I remembered. He was the former Las Vegas mobster, living under an assumed name in Palmcroft. One day in the fifties, he and his wife were killed at home in a mob hit. The house was still there, on Encanto Boulevard. I could barely make it out through the trees.

"The Greenbaums were cooking steaks," Wolfe said. "So after they were killed, the hit men sat down and ate their dinner. Bet you didn't know that."

"You ought to teach history," I said.

"Most of the good stuff happened before I got here." Wolfe said. "We had a good chief in the fifties. He was absolutely honest. So after he took over, things might still go on. But they had to go around the chief, do it where he couldn't find it. But this has always been a town for strange crime. Winnie Ruth Judd, the trunk murderess. The *Republic* reporter who was blown up. Bob Crane killed in Scottsdale, and then all his porn videos were found. Remember the woman who cuts off her husband's head and limbs and stuffs his torso in the dumpster? I'd rather that a lady just walk out on me. Remember the father out there in Mesa, takes his baby girl out on Christmas Eve to watch the lights, but he sets her on fire and kills her?"

"Yeah, no need to remind me." The music from the carousel no longer sounded innocent.

"So, if you ask me, 'Did Pilgrim kill himself?' Until now, I had no reason to doubt it. But this town is just weird enough that anything's possible."

A youngish blond man walked by and paused to lean over the bridge railing. He had peroxide yellow hair, long but slicked back over his ears. His eyebrows were blond, and his lips small and curled, like the mouths in eighteenth-century portraits. He was wearing a blue shirt and a tie as yellow as his hair. We stopped talking, and in a moment the blond man walked on.

Wolfe said, "I can tell you this. I remember a guy named George Weed."

I stared at him as if he had revealed the location of the Lost Dutchman Mine.

"Don't look so surprised, Mapstone. I'm old. I'm not stupid."

"Where? When?"

"I remember a guy named George Weed from the 1960s. Skinny guy. He ran the elevator at the old Greater Arizona Savings Building.

Remember, at Central and Adams? With the big radio antenna on the roof."

I nodded.

"Back then elevator operator was steady work. And he was one of my snitches. He'd tell me things, things he heard and saw. I had lots of guys like him around. You didn't need a whole day to drive across the city. You walked four blocks and talked to people."

"Did he have family? Where did he live?"

"Well, my memory's not that good. It's been forty years. He was the elevator man, Mapstone. Like the scissors sharpener and the guy selling candy in the courthouse lobby. I don't even know where those people are now. Maybe on welfare, or wandering the streets. Anyway, you saw him every day. He was part of the landscape."

"I had an address for him, an apartment on Second Avenue," I said.

"That's the guy," Wolfe said.

"What ever happened to him?"

"They automated the elevators—this was sometime in the early sixties—and there was no more need for elevator operators. So I think he went to work down in the produce district. Oh, where the hell was it? McMackin Produce, over at Buchanan and Second Street. Just cleaning up. The guy wasn't a brain surgeon, OK? He was nice enough, but seemed simple. He wasn't going to live out in Arcadia with the bankers and the lawyers."

"Did he seem like the kind of guy who would be wandering around with an FBI badge sewn in his coat?"

Wolfe snorted. "Nobody ever seems like the kind who will do what they eventually do. Just ask your common everyday serial killer. People will surprise you. I know one guy…see him at the bar every now and then. He's just some old man in raggedy clothes. He's a goddamned millionaire." Wolfe shook his head. "The guy drove a Greyhound bus for thirty years, and never did anything but save his money. He lives on oatmeal. So who knows what was underneath George Weed."

We both leaned on the bridge railing, watching the park. The crew was finished at the carousel, the music gone.

"My heart is shot, you know."

I stared at him, asked what he'd said although I had heard him perfectly.

"They won't let you have a transplant if you're an old bastard like me. So I'm sorry I can't do more for you."

"I'm sorry, Wolfe."

"Don't be." He shrugged. "I've had a hell of a life. And I'll tell you this, if I live long enough I'm going to be a real pain in the ass. I might just get Peralta to hire me as your partner."

I looked at him anew. Looking for signs. Was the skin around his eyes more ashen than I remembered it? I resisted an impulse to touch my own chest. We go through most of our lives thinking the old are a different species from us, that we won't become them. I said, I'll look forward to it."

It seemed time to go. I was about to shake hands when Wolfe's hard cop voice returned. "When I was first on the force we didn't allow that."

I followed Wolfe's eyes to a lump of dirty clothes on the grass that contained a dark-skinned man.

"They stayed in the Deuce or we ran 'em in," he went on. "It was a simpler world."

Chapter Fifteen

Driving east on Encanto Boulevard, I passed the brick mansion where the mobster and his wife were murdered. Another unsolved case in my town. The house sat amid lovely landscaping and innocence, its history brooding silently in the memory of a few old cops and crime aficionados. A crime that had happened before I was born, but after John Pilgrim had been dead for years. Harrison Wolfe had been a strong man in his prime, careless of his heart. Dan Milton would have been a promising postdoctoral student. A pair of kids would become Lindsey's parents, a troubled life before them. A pair of lovers in their late twenties would become my parents. Only the house remained.

The car swap was wearing on me. But I dutifully drove the Olds toward its hiding spot. Spring gardeners were out in Willo, despite the early heat wave. I resisted the impulse to drive down Cypress. Fifth Avenue took me south, across McDowell and into the older bungalow neighborhood of Roosevelt. This was where the rich and powerful leaders of Phoenix lived nine decades before. I wondered about George Weed. He ran an elevator in the early '60s, sometimes pitched tips to Harrison Wolfe. Did he carry the badge even then? Was he a cop wanna-be? I would have been satisfied to know how he got John Pilgrim's badge and why it was important enough to hide in a jacket he wore like second skin.

Yuppies from the apartments were out in the narrow grassy strip of Portland Park walking their dogs. As I slowed to let an athletic woman with short blond hair pull a golden retriever across the street, I noticed a black SUV about a half block behind me. It had been in my rearview mirror at least since I crossed Seventh Avenue. I coughed a little paranoia tightness out of my throat and continued slowly toward the entrance to the parking garage. The SUV followed at a distance.

The garage was several stories tall, meant to handle the apartments, Trinity Cathedral, and some retail shops. I swung into the first level and stopped. This was church and retail parking, and at this time of day it was nearly deserted. The Olds engine echoed off the concrete and I kept watch in the rearview. Maybe fifteen seconds later the SUV crept by, but didn't turn in. It was huge and black, a Hummer H2. The windows were tinted so dark I couldn't see anything inside. Then it was gone. I had a decision to make: drive around some more, or turn right up the ramp and swap cars.

Just then the Hummer reappeared in the alley to the south, heading into the other side of the garage. My hand was ahead of my brain. I slammed the gearshift into reverse and backed out onto Portland. I was being too careful, but I felt an irrational fear. Surely the product of two weeks spent in hiding, two weeks to contemplate the bloody work done to Lindsey's colleagues on the sidewalk in downtown Scottsdale. I laughed out loud at myself and the laughter dissipated into the noise of the air-conditioning. The blonde smiled at me and tossed the ball for her dog. I put the car into drive and slowly moved toward Central. The Hummer would be driving up the garage to park and disgorge its passengers. I would drive around the block and laugh at myself again. Then I would go home and teach myself to relax.

Only the Hummer came out of the driveway. Just enough for the driver to keep an eye on me. The big convertible was built for pleasure, not security. I felt a sudden rush of vulnerability.

I pressed the accelerator and the 442 engine responded instantly. A gray Honda was bearing down on me on Central but I slid in front of him and sped away. I blew through the yellow light at Roosevelt and followed the road as it swung over to a one-way on First Avenue. A block farther on I wheeled left and sped through downtown streets, crossing Central, First, Second, and Third Streets, then left and back across Roosevelt heading north. When I could refocus on the rearview mirror, the Hummer was a block behind me. When it crossed Roosevelt against the red light, I felt a stake of dread in my stomach.

What the hell was going on? I was half tempted to pull over and step out. Wait for the SOB to pull up behind me. He'd probably go around. It was probably some kids playing. At worst, it was some dumb carjackers scoping out my automotive relic. Pull over—why play games? And yet, something elemental stopped me. It said, Stay in the car. Keep moving. I thought about the blond man, improbably out of place at the park with his tie and shirt. Did I just imagine that his face appeared different, something Slavic in his features?

In a block I took the on-ramp to the Papago Freeway. The rush-hour mess was starting, but the big engine quickly had me up to seventy, sailing out onto six lanes of eastbound concrete. Overhead the wind became a gale rattling the ragtop. I crossed lane after lane, swerving past the thickening clots of cars, SUVs, minivans, and pickups. The Twelfth Street overpass swooped above me. Then we passed Sixteenth and bore into the Short Stack, where the Red Mountain Freeway hove off to the East Valley. Traffic was stopped, backing up. I slid over to the shoulder and ran around it, provoking a chorus of honking. Then I was past the jam-up, heading east. The speedometer said eighty-five, but the big car felt as if it were doing about forty. Behind me, I could see the Hummer trying to catch up. I fumbled for my cell phone.

Lindsey answered on the first ring.

"Are you OK?"

"Yeah, Dave. Are you?"

I told her what I knew. She promised to call the deputy down at the front desk. I promised her I'd alert the communications center and get some backup. I assured her I had the Python and some Speed-loaders holding extra ammo. It wouldn't come to that.

It was probably just a coincidence and a case of nerves. Still, I was glad that every second we moved farther away from the Central Corridor and the hideaway condo. I told her I loved her.

It was a beautiful day for a drive. One of the sad ironies of the urbanization of Phoenix was that the best place for average folks to see the mountains now was from the freeway. Camelback sat spectacularly off to the north, the afternoon sun making it glow in a rich red. The smog was light enough to see the gentle undulations of the McDowell range off to the northeast, and beyond them, Four Peaks soared through the haze. At the Fortieth Street exit, I raised the Sheriff's Office communications center and, after a long wait on hold, explained things to the watch commander. It looked like a hundred thousand other SUVs on the streets of Phoenix. No, I didn't have a license tag. By that time downtown Tempe was flying by on my right, and the black Hummer was a half dozen car lengths behind me.

Then it was gone. I swerved to avoid a slow-moving junk truck. Then I slowed to around sixty. I checked both mirrors and the Hummer had disappeared. As I updated the watch commander, I pulled off on McClintock and headed south into Tempe. She told me to keep the line open. So I set the phone on the seat and drove slowly across the Salt River, then turned west on University. My heart was still beating too hard. But the road behind me was devoid of anything that looked like my pursuer.

I cruised past the Arizona State campus, slow enough that cars sped around me angrily. Now I regretted not bagging the guy. He was gone and we didn't know what the hell he wanted with me. Another voice in me said it was just as well. The street behind me remained safe. I made a loop and retraced my route. How did he just disappear? I could have sworn he was still with me past the exit to Priest and downtown Tempe…Could he have exited at Rural? I cursed myself for not finding a way to get behind him, get his license number.

Then I took a sharp, involuntary breath. I told the watch commander I'd call her back, and hung up even as she was protesting. I speed-dialed Lindsey's cell.

The phone rang five times, and her voice mail picked up. I dialed again, irrationally checking the display to make sure it was, indeed, Lindsey's number. Still nothing. I pulled over into a parking lot, forgetting to signal or check my mirrors. I dialed the landline into the condo. It rang fifteen times. Next I tried the line to the concierge desk. Again, no answer.

I cursed under my breath. I almost mumbled aloud something about how this couldn't be happening. The car was already moving. I sped out of the parking lot and went north to the freeway. In a couple of minutes I was headed back toward the city, the sun in my eyes, my foot jamming the accelerator into the floor.

"There's no answer," I was yelling into the phone, trying to make the dispatcher understand me. I gave my badge number for the second time, gave the address. She put me on hold. I wanted to throw the damned phone out of the window.

The siren could be heard even above the wind coursing over the top of the car. Behind me, a DPS cruiser was closing fast. The highway patrol.

"Goddamnit!"

The speedometer read one hundred and twenty-five. The speedometer stopped at one hundred and twenty-five.

I flew low-altitude across the Short Stack and descended into the center city, staying in the HOV lane, heading to the Third Street exit. Now the trooper was right on me. I could see sunglasses and a grim expression. Another DPS cruiser was behind him. A buddy. Everybody ought to have a buddy. I held up my badge like a fool. I didn't slow down.

The Olds surged off the freeway doing a responsible eighty miles per hour, as I tried to raise the communications center on the cell phone. Behind me, the trooper's siren insisted I pull over. I gunned it through the yellow light at McDowell and heard screeching tires off to the left. I didn't want to look. Somewhere in my mind the moving violations were adding up: speeding, reckless driving, refusing to stop. I was half a mile from Lindsey.

Then I was at Central, heading north. A couple of Phoenix PD cars had joined the chase now, and I led a festive little procession up the northbound fast lane, past the Phoenix Art Museum, the Viad Tower, and the church where we had been married. Sure, something inside told me I wasn't thinking straight. I was thinking only of Lindsey right at that moment. And I felt like I had been kicked in the stomach when I could see emergency lights outside the condo tower.

Something wrong.

Something bad.

The palm trees hurtled past. Then I was slowing, stopping suddenly, slamming the gearshift into park, running toward the entrance to the building. Men were milling about. Men with guns. They noticed me and started out the door.

"Lindsey!" I yelled. "Where's Lindsey?"

Behind me I heard voices, commands.

Then a great weight fell on me from behind. The ground came up fast. I felt sharp pain, sudden force. I was losing altitude. Then I wasn't really there. It was only in a little closet of my consciousness that I noticed my arms being pulled in an unnatural direction, and I heard a sound that reminded me of handcuffs locking.

Chapter Sixteen

"You're gonna be OK. You just got the air knocked out of you."

"Do you know what day it is?"

"Don't try to talk. Just breathe."

"Do you want to go to the hospital to get checked out?"

"He's fine. He doesn't need to go."

People were having a conversation in a language I didn't quite understand.

"He's a deputy. He's on the job. Take those off."

I inhabited a hidden control room just behind my eyes, working an air machine of some kind, vaguely aware of things going on around me. I was attached to something heavy. Then everything turned sideways and my stomach was headed up my throat…

"Don't try to stand up. That's right. Keep your head down. Just concentrate on breathing."

"Lindsey!"

"She's OK, she's OK. Just sit there."

I came around. "There" was the grass in front of the condo tower. I was surrounded by redwood-sized men, a couple of paramedics, three Phoenix cops, two sheriff's detectives whose names I could remember if you gave me a few minutes without my passing out. A DPS trooper was glowering at me, putting away his cuffs. I squeezed my hands just to make sure they were still there. He must have weighed 280 pounds, and I suddenly felt every one of them on my back and ribs. My left arm was swelling painfully, in the grasp of a large man in a blue T-shirt.

I came around enough to notice the SWAT officers arrayed around the entrance to the building. Men in black jumpsuits, black Kevlar helmets and goggles, black bulletproof vests. My mouth thick with dread, I asked my question again.

"She's safe. She's gone. Just sit there and take it easy."

I focused on Chief Deputy Kimbrough, looking dapper in tan slacks, blue blazer and a rep bow tie on a blue and white striped Oxford shirt. The paramedic peeled the blood-pressure cuff off my arm and called out a number to his partner—at least I wouldn't die of high blood pressure.

"She's safe," Kimbrough repeated. "We had to move her. There was a security breach."

"What the hell?" I got on my knees and tried to stand, wobbled, then found a lamppost to support me. Every joint in my body felt swollen and stiff. I asked, "What breach? Why do you have SWAT teams here?"

"Somebody tried to get into the building," Kimbrough said. "After you called Lindsey she called down to the deputy in the lobby. He called backup, and they found a ladder leaned up against the building."

"What?"

"Just listen and breathe, Mapstone. You look like you're about to pass out. We found a ladder that had been leaned up against a second-story balcony. Nobody was home in that apartment, but the balcony door had been pried, and the door to the hallway was unlocked. We got her out. Now we're searching the building. Our friends from PPD think it might just be a burglary or a careless maintenance man. But the sheriff didn't want to take a chance."

I shivered in the warm breeze blowing down Central. "Show me."

I limped along the front sidewalk, then through some hedges to the south of the entrance. Sure enough, around a corner and just out of view, an aluminum ladder was raised to the balcony. A SWAT officer on the balcony glared down at me.

"So much for the safe house," I said.

"Peralta thinks Yuri found it by following you."

I stared at the chief, too sore to argue. He went on, "Whoever followed you this afternoon might have been trying to keep you away from here. So they could make their move. They want Lindsey."

"I guess they succeeded in keeping me away," I said quietly.

"Obviously it's not just Yuri. He's got help."

"And we can't seem to do anything to stop him."

"Did you get a tag?" Kimbrough asked.

I shook my head, a jolt of pain driving into my shoulder blades. I ran through what happened, from the time I noticed the Hummer on my tail. Then Kimbrough wanted it again, from the time I left the condo that morning. I was certain I wasn't being followed. Yes, I had gone through all the agreed upon procedures. No, I couldn't be sure that the blond man at Encanto Park was a bad guy. When I was done, I just wanted to go to Lindsey.

"You can't," Kimbrough said.

I asked why.

"It's a federal case. The FBI has taken over, moved her to a secure location."

"Sounds like a kidnapping."

"Don't be a smart-ass, this is serious. This was a close call."

"No shit," I said. "How do you know she's safe now?"

"I know!"

"Where is she?" I knew I was babbling. I couldn't stop myself.

"I don't know," he admitted. "They won't even tell me."

"Then how do you know anything?"

"My detectives took her to a rendezvous with the feds. One of our men will be with the federal agents. You remember Patrick Blair, from Robbery-Homicide Division? He'll stay with her."

"Damn it!"

"You don't have to shout," Kimbrough said.

Amid all that was coming at me, I realized my ears were ringing loudly. In a lower voice, I asked, "When can I see her?"

Kimbrough said nothing, and the frustration made every ache worse.

I tried it another way. "What if she's asking to see me?"

"She's being told the same thing," Kimbrough said. "Every member of her team is now in protective custody."

"So she doesn't have civil rights, just because she works for the Sheriff's Office? This is nuts. You promised this would be for two weeks. Now, she's gone God knows where, and you have nothing to say to me?"

"I don't have the answers, David. Wish I did. You're lucky you're not in jail after what you pulled on the freeway with DPS. You've got to be a professional about this. Lindsey is at risk, and any of us could bring her into danger without even realizing it. I feel like I had a role in this, too, finding a way for you two to stay together when maybe that wasn't such a smart thing. Now we've got to let the people with the real experience deal with this."

A city cop came up and told Kimbrough the building was clear. Whoever had used the ladder was gone. The cop was all of twenty-five, with a dirty blond crew cut, and he kept calling Kimbrough "dude." Kimbrough glared at him each time, but the kid was oblivious to social skills, protocol, or any breaches thereof.

Kimbrough watched the cop walk away. Then he reached in his coat, and his features relaxed into a benevolent smile. "Here's a voucher for the Hyatt. We're shutting down this safe house. You need some rest. The sheriff will get with you tomorrow. I know he's interested in the progress of your case. He's at a fund-raiser at the Boulders, or he'd be here now. I promise we'll get you some information about Lindsey as soon as possible."

I waved the envelope away. "Nothing personal, Chief," I said. "You're a good guy. But this situation is fucked. I'm going home."

Kimbrough gave me an alarmed stare. "You can't. . ."

"Yes, I can," I said. "I'm going upstairs to get the cat."

I pointed down Cypress Street, into the lush old trees of the Willo district. "Then I'm going home."

⟨⟩⟨⟩⟨⟩

A fleet of thunderheads over the South Mountains was set ablaze by the fading sun. The sunset seemed to electrify the prism edges of the Bank One Center, tallest building in downtown, until the tower was defined by the bright straight lines of reflection from the west. Airliners took off from Sky Harbor, two by two, flashing in the last of the sunlight as they made their turns. Gradually, the sky gave way to an infinite, India ink blue-black, silhouetting the palm trees against the incandescent twilight.

Under this vault of big sky, I was a puny human sitting on his front porch, in front of the 1924 stucco house with the big picture window. The porch was dark and the house behind it was dark. I was in a dark way, not feeling quite human, aware of the comforting bulk of the submachine gun on my lap. The grass needed cutting and mail had gathered inside the door. Lindsey's old Honda Prelude—the bumper sticker read KEEP HONKING. I'M RELOADING—needed washing. Otherwise, the house looked much as we had left it more than two weeks before. Just to make sure, Lindsey's old gray tabby, Pasternak, prowled every room. That left me to assess the damage of a large highway patrol trooper hitting me from behind at speed, sandwiching me in between him and the pavement. The knees of a pair of Tommy Hilfiger chinos were a lost cause, and beneath them David Mapstone's knees weren't doing much better. The small of my back felt on fire, with devilish little arsonists spreading the blaze to each vertebra. My earlobes hurt—go figure that out.

I thought about whether I had really put Lindsey at risk. Whether I had been protective or selfish in demanding to be with her after the Scottsdale shooting. "Protective," my heart said, for this was apparently an open-ended threat, and our friends in law enforcement had proven remarkably inept in dealing with it. My head stayed silent in the debate, preferring to concentrate on its headache.

All these SWAT cops in their paramilitary attire, what did this mean for the health of American civil society? Like surveillance cameras everywhere, pre-employment drug tests, and other subtle assaults on the Constitution. Was it this way with the Roman Republic, the gradual loss of liberty under the guise of continual warfare? Cicero, eloquent, impotent...(Yes, David, distract yourself with a Big Thought.)

A pickup truck roared down the street. It was one of those two-story-tall four-by-fours, and he was doing at least sixty. My finger went automatically to the gun trigger. He raced by, heading to Seventh Avenue, no more able to stop for a pedestrian or a wayward child than a supertanker. People drove with such rage in my town. Maybe it was true everywhere now. I wondered: was this the way we would live now, Lindsey and me? Under constant threat, mistaking any speeding blockhead for Yuri or his agents.

Patrick Blair. Patrick Fucking Blair. Some personal history here: Lindsey and I split up once. It was after we'd been seeing each other for a year, and under pressure of circumstances and personal griefs, we just stopped seeing each other. There was no grand announcement. But jealousy is a powerful, primal thing, and I knew at the time Lindsey was working with a handsome young detective named Patrick Blair. We had never talked about those two months apart. And my hands weren't clean, either. But that's another personal history story. . .

My eyes were on a big man lumbering west on Cypress, crossing Third Avenue. He was walking with a pronounced limp.

"Just sittin' on the porch with an automatic weapon, eh?" Peralta emerged from the heavy twilight. He was wearing brown uniform pants with oversize cargo pockets, and an MCSO polo shirt. The cargo pockets were so full they made him look a bit like a cavalryman wearing jodhpurs. He was holding something to his face.

"I thought you were schmoozing campaign donors in Carefree?"

He sat heavily in the other chair. "Stopped to help some deputies," he said. "Haven't been in a fight like that for quite a while." He was holding a cold pack to his left cheek, mashing the flesh against his temple. "Dirtbag was already arrested, and he broke out the window of a patrol car and took off. So they ran him down a little off Bell Road, and he's fighting like a son of a bitch. Bites a deputy. Hits me square in the face, I mean nails me. So I had to change and get cleaned up. Another one of your misunderstood homeless guys. . ."

He adjusted the cold pack and looked at me. "Did you tell her you love her this morning?"

"What?"

"Did you tell her you love her?"

"Of course."

"We do dangerous work, Mapstone. You, me, the same as these deputies this afternoon who had a prisoner fight them. I live with that burden for an entire department. Some days good men and women aren't going to come back."

"When the hell did you decide to become compassionate?" I was still feeling less than human. I stared out at the street, where the houses were starting to light up with a merry hospitality I didn't feel.

Peralta refused to take easy bait. Instead, he ordered me to fix drinks. So I set aside the gun and went into the kitchen. In five minutes I returned with a shaker and glasses, and filled a Gibson for Peralta and a martini for me. He had moved only enough to produce two cigars, his favorite Anniversario Padrons. He clipped one and handed it to me. We each lit a cigar in silence, watching the flame become a corona around the tip. I am only an occasional cigar smoker, mostly with the sheriff. We last smoked cigars after his father's funeral, smoked and sat in silence in Peralta's study.

Now I let the smoke waft across my palate, and my muscles relaxed notch by notch. Peralta lifted his glass and gently clinked mine.

"*Salud,*" he said. I added gin and vermouth to the taste of fine Dominican tobacco.

"Patrick Blair is protecting my wife," I said finally, instantly feeling adolescent and small.

He grunted. "Why, don't you trust her?"

"Fuck you."

He sighed and sipped. "David, sometimes you can be a real asshole. You probably don't even know when you're doing it."

Fair enough, I thought. I sipped the gin, feeling the cold liquid burn my throat. All my aches felt instantly better.

"Separation is good for a marriage," he ventured.

"Is that the way it is for you and Sharon?"

He ignored me. "You act like I'm all-powerful, like I can control and fix everything. . ."

"That's an impression you strive to convey," I snarled, angry from two weeks of hiding, two weeks of a toy investigation into the fate of an FBI badge. I was still nursing wounds from his angry lecture after Kate's press conference.

"Get it straight," he hit right back. "Yuri, the Russian mafia, the shooting in Scottsdale, Rachel Pearson's kidnapping—that's all new. I can't snap my fingers and fix it." He let an inch of fine ash fall off the tip of his cigar.

"So what you're telling me is that I may never see my wife again, and nobody can change that, and you don't give a shit."

Frustration was talking. And a little booze. Once again, though, he declined to escalate the war I was trying so hard to start. And, deep down, I knew I was safe bitching. Peralta's temper was like a nuclear weapon. You couldn't detonate it by hammering on it. You had to know the physics. You had to have the codes. So we drank and smoked, wrapped in a smoky haze as the neighborhood surrendered to full darkness.

By the start of the second drink, he asked about George Weed.

"The rummy, as you call him? I thought he didn't matter."

"You're being an asshole again, Mapstone."

So I drank, too fast, and told him what I knew. George Weed was sixty-six years old when he died. He'd been born in 1938. He had a Social Security number. All this came from a county hospital card he held in the early 1980s, when he was being treated for stomach ulcers. He was a native Phoenician.

His birth certificate said his parents were Aimee Jones Weed, sixteen years old, and Homer Weed, twenty-five, whose occupation was listed as "laborer." In between birth and his death in the green swimming pool, Weed worked as an elevator operator and a janitor. He rented an apartment for years just north of downtown. The apartment was now a vacant lot. He had been on the streets for years, at least a decade. The Reverend Card had watched him for three summers, said he was "paranoid." Peralta asked, "Any family?"

"No one has claimed the body," I said. "We've run his photo on TV and the Sheriff's Office Web site. As far as the old county hospital card, I couldn't find any corresponding records listing next of kin."

I knew what that meant: soon the sheriff's chain gang would take George Weed and put him in the potter's field by the White Tank Mountains, a desolate desert graveyard with numbers denoting the dead buried at the county's expense.

"Not bad, Mapstone," Peralta said slowly, speaking around the cigar in his mouth. "Pretty good detective work."

"I know it doesn't tell us how he came to have an FBI badge."

Deep in my head, I was only wondering where Lindsey was, how she was. I glance back in the house, half expecting her to come out with chips and salsa and join us. But Lindsey wasn't there. I felt her absence more painfully as we talked hour after hour, through three drinks.

"I have an offer, to go back to teaching," I said.

He stared into the night while I told him about the job at Portland State.

"It rains all the time." he said.

"Not that much, and I like rain."

"You'd be bored," he said. "Sitting around with Volvo drivers, using nonsexist language and hugging trees. Dip me in chocolate and throw me to the lesbians—I could never work in a university."

"I believe that."

"You won't go." Peralta said, hurting my feelings that he didn't try harder to talk me out of it.

Finally, Peralta rose to go. He looked steady as a tree trunk. "You're dumb to stay in this house," he said, his posture showing no evidence of having consumed a trio of sizable cocktails.

"You're here." I said.

He motioned to the east. "I have a security detail waiting for me over there." A pair of car headlights came on.

Peralta stared into the dry black sky, where you could see stars even against the city lights. He said softly, "You and I go back, don't we, Mapstone?"

I agreed we did.

He produced an envelope from the cargo pants and set it on his chair. "Those are tickets to San Francisco. On the county's dime. In that envelope you'll also find a name and an address. It's the son of Special Agent John Pilgrim. Why don't you go talk to him about his father?"

I stood, a bit unsteady. "What will Eric Pham have to say about that?"

"Leave him to me."

I didn't pick up the ticket.

"Lindsey is going to be fine," he said, "And you'll be climbing the walls."

"Why do you care?"

"About Lindsey? You must really think I am a bastard."

"You are a bastard," I said, draining my martini and setting down the glass. "But I mean the Pilgrim case, George Weed in the swimming pool. Why do you care?"

Peralta said nothing. The skin on his face hardened until, in the meager light reflected from city sky, he seemed to take on the countenance of a stone idol. Waiting for worship or sacrifice, I thought unkindly. I said, "You go to San Francisco. You can see Sharon."

"Not my kind of place," Peralta said. "Can't you just trust me for once? We go back, remember? Old partners?"

"Old partners are straight with each other."

"Thanks for the drinks, Mapstone." He ambled down to the street, his earlier limp gone, and a black Crown Victoria slid up to the curb.

He gave me a little wave with his big hand and disappeared inside.

Chapter Seventeen

The force of jet engines pushed me into the fabric and cushion of my seat. It was just enough G-force to keep my back from hurting. After several hours of looking at the airline tickets, I had decided to get out of town. Less than twenty-four hours after being taken down like any other scumbag fleeing from the cops, I had a diverse menu of aches and pains. For some strange reason, I was less nervous than usual about flying. Maybe after two weeks of keeping anxiety like an unwanted boarder I had become accustomed to being afraid all the time.

Out the window, the city fell away rapidly and spread out. It looked like a 1,500-square-mile semiconductor chip surrounded by dun and gray mountains. Down below, spring was almost gone. April had been a succession of days with above average temperatures. The sweet season that begins in October would be burned away by May, followed by the hellish summer. All the rich people fled to Coronado or Del Mar or the San Juan Islands. The rest of us suffered.

The jetliner climbed and turned northwest. Out the window, the urban organism that was Phoenix ate up the fields and citrus groves that had once separated the city from the desert. Farming was the oldest human activity in the Salt River Valley, dating back to the prehistoric Indians who dug the first canals. Now it was almost all gone. Home looks different from 15,000 feet.

I was on the airplane after spending one of those nights of the damned that produces artists or serial killers. Sleep brought nightmares of violence and loss. Waking brought its own anxieties. Every noise in the old house assumed a sinister tone. Closing and locking the bedroom door provided no security to my imagination. Nor did keeping on every light. So I lay down, turned from side to side, got up, prowled, came back to bed, over and over. I swore I could smell Lindsey in the sheets. That and lying on her side of the bed provided my only comfort. So I walked the floors, checking doors and windows, setting traps, finally turning off all the lights so I could watch the street. Pasternak, the old tomcat, watched me from Grandfather's grand old leather chair. The Russian mafia didn't come, but sometime after 4 A.M. I was lost in yet another nightmare, vivid and horrible. The clock said I had been asleep for all of fifteen minutes.

I was really hurting by that time. So I downed too many Advils and took up station in the study. There was nothing to do but try to work, so I put my mind on the world of John Pilgrim. In 1948, World War II had been barely over for three years but the Cold War was coming together. Harry Truman had won a surprise victory for another term as president. But a freshman Republican Senator named Joe McCarthy was accusing the administration of being riddled with communist agents. The Russians were about to acquire the A-bomb. It was a time of fear.

John Pilgrim would have arrived in a small farm town called Phoenix. It was an entirely different dimension, a different state of matter, from the sprawling city I was leaving, with its golf courses, world class resorts, endless subdivisions, and urban problems. Phoenix in 1948 consisted of about seventeen square miles. Those who weren't farming worked in the produce warehouses, the farm implement businesses, and the feedlots and slaughterhouses of the world's largest stockyards. The good jobs were on the railroads, or in the banks and offices that a small city could support. One of those offices was my grandfather's dental practice downtown on Washington Street.

The sense of newness and mastery of nature must have been overwhelming. The Valley had only been inhabited, in modern times, for eight decades. Before that, it was a vast wilderness, with the abandoned canals of the Hohokam sitting there for centuries as testimony that here was one of the most fertile river valleys in the world, provided you could add water. At the turn of the twentieth century, the federal government did add water, with the dams and lakes on the river east of town, and the desert bloomed. By the 1940s, the second miracle was coming into wide use: refrigerated air. A completely manmade environment became possible. Thousands of servicemen had trained in the Arizona desert during the war, and many had decided they wanted to return. So the sleepy farm town that John Pilgrim found was in the midst of big change.

Pilgrim's world would have been one of hopeless conformity to twenty-first-century eyes. If a man was lucky, he held one job all his life, a good union trade. And lucky was the word, for these people had been through a Great Depression when a quarter of the workforce was out of a job. In a little town like Phoenix, people lived conventional lives, went to church, knew their neighbors. This was the confining place John Pilgrim found.

But none of that told me a damned thing about why John Pilgrim ended up dead, and lost his badge. And I was right on the edge of a profound thought when I slipped into a heavy nap 30,000 feet above California.

<>◇<>

I took the new BART line from the airport into San Francisco. The train was filled with all the characters that make a real city. A pair of Anglo men in their twenties held an intense huddled conversation about who really killed Tupac Shakur. A hulking dark-haired man carried a flamboyant tropical bird on his shoulder. Miniskirted coeds danced through the car, changing seats with arthritic old women. Street kids bummed change. But there was no mysterious blond man with the Slavic face, no one paying any attention to me. I felt anonymous and safe. By 4 P.M., I had checked into a little hotel on Grant Street, right at the gate of Chinatown. Lindsey and I had discovered it years ago. I didn't stay long, changing into a navy suit with a blue

Ben Silver tie, checking a street map, and heading out into the heart of the city. The air was cool and healing, with fog starting to congregate over Mount Sutro.

Richard Pilgrim lived on Washington Street in Pacific Heights. It was one of those fabulous city neighborhoods with everything you could want in walking distance. There was nothing like it in the 1,500 square miles of Phoenix sprawl. The address went with a five-story Victorian job with big bay windows jutting over the street. Richard was on the fifth floor, and after explaining myself over the intercom, he pressed a buzzer and I went up.

The man who met me at the elevator and studied my ID was nearly a head shorter than me, with a slight body and black forearm hair curling out of the cuffs of a simple but expensive-looking gray turtleneck. He had a clerk's face, mild and unquestioning, with small brown eyes, a comb-over of thin straight black hair, and a mouth too broad for the too narrow lower part of his skull. His skin looked draped and unhealthy, like sun-bleached tent fabric.

"This is a very unexpected visit," he said, once we were seated opposite each other in a high-ceilinged living room. The room was large but cramped with too much furniture, upholstered in very loud reds and greens, and stacks of books and newspapers. I noted art books, science—physics and astronomy—investing primers, children's books, coffee-table photography books. A polymath.

"I didn't know if the FBI had been in touch," I explained. "A little more than two weeks ago, your father's badge was found in Phoenix. It had been missing since his death." I was calm and measured, using my counsel-the-victims voice that had also been useful with neurotic graduate students back in my professor days. The small eyes watched me. They seemed permanently wet. I went on: "The badge was being carried by a homeless man who was found dead in a swimming pool. We don't know why this man was carrying your father's badge."

The broad mouth smiled. "Sounds like the perfect macabre Phoenix crime," Richard Pilgrim said. "Is that all?"

I looked him over. He sat across from me perfectly compact, folded in on himself as neat as a shirt back from the cleaners. "That's all," I said. "Except for a few questions."

"Always questions." He sighed. "You'll have to excuse me, Deputy, if I'm not playing the role correctly. My father was killed over half a century ago. I was ten years old. I have few memories of him, and those I have aren't particularly…savory." He was a man who chose his words. "You see, Deputy, there was a general once named Douglas MacArthur, and he had a son."

"Arthur," I said, more from reflex than a desire to be a show-off.

"One doesn't expect a policeman to know such obscure knowledge," Richard Pilgrim said.

"I play a lot of trivia games," I said. "Arthur disappeared as an adult, lived a life of obscurity. Very different from his father's grandiose life."

"Exactly." Richard said, tapping his slight knee. "In my small way, I was touched by that story. My father was a hero, so they said. A hero on a small scale. He was a tough guy. Loud. Athletic. I wanted none of that. In fact, I spent my entire life trying to get away from my father's influence.'

"And here I am, waking the dead."

"Exactly."

"Seems as if you succeeded," I ventured. "In getting away. What exactly do you do for a living, if you don't mind my asking?"

"Live each day gratefully." He smiled. "I'm a freelance editor. The book business is awful, but I've managed to make a good living. I never have to leave my flat if I don't want to."

"That would be a pity, such a nice neighborhood."

"Yes, you're from awful Phoenix, so I'm surprised you can appreciate it."

"I thought about what it would look like as a giant surface parking lot and Home Depot store." He didn't smile. Back to business. "Mr. Pilgrim, does the name George Weed mean anything to you?"

He shook his head. I told him who Weed was.

"Sounds like an alias," the G-man's son said.

"I realize you were only a kid, but do you have much memory of the time when your father died?"

"I remember everything," he said simply. "They came to the door after we were asleep. Mother talked to them in the living room, I knew it was bad. We were living in a little duplex on…I think it was Culver Street. I'd been in four different schools by the fifth grade, he was transferred so much. I hated being in Phoenix. I hated the heat. They closed his coffin for the funeral, and I was afraid to touch it. They folded up a flag and gave it to my mother."

"You said some memories weren't so good."

"I used the word 'unsavory.' My father had a drinking problem. He and Mother fought. He hit her. It's not fun to see when you're a little kid. He'd stay out, whoring around, I suppose. There were money problems. I remember once I followed him on my bike to one of his bars. Who knows what the hell I was thinking. Maybe that if I caught him everything could be made happy for us. The Pla-Mor Tap Room. I never forgot that name. When he realized I was behind him, he didn't get mad, didn't hit me—and believe me, he was capable of it. He took me in and bought me a beer, shot some pool, made me feel like a little man. I was ten years old. He was like that, too, could be fun as hell. Very charming. I didn't know until years later it was classic drunk behavior."

"What was your mother like?"

"She was small and pretty and kind," he said, speaking rapidly. "She deserved better. After he was killed, she wanted to move us to Los Angeles, to live with her brother. But she took up with a man there in Phoenix, another version of my father." He rubbed the loose face skin. "None of that matters to whatever investigation you're pursuing."

"Do you have any siblings?" I looked around for family photos, found none.

He shook his head, staring intently at the floor. "There was a lot beneath the surface. In his life. Don't ask me what. Little kids pick up on these things, even if they lack the sophistication to know the specific details."

"Did he ever mention his work? Anything you might have overheard."

"Somebody named…Duke." He raised his forefinger in a triumph of memory. I waited. "Duke somebody. I remember this terrible fight my parents had just before he walked out, for the last time. It must have been just before he was killed. They were yelling like furies, and this Duke person kept coming up."

"A friend? Somebody your father was investigating?"

"I just don't know," he said, shaking his bony head, deflated.

"What did they tell you happened to your father?"

"He was killed in the line of duty," Richard Pilgrim said. "And he was a hero. I never believed it. I thought he drank himself to death, or got into some kind of trouble. You need to believe me, Deputy, that I haven't spent my life obsessing about this, like some low-rent Hamlet."

He walked me to the door. "I'm sorry your trip was for nothing," he said. "But maybe you'll have better luck when you talk to Renzetti."

I raised my eyebrows.

"Didn't they tell you? His old partner is retired in San Jose. Vince Renzetti. The old guy's got to be ninety-five, but he's still alive. Still wants to be the good FBI man, looking after the windows and orphans. I talked to him not more than a month ago."

Chapter Eighteen

Vince Renzetti, John Pilgrim's old partner, lived in a comfortable vest pocket of a neighborhood just north of San Jose's small downtown. On the train down the Peninsula from San Francisco, I got eyefuls of the squat flat-roofed, glass-skinned office parks from which Silicon Valley rules the world. But the center of San Jose seemed like the prosperous farm town that it would have been decades ago, when canning prunes meant more than thinking up software. At the least, the architecture was more appealing: a charming Spanish colonial railroad station, where I transferred to the light rail line; a handful of interesting old hotels and office buildings, well restored; an imposing old cathedral, and a sign that pointed to Peralta Adobe Historic Park. That last one brought me back to the business at hand.

Renzetti had one of those "go to hell, telemarketer" devices on his phone, which required you to dial in your phone number in order to complete the call. When I did, he had no reason to know who was calling or why—so, not surprisingly, he didn't pick up. So there I was on his street. The address went with a little gray Deco Moderne house, all Buck Rogers curves and streamlines, deep in the shade of hundred-year-old trees. It was about two blocks off the light rail line, and the walk felt fine in the warming morning air. I didn't know whether I would like this town or not—I didn't know the way to San Jose and had never been there before. But I liked the vistas, yellow-brown hills lifting up in the east, and in the west a brooding line of blue-green mountains. The map told me the ocean was on the other side. An airport must have been nearby, as a succession of jetliners, silver bellies close, swooped across the sky.

I walked up a narrow brick sidewalk. You never know what you'll find when you go calling on retired cops. The stereotype of the lawman who puts down the badge and ends up putting a gun in his mouth has more than a little truth to it. Cop work is a consuming calling, and some cops lose too much of themselves in a world that can be very insular and destructive. Sounded like universities, when you thought about it. Of course, there were happier outcomes. Two of the retired cops on my street had taken up art, one working in metal and the other in woodworking. Hell, they seemed healthier minded than me on a good day.

Vince Renzetti's mailbox told me I was probably dealing with a by-the-book guy. A prominent decal proclaimed "Retired Special Agents of the FBI—Gold Member." On the door, a hand-lettered sign said, "In the garden, to your left."

Sure enough, another narrow brick sidewalk took me to the west side of the house, through a gate, and into a walled-in side yard. I stepped into an outdoor room: walls and ceiling of limbs and vines, wainscoting and floor of stalks, ferns and flowers, a vault of deep green, with splashes of purples, reds, and yellows. I don't know much about gardening, aside from enjoying Lindsey's handiwork back home. But it seemed as if this side yard could pass for a small city's prized botanical garden. The rows of plantings and sandy pathways had a military precision that was very different from the cultivated wildness of Lindsey's garden. I heard a loud snipping noise behind an extravagant stand of irises.

"Agent Renzetti?" I said to the back of the man making the snipping noise.

"That's me." The voice didn't go with an old man. It was a powerful baritone. The man stood, unfolded himself, and looked me over.

"You don't look like the man who's supposed to be delivering my dirt."

I held up my badge and ID card and told him who I was.

The man who took my badge case certainly didn't look in his nineties. He looked like one of those heroic comic characters come to life: muscular chest sprouting out of a tiny waistline, thick jaw, gray hair combed in a Brylcreem pompadour. Only his hands seemed old: mottled, bony, arthritic walnuts where the knuckles used to be. And where his upper arms disappeared into his T-shirt, pale crepey skin draped down. He was tall and stood with an officer's bearing. His eyes were a strange yellow-green—was that called hazel?—and they didn't like what they saw.

"Maricopa County?" the baritone boomed. He held his garden shears as if he might use them on me. "What's your business here, deputy sheriff?"

"I'm investigating the John Pilgrim case."

"John Pilgrim?"

"I understand he was your partner, when you worked in Phoenix in the 1940s."

"That's an FBI matter," he said. His lips barely moved when he talked. It was more a gentle bobbing of the jutting square jaw. "I can't talk to local law enforcement about that."

He handed back the badge case and turned back to his work, the comic book hero body kneeling down to a flower bed.

"Agent Renzetti, we found his badge."

He stopped, then the bony hands resumed their snipping, picking up each dead stalk as he worked. "What are you talking about?"

"The missing badge. We found it a few weeks ago, on a homeless man who had died. I was hoping you could give me some insight into what Agent Pilgrim was working on when he died."

"How the hell did you find me?"

I told him about Pilgrim's son.

He turned his head toward me. The eyes studied me with disinterested hostility.

"What's your name again?"

I gave it to him.

"Badge number?"

"I've been working with the Phoenix FBI."

"Then you won't mind giving me your badge number."

I gave it to him. I was wasting my time in this pleasant little neighborhood a long way from home.

The hero turned back to his flowerbed. He just let me stand there. I watched a hummingbird, just over his shoulder, levitate amid some yellow trumpet-shaped blossoms.

"Good day, deputy."

"Let me give you my card, with the number where I'm staying in San Francisco." I pulled a card out of my blazer pocket and dropped it on a nearby potting bench.

As I walked away, I heard, "Please don't bother me again."

‹›‹›‹›

When I got back to the hotel there was a message from Eric Pham. Please call. I thought about calling—maybe it was about Lindsey. But I knew it was about Renzetti, as in, what the hell was I doing? If there were trouble with Lindsey, Peralta would call. I could count on that, couldn't I? I ignored the message and called Sharon Peralta. We agreed to meet for dinner.

We met at Tadich Grille, a walk down a hill from the hotel on busy city streets. After a long enough wait in the noisy bar for me to finish a martini and for Sharon to sip a cosmopolitan, we were shown to a secluded booth in the back. Sharon was turned out elegantly, as always, in a black pantsuit with a simple turquoise pendent dangling from her neck. Her hair was pulled back in a chignon. Those huge, lovely dark eyes looked as they had when she was twenty-five. I hadn't seen her for months, since she began commuting to San Francisco.

"So how is Mike?" she wanted to know. It was an odd question coming from his wife of, what, twenty-nine years? But, as she had said before, I had been his partner on the streets, and partners sometimes knew more than spouses did.

I settled for, "OK, I guess." I wasn't going to engage in special pleading with the sheriff's wife, even if we had known each other for what seemed like forever. I had known her when she was my partner's shy young wife. But her gradual transformation hadn't surprised me. From persisting in getting her degrees, to establishing her practice in Scottsdale, to her debut on radio and writing the self-help book that was to become her first best-seller—I'd like to say I always knew it would happen. Sharon had grit.

"I know it must be frustrating for you, not being with Lindsey," she said, reading me pretty well, as always.

"I don't understand his obsession with this case," I said.

"He's not comprehensible by us mere mortals, David. You know that. I'm still waiting for him to mourn his father's death. Not Mr. Tough. Frankly, I'm surprised you've put up with his moods for the past five years."

"You wanted me to come home to Phoenix as much as he did," I said.

"I know," she said, her huge liquid black eyes studying me. "But I've come to hate Phoenix. They've ruined it, David. We natives remember when it was wonderful. But now Phoenix has all the problems of a big city, and none of the culture, none of the edge. The politics are insane. There's no economy. The heat is worse and worse."

"But it's a dry heat…"

She grimaced. "Oh, God. No I had to leave, David. That's one reason I'm here."

"Here is nice."

"I could see you here, David." She gave a mischievous smile. "You're cultivated and quirky. You are such a big-city person."

"Thanks, I guess."

"Your Little Miss Perfect would like it, too."

"Lindsey," I said.

"Mmmmm. OK, no cattiness, I know you're worried. And I must admit she's been good for you."

We ordered, and I ate too much. Sharon told me how her old practice had dwindled in the years she was doing her radio show, so she felt free enough to work from San Francisco and commute to Phoenix twice a month. "I'm not sure, after twenty years of practice, that I was doing most of my patients any good," she said. Here she could focus on her radio show—"I know it's entertainment," she said—and writing. She was teaching a class at San Francisco State.

Then she wanted to know more about me, and I told her about Dan Milton's death and my own questions about whether I should go back to teaching, my growing discontent with my hometown.

"Maybe it's my midlife crisis," I said.

"You should go to Portland," Sharon said. "You need to be around smart, stimulating people."

I just listened.

"Do you still have panic attacks, David?"

I hunched deeper into my seat. It wasn't something I was proud of, despite the New Age of nonjudgmentalism. I said, "Not so much now."

"See, I told you Lindsey was good for you." She patted my hand. "You're a Renaissance man, David. One of the last. You needed to come back to Phoenix when you did—you found Lindsey there, didn't you? Somehow you needed the adventure of the sheriff's office. You're a man of action and a man of the mind. A thinking woman's deputy." She laughed, her full crystal laugh that I realized I had missed. "But you were gone from Phoenix for years before you came back. You just outgrew Phoenix. I did, too, in my way. Whatever comes next will become clear soon enough. I've lived long enough to know every day is a gift. I'm damned if I'll mortgage my happiness to the future a day longer. That's another reason I'm here."

"And what about the sheriff?" I ventured cautiously.

She shrugged and made a little face. "He's got his dream," she said quietly.

Unease descended over me. God knows they'd had trouble before. But Mike and Sharon had always been together. All my adult life, really. I started blathering about my case. Then the check came.

<>⟨>⟨>

Outside, a misty rain had begun. I started to hail Sharon a cab, but she put a hand on my arm.

"David, you need to know."

"I don't, Sharon."

"Yes, you do. I have someone here. Someone I'm in love with." She studied my face. "Don't hate me," she said.

"You know I don't," I said. "I'm just listening. Does Mike...?"

"No," she said. "I don't think he cares. He doesn't want to be here. And he had a fling years ago. But this isn't payback. I really want to be happy, David. Nobody knows this yet, but I'm going to end the radio show. Money isn't an issue now. I just want to finally live my life. My daughters are here. And now I feel like I have a real shot at something good."

Sharon's black hair glistened in the misty rain, and I saw clearly how it was shot through with gray, how her face was now a scrimshaw of subtle wrinkles. We'd all gotten older together, me and Mike and Sharon. But the world was moving at a thousand miles a minute. I felt a wave of love and sadness. I pulled her into me and hugged her. She cleaved close to me, and I could feel her tears on my neck.

"Time to get you out of the rain," I said, holding my arm up. In a few seconds, a yellow cab pulled over.

⟨>⟨>⟨>

I buttoned up my trench coat and walked, happy to be surrounded by the tall buildings and the lights. The detached scholar in me absorbed Sharon's news with equanimity, while the edgy David was thrilled. A few couples walked by covered by umbrellas. Men and women. Women and women. Men and men. Better to muse on the many wonderful varieties of love in a beautiful city. The windows of an art gallery shimmered in the night, well-dressed patrons inside laughing and drinking wine. The narrow, crowded streets of Chinatown beckoned on one side. The towers of the financial district rose above me. Sharon was right, I could see myself here.

I turned onto a darker sidestreet and heard voices singing. Singing well. They seemed weirdly out of place on a deserted sidewalk. I recognized the grand nineteenth-century hymn, written before modernity and doubt: "Oh God, Our Help in Ages Past." A church hulked against the street, its stones black from age and soot. But a stained glass window was brilliantly lit, and it let out the voices of the choir practice inside. It took me a moment to realize that one of the voices was closer, coming from a darkened portal into the church. My eyes adjusted to a raggedy man standing against the sooty stones. He had a beautiful voice. "'Time, like an ever rolling stream, bears all who breathe away,'" he sang to the street.

At his feet was an upturned hat. I pulled out a bill and dropped it in. I walked on slowly, letting the rain mend my desert skin, hearing the voices fade.

When I got to the lobby, the desk clerk handed me a message. It was from Vince Renzetti.

Chapter Nineteen

What is it about old photographs? Did they always look old? On a shelf at home, my grandmother and grandfather look out at me from a sepia print. He wears a thin tie and suit coat, she a simple, light-colored blouse. He is blond, with a wide, sensual mouth. She is black Irish, her eyes brooding and intelligent. Both wear serious expressions—the style of the day, and, as Grandfather told me much later, a style that helped conceal the dental problems that were rampant then. Those days were 1910, and Grandmother and Grandfather were newlyweds, twenty and twenty-four years old respectively. And of course that photo was the leading edge of technology of that day. They didn't sit for the photographer in dusty territorial Arizona knowing that many decades later they would look like a museum piece to their grandson, who lived with everyday miracles such as jet travel, air-conditioning, biotechnology, and computers.

I reminded myself of this as I sat in Vince Renzetti's parlor and took in a lifetime of old photos that sat on tables, shelves, and walls—everywhere that didn't house a plant. He was one of those men who were told "You haven't changed a bit!" at reunions. So he was instantly recognizable in the Army Air Corps officer's uniform of World War II. Same in the photo with J. Edgar Hoover, both men wearing double-breasted suits and expressions of straight-mouthed seriousness. And another picture showing him with a young man who had a thin nose and an earnest Kentucky face: John Pilgrim. They were walking with their hands on the arms of a fleshy-faced guy who tried to look away from the camera.

"That was just after we were assigned to Phoenix, in 1947," Renzetti said, noticing me noticing the photo. "Everybody wore suits, ties, and hats back then. Even the bad guys."

He sat in a straight-backed chair opposite me, drinking green tea. This day he wore a blue blazer and red and white rep tie. Outside a screen door the weather was chill and rainy. Inside, it was uncomfortably warm and smelled vaguely of dill and Williams LectricShave.

"I've checked you out, Mapstone," he said in the booming master-of-ceremonies voice. "You worked as a sheriff's deputy when you were young. Then you got your Ph.D. in history and taught for fifteen years. When you failed to gain tenure, you went back home to Phoenix. You got a job from your old partner, who was the chief deputy."

"Now he's the sheriff," I interposed.

"You use the historian's techniques to solve old cases," he went on. "Very innovative."

Renzetti's eyes never left me. His hands didn't move from the teacup he held in his lap—no gesticulating Italian-American stereotype in Vincent Renzetti. His posture was relaxed and businesslike. Only his sentences, short, chopped, conveyed any sense of energy or agitation.

"You were raised by your paternal grandparents," he said. "Why?"

"My parents died," I said, trying to force down a feeling that we were playing a game of personal manipulation, maybe just as he played it as a G-man. "They were in a small plane."

"I'm sorry," he said, and a little warmth took his voice down a few decibels. "My wife and child are dead, too." He motioned to a shelf of family photos, a black-and-white of a fair-haired woman with merry eyes and a wide, glistening forehead, and a color photo of what seemed like her clone in long hippy hair—a daughter. But he offered no explanation.

"I gave my life to the Bureau," he said. "I don't regret it. Most of the time."

And he told his story. He was a kid from San Francisco, North Beach, born in 1919. His parents came over from Naples before the Great War. His father, who couldn't read or write, delivered milk with a horse-drawn wagon. But young Vincent was forced to stay in school. He went on to Cal-Berkeley. When World War II broke out, he enlisted in the Air Corps, and flew P-51 Mustang fighters in Europe. He didn't say it, but I noticed a Silver Star pinned on the uniform of the young officer in the photo. After the war, he went to law school and then joined the FBI. He was a rookie when he came to Phoenix.

"My point is that I've decided to take a chance on you, Mapstone," he said. "The Bureau was good to me. I've had a good career, and a good life. The only thing I regret is what happened to John Pilgrim."

He sipped his tea and I watched, afraid even to breathe.

"Nowdays, I read these stories about a special agent who was passing secrets to the Russians. Another one who was selling information to the Mafia. Then the agents who warned about terrorists, and they were ignored. That hurts, personally. It makes me wonder why I stayed silent all those years."

The room grew large with expectation. Outside the screen door, I could hear soft rain, and beyond that, a siren. I asked quietly, "Did Pilgrim kill himself?"

"No, hell no," Renzetti said, his nostrils flaring. He set the teacup aside and shook his head in short, exasperated jerks. "That's just nonsense. John loved life. He loved everything about it. Maybe too much."

"So why...?"

"Why? Because John was a maverick. Because John made his bosses look bad when he solved cases his own way. Because they didn't know what the hell happened, and saying he was a suicide tied a neat little ribbon around it. Even if that ribbon was only for internal consumption. Look, the Bureau probably told you John was a head case of some kind, that he was sent to Phoenix to get one last chance. That's bullshit. He was a top agent. He was sent to Phoenix to trap a spy." He sipped his tea and watched my reaction. "That's right. The Soviets had moles at Los Alamos. People working on the nuclear program. All this has come out the past few years, Moscow releasing documents, American papers declassified…"

"The Venona documents."

"Very good. So in the late forties, the Bureau moved against these spies, and it became too risky for them to meet their handlers in Santa Fe or Albuquerque. But Phoenix was a day's train ride away for someone working at Los Alamos. It was big enough that you could go unnoticed. We got a tip that a Russian had set up shop in Phoenix, a guy named Dimitri. He spoke good English, and passed himself off as a hard-working immigrant. His real mission was to pass along atomic secrets."

I eased back in my chair, trying to take it all in. My case of a homeless man carrying a missing badge had suddenly catapulted me into the dawn of the Cold War. The Red Scare.

"There *were* spies," Renzetti said emphatically, fixing me with the yellow eyes. "It wasn't like that cocksucker McCarthy told it. But Soviet agents had penetrated parts of the government. John was transferred from Los Angeles to Phoenix to shadow this Dimitri. And I was just some shavetail kid who was assigned to go with him."

They had arrived in Phoenix in the summer of 1947, and soon found themselves handling more than the Russian. "It was a wide-open town," Renzetti said. "Like the old West meets Tammany Hall. Phoenix was run by a city commission, and the commissioners were dirty. One of them was running prostitution and drugs on the south side of town. There were allegations that some of the local contractors who had built the training bases during the war had defrauded the government of huge amounts of money and material. There were problems on the Indian reservations. On top of that, the Mafia started to move in, buying land, selling protection. The Chicago Outfit set up a little satellite operation, and they started taking over the rackets from the locals. Lot of bloodshed. We had a six-man field office, and we could have used a hundred agents."

"Sounds like Pilgrim could have made a lot of enemies," I said.

"He did. Look, Pilgrim was no saint. He liked drink and he liked women. Hell, he *loved* women. It was a different kind of world then. But he was a damned good agent. We got an indictment against the one commissioner, Duke Simms. We sent some of the local cops to prison, and we slowed down the mobsters."

I noted the name Duke—Pilgrim's son had mentioned a Duke. I said, "What about Dimitri?"

"Disappeared. After John was shot."

"And you don't buy the suicide theory."

"No."

"His son seems to believe it. The Bureau definitely does."

"They didn't know him the way I did. Look, Pilgrim told me he was going to meet a guy. Somebody who had information about Dimitri. That was the last I saw him. He turned up dead two days later."

"Why didn't you go with him?"

"I was a newlywed, Mapstone. It was the weekend, and I wanted to be with my wife."

I unconsciously looked at the photo of his wife. Renzetti continued. "If it was a suicide, why did Pilgrim's car turn up in downtown Phoenix, miles from where the body was found? Why did his badge and gun disappear?"

"Wait," I said. "I didn't know his gun wasn't found. That wasn't in the report."

"I know," Renzetti said.

"So you're saying the FBI covered this up?"

Renzetti stared at his bony fingers folded in his lap. "I'm saying they didn't know what happened. Everything about this case was embarrassing, and the Bureau under Mr. Hoover was very averse to being embarrassed. Get it? We interviewed over a thousand people, and never could even find a suspect to bring in. The guy we came to bag escaped, maybe back to Russia. But there's more to it. John was his own man, did things his own way. The bosses didn't like him, and there were things I didn't like, either. Maybe the brass was afraid they'd find he was dirty, and they didn't want to know."

"Was he?"

Renzetti's head moved from side to side with finality. "No way. John drank too much and womanized way too much. But he was a great FBI man."

"So Dimitri killed him?"

"Yes," he said emphatically. Then his arms slowly extended, hands palms up. "I can't prove anything. It's always haunted me. After John was killed, I was transferred to the Bay Area, and I spent my career here."

Here seemed a lonely place now. A picture palace of beloved dead. Men like Vince Renzetti had always made me feel small, in an admiring way. They had served their country in combat in a great cause, something most Baby Boomers would never know. Strong, taciturn men who knew whether they were cowards or not. They walked to a Sousa march, "Semper Fidelis," perhaps. Peralta was such a man. Finally, I was always dumbstruck in their presence. When nothing more could be said, I was tempted to ask if there was anything I could do for him, anyone I could call. But he hadn't invited that intimacy. So I gathered up my trench coat and, thanking him, walked away into the rain.

Chapter Twenty

I rode the train back to San Francisco feeling the weight of too many Russians in my life. Yuri, the shadowy cyber-criminal who had a contract out on my wife. Dimitri, the spy, who may have killed John Pilgrim. But my list of questions was only growing, topped by: how did the badge get from the murdered G-man to the jacket of the dead homeless man? Had it been passed from person to person over the years, perhaps bringing a cursed fate to the bearer? Or had it always been on George Weed? Rainwater dashed against the train's windows, spreading and trailing back. I studied the geography of the clouds, feeling further from the answer than ever. The only thing to do was fly back to Phoenix and face Peralta's wrath.

I must have been dozing. The car rocked a little as another train swept past us. I opened my eyes enough to see the Palo Alto depot washed by the rain. Maybe I could get a job as a lecturer at Stanford. Lindsey and I could live in the city, and I could ride the train to work. Maybe pigs would fly. Maybe I was a protégé of Dan Milton, but the world had too many well-credentialed history professors wanting to find sinecures at top universities. Still, it was a nice daydream. I let my head settle into the softness of the seat and closed my eyes again, day-dreaming about Lindsey. Nicer daydreams. Taking her out on the town. Having her read me a classic in bed. The times she would wear black pumps and nothing else...

But when the train lurched forward again my eyes fluttered open just enough to see the face in the window of the door that led to the next train car. The face was looking at me. It was a blond man, with his hair slicked back. I kept my head down and my eyes nearly closed. I didn't believe it. Maybe he had just intruded in my dozing. I closed my eyes tightly for a second. But when I opened them again, he was there.

It was the blond man from Encanto Park. He saw me see him. The face disappeared and I could see the door to the next car open and close. A burst of adrenaline lifted me to my feet and propelled me toward the door.

The train was picking up speed, gently swaying side to side. My feet found purchase with the rocking motion, and I slipped quickly to the end of the car. Then I opened the sliding metal door that went into a small, enclosed vestibule where the cars connected. Around me, the train sounds were louder, the air cooler. I looked through the glass of the next door. The car was full of Silicon Valley commuters going home to towns on the Peninsula or in the city. Faces regarded me with the wary disinterest of city people. I stayed in the vestibule, watching. No blond man. For reassurance, I felt the Colt Python in the nylon holster on my belt, and then I pulled the door open and stepped into the next car.

These were double-decker commuter cars. So I had the best view of the people sitting on the first level, where the seats were two abreast on either side of the aisle. Stepping forward, I could also see the seats above, single chairs that overlooked the car's central hallway and were set off by a railing. It became clear what I couldn't see: the stairways up to the second level.

I moved quickly up the winding stairs. But just as my head came up enough to see down in the car, a figure moved out of the staircase at the opposite end, pulled open the door, and disappeared forward into the train. It was the blond man. He was again well-dressed, in a dark blue suit, red tie, and white shirt. His suit coat was roomy enough to conceal a large firearm. I fought to slow my breathing as I crossed the carpeted aisle on the second floor, tramped down the metal stairs, and followed him through the next door. I could hear a conductor calling out the stop at Redwood City and the train was slowing. I couldn't let my blond-headed watcher get away.

Then I was face down, my nose mashed into the cold metal floor of the vestibule. My brain was about two steps behind events, fighting desperately to catch up. He'd used a neat move on me, waiting just the other side of the vestibule, then coming at me from behind once I stepped through. He must have stepped into the back of my knee to bring me down, then pulled my trench coat and suit coat over my arms to disable me while shoving my face into the floor. I admired the hell of out his little move as I struggled to swing myself around, worried that a bullet might come into the back of my head, my hand struggling to feel the butt of the Python, my mouth full of cottony fear. I was conscious of all the metal grinding against metal around me, as the train cars rubbed against each other. But I was alone in the vestibule.

By the time I got on my feet, the blond man could have been a mile from the train. We were moving again, and I could see nothing out the window but drizzle-mussed lights fading rapidly behind us. I limped back to my seat, avoiding the eyes of a conductor who was paying too much attention to me. My knee was feeling as if it were constructed of Jell-O, and for some reason my stomach was queasy, too. I slumped into my seat, feeling foolish and vulnerable. The blond Russian slimebag had played me like I was a rookie. No, like a civilian. I was a joke.

Then I became conscious of the frantic pounding against my breastbone, a sense of constriction, my breath gathering inside me. The old familiar sense of dread, that death could be at hand. But I knew this was no heart attack. It was a bad brew of brain chemistry, that's all. Or maybe it was the melancholy and fatalism of Celtic and Welsh genes stewing around inside me, the knowledge that history would eventually work against me. I tried to ignore it.

My injured pride rocked along with the train as we passed through Hollister, San Bruno, and the grassy empty land that was once the city's main rail yard. The car was silent except for the beat radiating from the headset of the kid sitting across from me. The Russian couldn't be after me to get to Lindsey—unless he thought she was in San Francisco with me. Or his mission was somehow to grab me as a bargaining chip. Either thought was unsettling. At least she was safe. I prayed she was safe. Wherever the hell she was. With Patrick Blair, with his waterbed eyes. I visibly shook the junk of brooding thoughts out of my head as the train slowed. We stopped at a forlorn little shelter at the foot of a hill. We were back in the city now, but outside the landscape looked abandoned. Gentrification had apparently not reached this far into San Francisco's underbelly.

And a well-dressed man gingerly stepped off the train and walked toward the shelter.

The Russian.

David has good judgment—that's what people always said. As a teenager, I was mature and careful. The older cops appreciated that I wasn't a hotdog, and the older professors commented on my thoughtful nature. As a bachelor, I never radiated the danger that can attract so many women. Nope, I was predictable, prudent... ponderous, as one old girlfriend said as she was getting restless. Yep, David doesn't do stupid impulsive things. Usually.

I bolted up and ran for the exit, nearly flattening an elderly Asian woman trying to find a seat. The door was just about to shut. I jammed my fist against the rubber edge and the door stopped and opened again. A little alarm rang. My foot was already on the wet asphalt. I stepped out of the streetlight and felt the train pull away. Then the spot became as silent as the primeval forest.

I surveyed my surroundings. The shelter sat in a little depression, down a hill from what looked like some apartments. A long footpath ran down the hill from the apartments to the station. In one direction the tracks ran into a tunnel, and above that some darkened industrial buildings. Behind me, old warehouses crowded right up to the tracks. The air smelled of the bay and something heavy and sour, maybe an oil refinery. There was not another person or car within sight. Then I saw the Russian.

He was already two-thirds of the way up the footpath, passing through a cone of light, walking rapidly.

There was only one way out: the footpath. I took the chance he wouldn't look behind him, and ran as fast as I dared along the rain-soaked concrete. He was already past the buildings and out of sight by the time I had covered the hundred yards that took me to the cone of light where I had first spotted him. It was a tough climb from the tracks, and the moist heavy air burned in my lungs. When no gunshots came from the direction of the apartments, I continued on, hoping he hadn't seen me get off the train.

In minutes I was on a street. Looking right, I saw the Russian was two blocks ahead, walking slower now, his shadow bobbing off a wall. This was definitely not the part of San Francisco the tourists saw. From cracked pavement on the street and sidewalks to the big empty buildings with their broken windows and graffiti-stained walls, it had seen better days. The historian in me appreciated what I was seeing: the remains of the old industrial city, when railroads and manufacturing and union jobs defined upward mobility for most Americans. The buildings around me were substantial, brick and stone, several stories tall, with elaborate machinery sprouting out of roofs and sides. One wall had collapsed, revealing a nave and transept of an abandoned industrial cathedral. Remains of railroad tracks ran down the middle of the street, and the cracked curbs were matted with old trash. Here and there, a working warehouse remained, trucks coldly illuminated by harsh yellow-orange security lighting. Elsewhere, sparse streetlights radiated a cool gloom.

As I walked, I became aware of old cars parked in empty lots. But they weren't abandoned. I saw movement inside. A cook fire flared beside one ruined van. People living in their cars. A little colony, in sight of the soaring towers of downtown. And two men in suits walking past.

I drew closer to the Russian. If he had seen me he wasn't show-ing it. At one point he looked behind him, but I had stepped into the dead space of a wall that jutted close to the street. It was dumb luck but I took it. Then there was the matter of what I would do when I caught up with him. Or, my panicky insides reminded me, what he would do with me. My cell phone was in my trench coat. So easy to call the local authorities and…what? I couldn't prove anything. And considering that I was wandering outside my jurisdiction without having checked in with the San Francisco PD…I let the cell phone be.

At an intersection overgrown with weeds, the Russian pivoted on his heels and turned left. I was close enough that I could hear the broken glass and rocks grinding under his shoes. The panic attack was long gone. All my nerve endings were back in service and focused on the moment. I took a chance and sprinted up an alley that ran behind a brick warehouse. Alley cats and other critters scattered in my wake as I really put on the gas. My hamstrings and calves burned in protest. I pounded across chuckholes and broken concrete, then slowed to a walk and consciously made myself breathe normally. Trying, this time, to recover a little of my long-ago training. I was conscious of the whiteness of the fog moving high above.

Then I had the Python out and in his face. This time the nice little move had been mine, cutting him off as he started up the new street. I dropped into a combat stance, both hands on the revolver.

"Move and I'll blow you to the fucking moon."

The Russian stared open-mouthed, his hands in front of him as if he had just struck an absurd pose. Even in the streetlight, his hair was almost surreally yellow, and his skin was pink. His swimming-pool blue eyes orbited under yellow slashes of eyebrows. His mouth was small, but his lips were delicate. This was definitely the guy from Encanto Park. Presumably the one who followed me in the Hummer, who lured me away from Lindsey while his crew tried to get into the condo.

We just stared at each other. Finally, I was able to generate enough saliva to get my tongue to order him onto the ground.

"Deputy, you're making a mistake," the Russian said in English. Indeed, it was the best imitation of a Mississippi accent I could imagine.

"I'm FBI," the Russian said. "I'm on the job."

My brain heard that but I stayed in the combat stance. I let him reach slowly into his coat and produce an oversized black wallet. Inside were credentials, and a badge that looked very much like the one we pulled from the pool in Maryvale.

"Good forgery," I said.

"No, listen…" he fumbled. I could see sweat shining on his pink forehead. Being on the business end of the Python will do that. "I work for Eric Pham," he blurted.

"Why?" It was all I could think to say.

"He just wanted me to keep an eye on you. That's it!"

"You were at the park," I said.

"Yes."

"And you followed me, in a black Hummer?"

"What? That wasn't me, man. You think the Bureau would spring for a Humvee?"

"You're sure? You didn't follow me out on the freeway?"

"I know what I did. I broke off contact after you left the park."

I kept the gun on him but snatched the badge case and examined it under the light. The credentials had all the holograph stuff shining through that I had seen on Pham's men in Maryvale. This ID said the blond man was Special Agent Danny Maddox. I relaxed my stance and handed back the badge case. I holstered the Python and cursed.

"He just wanted to keep you out of trouble," Maddox said.

It was just another way to say he wanted someone spying on me. I was learning fast why local cops mistrusted the feds.

‹›‹›‹›

Maddox and I shared a cab downtown. He was just a guy doing his job. Then I walked alone past the shining shop windows of the stores around Union Square, still mad as hell—at Pham, at Peralta, at everybody. I ended up in a bar called John's, where the menus proclaimed some tie between the place and the Maltese Falcon. I let the bartender make me a martini, then another.

More than ever, 1 didn't want to be on this case. More than ever, I wanted to find Lindsey and run away. Maybe to Portland, where Dan Milton spent happy years. She didn't like the rain as much as I did.

An envelope was waiting for me back at the hotel. Inside was a sheet of fax paper, with my name and address in the upper right corner of the page. As I unfolded it, I saw it was blank except for a prominent smudge close to the center. Exactly the shape that lipsticked lips would make if they kissed the paper. Exactly the shape of Lindsey's sensual lips. Exactly off center, from a woman who mistrusted symmetry. That was all—not a word written. The margins, where a sending fax number might appear, only held a series of dashes and asterisks. But my lover had found me nevertheless. I touched the kiss, folded the paper into my jacket, and went upstairs.

Chapter Twenty-one

They met me just beyond the security checkpoint at the Gold-water Terminal at Sky Harbor. While other people were greeted by expectant friends, smiling lovers, or goo-gooing children, I was welcomed back home by two FBI agents. They were generically good-looking—he had been the dark-haired high school quarterback, she the blond cheerleader who had also led the honor society. All they wanted from me was a quiet walk to the car. I kept my firearm. We were all conspicuously armed. A half dozen white-shirted TSA guards were chatting amiably with each other, occasionally glancing in our direction.

Then we were speeding along the freeways and surface streets, heading north. The jacaranda and palo verde trees were blooming, but the cityscape was unavoidably Phoenix, all seven-lane streets, suburban setbacks, and soulless commercial buildings. Big-box drugstores and gas stations seemingly on every corner. The signs of our strange local economy: check cashing outlets, bankruptcy lawyers, used cars and mortgage refinance companies, in English and Spanish. Piestewa Peak angled out of the smog, a dark mass in the brownish air. The sun radiated heat through the windows, and soon I was covered with a sheen of sweat. We weren't going downtown, and I felt a jolt of unease, as if Yuri's mobsters had forged those complicated Bureau credentials and the agents in the front seat were really Ivan and Ludmilla instead of Biff and Muffy. But the real estate became steadily nicer, and then we were winding into the lush preserve of the Arizona Biltmore. It was too pricey a joint to use for killing one history professor.

Five minutes later, they deposited me in a large suite with an expansive view of the golf course and the red-rock head of Camelback Mountain. But to get that view, I had to look past the crowd of feds seated and standing as if they were a theater tableau frozen by my entrance. Unlike well-suited Biff and Muffy, this bunch was outfitted in a kind of overdone resort casual, as if they had all suddenly been ordered to serve search warrants at Tommy Bahama. Of course they looked utterly conformist, decidedly un-casual. They were all looking at me. Eric Pham gave me a prim, sad shake of the head.

I said, "I'm glad to see my tax dollars at work."

"Shut up, Mapstone." This from a female voice. The woman attached to it was somewhere around fifty, with a round face and frosted short hair. She introduced herself as Assistant Director Davies, beckoned me to sit, and for maybe a minute we all just watched each other. The feds' faces eyed me like junkyard dogs ready to pounce on a cat burglar. We were in one of the new suites, heavy on Indian art and Southwest colors. But it still had the deco touches of the old hotel, the creation of a Frank Lloyd Wright disciple and for decades the province of visiting bigs. Go down in the lobby, and you can see the photos of the Biltmore when it was alone in the pristine desert, miles from the city and nestled against untouched mountains. Now it was about in the center of the metropolitan area. I was pretty well gone in this reverie when they started firing questions, semiautomatic.

"What were you doing in California?"

"Who authorized you to contact Pilgrim's son?"

"Why did you talk to Vincent Renzetti?"

"What did you tell them?"

"…a detailed report on your actions…"

I let them run down and finally said, "But I thought 'alliances are the way to get things done in the New Economy.'"

"What is he talking about?" Davies demanded. Pham stared into the deep piles of the cream-colored carpeting.

"I'm talking about the naïve idea we're on the same side here," I said. "I'm trying to find out what happened to your agent."

"That's the problem," said a sausage-faced man who stood behind the assistant director. "You have no authorization."

The words dropped into the room as if Robespierre had sentenced me to the guillotine. All that was missing was a basket to receive my severed head. But the crowd nearly gasped.

All the attention made me alternately frightened and amused. I tried to go with the latter feeling. "You guys…" I shook my head. "You're still trying to cover your asses."

"Hey!" A man's voice. Assistant Director Davies held up a hand.

"This is serious, Mapstone," Davies said. "What did Renzetti tell you?"

"Not a damned thing," I lied. "He's a lonely old man. You ought to invite him to a retirees party every now and then."

"He's talked to us," Davies said.

"So." I said, "you know he didn't tell me anything. He's a stand-up guy." Stand-up enough to keep my confidences, I hoped.

The Feds looked at each other.

I asked, "What are you afraid he'd tell me?" They easily ignored this foolish civilian entreaty.

Another Fed: "Special Agent Maddox said you went to Renzetti's house twice. That's a lot of trips for nothing."

"That happens sometimes in law enforcement," I said. My career had been built on lots of trips for nothing.

"And the son?"

"He was a kid when his father died," I said. "He doesn't know anything."

Sausage Face demanded, "Why did you remain in San Francisco four additional days after you assaulted Special Agent Maddox? You were gone an entire week, Mapstone."

"I assaulted him? Jesus!" I wished I were facing toward the window. As it was, all I could see were hostile faces in golfing shirts. "You assholes decided to have him tail me—how smart is that?"

"Answer the question, please."

"I was sightseeing," I said. "Am I under arrest?"

Silence. Bureaucratic brains processed. I was sure if I tried, I could hear the clanking. Assistant Director Davies' makeup looked odd, with rough meeting points for base and rouge. Hell, I was no expert. I stood and walked to a window. The gigantic pools were stocked with beautiful people and not so beautiful people with fat bankbooks. Others meandered on the putting green and bowling lawn. They were loving the ninety-nine-degree weather—back home it was probably forty-five degrees and the sun hadn't shined for a month. If you could spring for several hundred dollars a night, you could live better than a Roman emperor.

I tried again, "What are you guys afraid of? That I've found photos of J. Edgar Hoover in a dress plotting the Kennedy assassination?"

That set them all off.

"…highly sensitive…"

"Who have you told about this case?"

"…national security…"

"…court order to check your hard drive…"

"OK," Davies said. "Let's hear it from the top. From the moment you last met Eric. Everything you've done. Including your meeting at the park with the retired Phoenix detective, Wolfe."

I gave them a sanitized version, but even so it took about an hour with their questions. I left out some of Wolfe's conversation and lots from Renzetti. I didn't tell them my sightseeing was across the Bay, to the University of California library's special collections. One of the archivists was another protégé of Milton. It was a valuable connection. When I was finished telling the story, it didn't seem as if I'd accomplished much at all. They seemed to agree, if you could judge by the bored faces in the room. All except Pham, who looked as if he had been constipated for a month.

But Davies wasn't done.

"Weren't you once involved romantically with a newspaper reporter?" she demanded.

"Yes, about twenty-five years ago," I said. "Is that the best you can do? What the hell are you so afraid of?" My worry instincts told me these folks could use some new antiterrorism statute to toss me in jail forever. I pushed past them and said, "I thought the Bureau was convinced that John Pilgrim was a suicide."

"That's correct," Davies said, a note of discomfort creeping into her voice.

I continued, "So I'm just looking for the way his badge ended up on a homeless guy in Maricopa County. And right now I'm not making any progress."

Davies gave a chilly smile. "I don't know if there's progress to be made, Dr. Mapstone."

"I could make more progress if I could get Bureau help in tracking down records on Pilgrim's death."

She shrugged. "Sometimes we just have to live with mysteries." Then she nodded toward Biff and Muffy, who put hands on my shoulders. "These agents will drive you home, Dr. Mapstone. Thank you for your time."

‹›‹›‹›

I had just lugged my bags inside the house on Cypress Street when there was a banging on the front door. I clipped the holstered Python on my belt and walked quietly in the direction of the banging.

It was Peralta in full dress uniform, his star gleaming in the sun.

"Let's go."

"Where?" I was tired and annoyed.

He was already halfway to the street, where his familiar black Crown Victoria was idling.

"So what'd you do to piss off the FBI?" he asked, once we were rolling. After I told him a Reader's Digest version of the past week, he said the Feds were demanding I be taken off the case. He was smiling.

"I thought you said not to worry about Eric Pham."

"They're pretty mad," Peralta said. "You can make people mad, Mapstone."

"I just have an inquiring mind. John Adams said an inquiring mind is God's greatest gift."

Peralta grunted.

In thirty minutes, we were on the far west side of the city, past the old suburb of Maryvale and into the new sprawl of Avondale and Goodyear, heading toward the White Tank Mountains.

"Where are we going?"

"Are you ready to offer a theory?" he demanded.

"Not yet. Where are we going?" The sun sent heat waves off the freeway, the mirages of the auto age. Late April and the newspaper said every day of the month had been above normal temperatures. I angled some air conditioner vents on me and finally started to cool off.

His deep set, lively black eyes looked me over, then returned to the road. He said, "Patience." That was to my question. He had none. "How does all this connect with your homeless guy?"

I said, "Patience."

He shifted his bulk in his seat. "We don't have a lot of time, Mapstone…"

"What?" I said. "My wife is being chased by the Russian mafia and I can't even see her. I don't have a clue how our life is going to be from now on. That's urgency I can understand. This fifty-year-old murder case is—"

"Important," he said.

Then we were at the gate of Luke Air Force Base, where heavily armed Air Police in camouflage fatigues waved us through the maze of concrete barriers.

"I've had my fill of feds today," I said. Peralta ignored me as we passed the main administration buildings, then anonymous brick maintenance and barracks buildings. Luke was the largest fighter training base in the world—but the subdivisions kept creeping closer, and soon it would be forced to shut down. We eased the car past more guards, barriers, and concertina. Peralta stopped the car and we both were ordered out for a search. As an airman used a mirror on wheels to check the underside of Peralta's cruiser, we handed over our firearms and signed on a clipboard. The Air Police were young, superbly fit, and unsmiling. Then we were loaded into an olive Humvee—not the luxury civilian kind that had chased me. An Air Police officer in back slid a hood over my head.

"What the hell?" My heart rate shot up instantly.

"Just relax, sir. Please leave the hood in place for security reasons."

"I'm not relaxed."

"C'mon, Mapstone." I heard Peralta's voice. "Do yourself a favor."

I felt movement, air coming through the open windows, the distant blast of F-16 jet engines. The fabric of the hood was rough against my face, and it was hot. Things were getting too strange. What secret history had I stumbled onto in the embalmed living room of Vince Renzetti, in the archives at Cal-Berkeley? What unlucky amulet was the lost badge of John Pilgrim? Somehow it fit together: the Russian agent in dusty old Phoenix; the Chicago Outfit, consolidating their crime empire; the young FBI man with a love of trouble and women, who nevertheless was very good at his job. A single shot beside an irrigation canal. A missing badge. And then five decades…

Lindsey would help me make sense of this. Lindsey would shield me from my dark moods and my night fears and the consequences of my inquiring mind. I needed Lindsey right then, right that second.

And when the Humvee stopped and they pulled off the hood, she was there.

Chapter Twenty-two

My federally arranged conjugal visit lasted a little less than sixteen hours. Too soon, I was in a sheriff's cruiser, piloted by a quiet young deputy, headed back to the center city. I used the silence of the ride to think about how welcome Lindsey's flesh had been against mine. I noticed how thin and even frail she seemed to feel in my arms, how the hours let things shift back and forth between us, who was strong, who was scared. She felt guilty over Rachel Pearson, that she was somehow responsible. She dreamed about Rachel's death.

Clouds had come in from the west overnight, and little hints of rain floated into the windshield. It would be the first trace we'd gotten all year. For a few hours, everything seemed a little better. When the deputy deposited me back on Cypress Street, I went inside and showered reluctantly, wishing I could keep the physical evidence of her on my skin and in my hair for the days to come. I had no idea when I might see her again.

But it was a workaday Tuesday, if your workaday included a wife who had been kidnapped by the national security state, the threat of Russian mobsters, and the deepening mystery of John Pilgrim's badge. It had been nearly a month since Weed's body was found. At least it was raining. I took comfort from the drops hitting the convertible top as I drove down to the old courthouse. Inside, I walked past the new guard, a slight kid named Alfredo, who nodded and looked away. I took the winding stairs two at a time, feeling some wonderfully sore muscles in my legs and abdomen. I missed Lindsey already.

The old courthouse was slowly being restored, floor by floor. Four years earlier, when I had taken that "temporary" job for Peralta, the imposing brown masonry building had been nearly empty. The marriage license bureau was in the basement. And I set up my history shop on the fourth floor, in an office that had once held the sheriff. In the 1940s, the building was also home to Duke Simms and the corrupt commissioners investigated by John Pilgrim. A floor above me was the old jail, which shut down in the 1960s. When I worked late, I tried not to conjure the ghosts of prisoners and jailers. Now, the county wanted the old building back, and was slowly refurbishing each floor. Soon, I suspected, I would be forced to find a new office. But while the county suffered through a fiscal crisis, the restoration had stalled on the third floor. And the fourth floor was my private sanctuary.

I reached the top of the staircase and crossed the polished tiles of the atrium, then turned down the hallway that led to my office. But even at the head of the hallway, I could see my door was ajar. I instinctively moved to the wall and stopped to listen. Now the feeling in my legs was sudden fear, a rubbery sickness in the muscles. The dryness in my mouth was unrelieved by the tapping of rain on the big windows behind me. Nothing moved in the dimly lit hallway. No sound came from beyond the glass of my office door, and the only light came from the windows beyond. But the door stood open maybe two feet. I edged down the marble floor, past the dark glossy wood frames of other doors and transoms. I always locked my door. The courthouse janitorial staff, alas, never made it to four unless I called them for a special trip.

I paused ten feet from the office door and slid the Python into my hand. Then I took a handful of quiet steps and settled against the wall of my office. DEPUTY DAVID MAPSTONE, SHERIFF'S OFFICE HISTORIAN, the sign said. No sounds came from beyond the open door. Looking in, I could see changes. Someone had been in there. Gripping the magnum in both hands I went through the door and swept the big room with the barrel. I had no doubt that I looked vaguely ridiculous.

The office was clear of danger, but it had been visited. Turning on the lights, I saw the extent of it. Drawers weren't quite closed. Files were lightly tousled. The Pilgrim case bulletin board was moved several feet from where I left it. Whoever had been here made little effort to conceal their visit. Then I heard footsteps and wheeled, sighting down the barrel at the guard.

"Take it easy!" he said.

"Somebody broke in," I said, holstering the gun.

"I had to let them in, sir."

I stared at him.

"It was the FBI. Three of them. They showed me their IDs."

"When?"

"They were here about an hour ago."

I eased myself down into the wooden swivel chair.

"FBI?" I asked. He nodded. "And they just walked into a county office? Wait until Peralta hears that."

Alfredo coughed softly. "The sheriff was here. He told me to let them in."

I felt a heaviness in my feet and let him say it again.

"Who else was here?"

"Well, a woman detective was with them, too," Alfredo said.

"Kate Vare?"

"They all seemed in a hurry. I thought they were just waiting for you. I didn't think…"

I just glowered at him.

"I'm sorry, sir." he said. "What does it mean?"

I said softly, "I wish I knew."

When I didn't say anything more, he disappeared out the door and I heard his footsteps in the empty hallway. I was left alone with my paranoia. Outside the expansive arched windows, rain bathed the bland skyscrapers of downtown. The raindrops made a soft roar in my ears. I picked up the phone and called Peralta's office. His secretary said he had gone out on a raid.

I took down the location, thought for a few moments, then turned out the lights, locked the door, and walked loudly back toward the staircase.

Forty-five minutes later, I pulled off Interstate 17 and followed the directions Peralta's secretary gave me. They led to a trailer off in the high desert northeast of New River. But this was no wilderness idyll. The place was littered with junk cars, old refrigerators, and anonymous castoffs from the machine age. Trash sat in six-foot piles, and dangled from the branches of palo verde trees. Now it was also cluttered with sheriff's vehicles. I showed my badge and a deputy in a yellow slicker waved me through the perimeter. It was slightly nastier than the usual meth bust. Another deputy told me that in addition to the illegal substances, the bust had yielded a half dozen starved horses, a goat, twenty wild dogs, and six emaciated children. Let's just say it was a piece of Arizona that the chamber of commerce didn't want the tourists to see.

Peralta wasn't there. So I bumped back over the muddy dirt road to the interstate and got on the cell phone. I tried his private cell, a highly classified number. But it only rang and beeped, not even a greeting on the message system. I told him to call me and hung up. I was tempted to call Eric Pham, Kate Vare. Demand to know what they were doing searching my office, what hidden agendas were being played out at my expense. But an interior voice stopped me. I drove back to the city with a head full of thoughts and questions, none of them good.

Chapter Twenty-three

The phone rang once. Just enough to wake me. No more rings followed, but the ring's echo seemed to linger in the room. When I picked up the receiver, only a dial tone waited on the line. The clock by the bed said 3:13. I hadn't been afraid of the dark since I was a little boy. So why was my heart hammering against my chest? Lord Nelson had suffered from panic attacks and night sweats. That was no comfort at the moment. Around me was the familiar old bedroom, where Lindsey and I played, laughed, and read to each other. The nightstand on my side of the bed held a thick volume with a royal blue binding: Woodrow Wilson and the Decline of the Progressive Age, by Daniel J. Milton. Autographed by the author. I knew the inscription by heart: "To David Mapstone, who is gifted with a fine, if fey, mind." Tonight the fey ruled. I reached beside the book to find the comforting bulk of the Colt Python, and I slid out of bed.

I prowled the house, nude except for the big revolver, conscious of how often I was drawing down lately. "Size matters," I would have joked to Lindsey. But Lindsey wasn't there. Pasternak met me outside the bedroom door and followed me, agitated just like me. Only a fool would keep living in this house after his wife had been targeted by the Russian mafia. We didn't even have an alarm. I stepped into the living room and leaned against the wall, listening. The light flowed blue-white through the picture window. Everything looked normal, the high ceiling, the heavy iron chandelier, stairs that opened onto a walkway that led to the garage apartment, the floor-to-ceiling bookshelves.

Grandfather had built this house only twelve years after Arizona became a state. It had been the physical manifestation of his flourishing dental practice. And the place where he would bring his baby son, named Calvin because Grandmother liked the name, and it was the president's name. Grandmother, whose first name was Emma, had come to Arizona from Indian Territory in 1910, because her brother was farming near Phoenix. She was black-haired and vivacious. By the time I knew her, her hair was white and the sun had turned her skin into a wrinkly parchment, but she still had the spirits that beguiled Grandfather. They had loved this house.

Cal Mapstone had flown B-17s in World War II, and came home to take his part of the great Arizona boom. But schooled in Grandfather's ideal of service, he became a physician, attending medical school in Los Angeles. He came back to Phoenix in the '50s and worked in the VA Hospital. He had married late, by the standards of the day, at age thirty-two. His bride was named Laura and came to Phoenix to be near her father, who was dying at the VA. They married in 1958, and a year later I came along. A year after that, my father and my mother were lost in a small plane on a trip to Colorado. Grandfather always said the plane would have been safe if Cal had been flying. But it had been another pilot. And the baby David came to this house, where he had been raised by his grandparents. Death and loss attended this house tonight.

Tread carefully in the past, Dan Milton told me, more than once. And so when I came back to Phoenix, I knew ghosts would be there to welcome me home. Mostly, they had been a comfort, with only the occasional heartache. But as I leaned against the wall, I realized that all the feelings that had been gathering inside me for the past two months were watered by more than the Russians and a vague sense of restlessness. It was more than a yearning to be a "real" historian. More than the sense it was time to let Phoenix go and move on. It was the terrible truth that adults hide from children, that drives the reflective soul to religion or philosophy. We are born to die. Our time here is so brief. Dan Milton, Judge Peralta, George Weed. Lindsey's colleagues who went off for a fun night of drinks in Scottsdale and ended up dead. Vince Renzetti, with his fading photos and the awful knowledge that when he died all those memories would die with him. Now I faced the real possibility that Lindsey could be killed. Or I could. This will never be over, Lindsey had said. I wanted to believe that I only wanted to survive to take care of her, my wife who knew some measure of grief and loneliness before we found each other. But, in truth, I was afraid, too.

I made myself walk. Better to walk than to dissolve into self-pitying existentialism. Out the window, the street looked safely deserted. The rain had moved on earlier in the evening, allowing for one of those Phoenix sunsets that make you weak in the knees. This one began with wavy scarlet streaks across the sky, and ended thirty minutes later with an emphatic red and purple vortex on the western horizon, precisely at the foot of Indian School Road. I was a connoisseur of Phoenix sunsets, but I had never seen anything like this. It looked as though if I could drive fast enough, I could enter the expressionist dimension of that sunset moment. Phoenix sunsets inspired such thoughts.

Into the study, I found nothing but the small light indicating Lindsey's printer was plugged in. The enclosed courtyard in back needed sweeping, but otherwise looked benign. The house was silent except for the familiar creaks and plumbing noises. I walked halfway up the stairs and sat, perusing book titles and petting the cat. That's when I saw it.

Out the window, on the street, just beyond the low hedge of the house next door. A glow. A cigarette glow. I closed my eyes tightly, not believing it at first. But the glow came again, unmistakably.

I made myself descend the stairs silently, as if any errant step would instantly be heard outside. In the bedroom, I pulled on some sweats and running shoes. I needed to be ready for anything. Still carrying the gun, I went to the bedroom window, which had a better view of the western end of the street. But the glow was gone. I stood in the dark, with the curtain barely pulled back, watching. A long minute went by, and I thought I had talked myself into seeing things. Then, just beyond the black bulk of the hedge, an orange tip flamed again. Someone was standing there, smoking. At 3:30 in the morning.

I reached for the phone and started to dial 9-1-1. I only got to the "9" and stopped. What if it was my neighbor, outside smoking. Only she was seventy and didn't smoke. I placed my hand on the phone. The worst that can happen is the cops find a vagrant sitting by the curb. Or a Russian hit team ready to take me out. I picked up the phone. I set it back on the nightstand.

"I can't live in fear," I said aloud, walking to the back of the house.

I let myself out the back door, crossed the yard, and then unlocked the gate that led into the alley. It was so dark it took a few minutes for my eyes to adjust. But then I was able to make good time down the gravel that led to Fifth Avenue. Once on the sidewalk, I quickly doubled back to Cypress Street. Somewhere in the distance I heard the rhythmic whisper-clack of a lawn sprinkler, the timer ignoring the recent rain; a train whistle coming from the Santa Fe line by Grand Avenue. I moved into the lawns, close to the fronts of the houses, and walked back toward the source of the glow. The grass gave way under my tread, but I moved quietly enough. The air was cool and dry, just the hint of a breeze from the High Country. As I got closer, I discerned the form of a man sitting on a motorcycle, watching my house. I had the cell phone in my pocket. But I held the Python in my hand.

"Don't even breathe," I said, making a show of cocking the Colt, an unnecessary piece of theater to actually firing a double-action revolver. But the decisive click of metal on metal carried its own important information.

"Dr. Mapstone, what are you doing out at this hour?"

It was Bobby Hamid.

His feline eyes glittered from the light of the street lamp. His casual posture on the motorcycle barely changed. He was wearing a supple leather jacket that on anyone else would have invited touching. A black knit top and black jeans completed the ensemble. I let the gun's hammer down and slid it into my waistband.

"No sleep tonight, Dr. Mapstone?" he said. "Virgil called sleep the brother of death. That has always stayed with me."

I didn't know whether to be worried or angry or relieved. "What if I told you the police are on their way?"

"This is a public street," he said. He took a drag from a small cigar, producing the glow I had seen from the house. "And I am talking with my friend, the history professor."

"I always wanted to have a gangster as a friend." I sighed.

"Oh, David, those are old wives' tales from the cop shop— one of those wonderful Americanisms, 'cop shop.' Sheriff Peralta doesn't understand me."

"He understands your connection to half the meth operations in the Southwest," I said. "Along with assorted murder and mayhem."

"And you know," he said amiably "that I have never been convicted, despite Sheriff Peralta's best bigoted efforts. These may be bad times for men with Middle Eastern backgrounds living in America, but as you know, Dr. Mapstone, I am a naturalized citizen, an Episcopalian, and a venture capitalist. All quite legitimate. I never even bought Enron stock."

I didn't laugh. "What are you doing here, Bobby?"

He adjusted one of his rich locks of hair. "Looking after you. It's no secret the Russians are after Miss Lindsey. You must be missing her. And who wouldn't? So beautiful, with that watchful, poetic quality to her. I can see her, before she found you, of course, as the smart girl surrounded by good-looking but stupid men. Thus her armor of irony and sarcasm…"

He watched me and paused.

"I don't quite understand why you are being so reckless," he went on. "Yuri's brigade—they call their cells brigades, so many are former Red Army officers—Yuri's brigade is known for its ruthlessness."

I let my eyes sweep the street. "For a venture capitalist, you know a hell of a lot about Yuri."

"I am an inquiring man, Dr. Mapstone, as are you. We live in momentous times: the great contest of the Cold War, the sudden collapse of the Soviet Union, the former Warsaw Pact joining NATO…things we never would have believed possible. The revolution that ruined Persia, that killed my family. Look at your hometown, David, utterly changed from when you were a boy. The clash of civilizations, Islam versus modernity. A new age of lawlessness, so many soldiers from the losing side with nothing to do but become mercenaries on the marketplace."

I declined to let myself be drawn in. I said, "What were you doing at the towers that night? When we shared the elevator?"

Bobby's economical features gave way to a thin smile. "Visiting a friend," he said. "I might ask what you were doing? You seemed very nervous. Maybe it's this case of the poor homeless man you're so obsessed with."

"Goddamn it!" I said, loud enough to wake some neighbors. I ratcheted my voice down. "No games, Bobby. I don't have time. If you want to help, you'll tell me where Yuri is."

Bobby's voice was calm. "Like the sheriff, you ascribe much more of a connection to the underworld than I really merit." He dropped the cigar to the street and crushed it with his boot.

"Wonder why?"

"How is Sheriff Peralta?" Bobby said. "It must have been a blow to lose his father. And his wife moving out."

I tried again. "Why is Yuri trying to kill cops? Seems like a ticket to prison or the morgue, even for a Russian."

"Maybe he doesn't see it that way," Bobby said. "I only know what I read, of course. Some say Yuri was a Red Army captain, decorated many times for bravery. That he served in Chechnya in the Russian Army, and he was so effective that the Chechen guerrillas tracked down his wife and daughter, raped and murdered them. But others say Yuri is not a Russian at all."

"None of this is helping," I said.

Bobby absently pulled a handkerchief out of his pocket and polished the chrome on the bike, a Harley that nevertheless had a kind of sinewy sleekness to it that seemed to go with Bobby Hamid.

"David," he said, fixing me with a new intensity in his eyes, "if I were in your position, I would get as far away from here as possible. I would let the government do whatever it will do to protect you and Miss Lindsey." He daintily adjusted his leather jacket. "You see, Miss Lindsey cost Yuri and his brigade many billions of dollars. And Yuri has creditors of his own, creditors who won't be willing to just send impolite letters and ruin his credit report. This is capitalism for keeps, Dr. Mapstone. This is the real global economy." Bobby licked his lips. "I would say Yuri's potential for vengeance is unlimited."

I watched him talk, feeling something cold on the back of my neck. For a moment I felt my legs were paralyzed in place, rooted into the cool sidewalk. But then I thought about Lindsey, and a different feeling came over me. I'd never been given to tough-guy speeches, but it came out with a certain cold anger.

"Bobby," I said," "do you know if I thought you were Yuri, and you meant any harm to Lindsey, I would kill you right here?"

Bobby watched me for a long time, something new in his opaque eyes. At last, he said, "Yes, David, I believe you would."

I was still standing on the street a long time after the noise from Bobby's Harley had faded from the neighborhood.

Chapter Twenty-four

I was on the freeway by nine that morning, making good time going south while in the opposite direction the army of suburbanites from the East Valley and Ahwatukee—the cops and firefighters call it "All-White-Tukee"—crept toward the city. As much as I loved riding trains and trolleys in Portland and San Francisco, in spread-out Phoenix I sometimes needed to drive in order to clear my head. After Bobby had left the neighborhood hours before, I had gone out to the Olds, put down the top, slid in a CD from Frank Sinatra's Columbia years, then I had driven slowly through darkened city streets.

Walt Whitman's "huge and thoughtful night" was all around, but Frank sang "One More for My Baby." "Let's just leave," my baby had said, as we lay nude, legs entangled, surrounded by barracks walls, and beyond them armed guards. "Let's just leave and start over, in a wonderful place. The government will have to resettle us, give us new identities. Can you leave Phoenix, Dave?"

"Can you leave your garden, Lindsey?"

"It's your home, Dave."

"I came home by accident. I had to find you…"

"I found you." She laughed. "You were too shy." It was nice to hear her laugh again. She said, "We can do anything we want. We can make a new future."

Our future would have to wait. I let the towers of Central Avenue sparkle down on me while I tried to figure out why the FBI was digging through my office, with Kate Vare in tow and with Peralta as tour guide. Too bad for them: most of my Pilgrim notes were in my old briefcase, sitting next to me on the car seat. Maybe Peralta was looking after my interests—but if that were true, why didn't he call me? Peralta had gone from badgering me with ultimatums to ignoring me while…what? It was enough to make you listen to talk radio and believe the conspiracy kooks who called in.

I let the big car take me through the forlorn streets of the inner city. People were sleeping in vacant lots and on street corners. They could have been mistaken for piles of rubbish. I idly looked for the woman named Karen. I had fresh questions about George Weed and his precious jacket. The Reverend Card's building looked dark and shut down. Prostitutes beckoned me from the gloomy sidewalks of Van Buren Street. I turned north, past streets that reminded me of a small safe town sheltered by citrus groves and pristine mountains: Mariposa, Cheery Lynn, Glenrosa, Montecito. A sign painted decades ago pointed to "Susan's Apartments." Gangbangers looked me over, seeing if I might be an easy victim. I drove and brooded, and that finally led me to another drive, this one out of town.

Once I got past Green Valley, the retiree tract houses and golf courses gave way to clean air and blessed emptiness. It was the West of my youth, rather than the overcrowded West of my adulthood. By noon, I had reached Tubac, the storied town north of the Mexican border. The land east rolled out to the massive Santa Rita Mountains. On my right was another rugged range, which I recalled as the Tumacacori. They were not my familiar Phoenix mountains. The history lay deep and fertile here, the conquistadors and padres and Piman peoples. Silver strikes and gunslingers and the coming of the iron horse. Off the interstate, I felt the high-desert air as cool tickling around my eyes.

My journeys of late were tying history into neat circles: San Francisco was founded by Spanish colonists from Tubac. In 1774, they were led by Col. Juan Bautista de Anza across El Camino del Diablo, the Devil's Road, west to California. The great world city that I had enjoyed lately was seeded by the little Arizona town sitting quietly off Interstate 19. Neat circles except in the history I was trying to understand.

I was down to playing hunches, and remembering tips. I remembered that Lorie Pope had told me I would find A.C. Hardin, crime buff, obsessed by the Pilgrim case, here in Tubac. In the chaos of the past month, I had forgotten Hardin. But I was a little surprised that he hadn't called me after the media exposure the case had received. Maybe it took awhile for the news to reach Tubac.

The place was not "done" like a Taos or Sedona, but it had aspirations. Art galleries lined the old dusty streets, a subdivision uglied up the south edge of town and the local paper promised rising property values and development. Tubac had survived 400 years of history, often bloody, but I found myself wondering if it could survive the Arizona growth machine. I asked directions at a coffee shop and used a little bridge to cross the Santa Cruz River. There was water in the river. A dirt road diverged through a thick stand of cottonwoods, then rose up a slight hill covered in brittlebush. Through the brush, I could make out a shack—it was no more than that. Four unpainted adobe walls, a window, a door, and a dilapidated roof. A rusty mailbox sat sideways on an old railroad tie, with "Hardin" painted in black letters. It looked like a scene out of one of those "forgotten West" books. But it made me feel uneasy. I was a man with ambiguous relations with the FBI and maybe with the sheriff of Maricopa County. My relations with the Russian mafia were fatal. I came unannounced.

As it turned out, A.C. Hardin was a she. Later I learned that A.C. stood for Amelia Caroline, and she cared for neither name. At that moment she didn't care for the tall stranger walking toward her house, and her displeasure took the form of a double-barreled shotgun aimed at me. She was twenty feet away but the barrels looked only slightly smaller than a pair of howitzers. I felt a huge pool of sweat gather on the small of my back. I wondered whether I stood a better chance if I identified myself as David the historian, or Deputy Mapstone the cop.

"I know who the hell you are," she shouted. Her voice had a little trill—did I detect just a hint of hysteria in the vocal cords? I noticed her finger was inside the trigger guard, putting me one spasm of her knuckle from kingdom come.

I said something about putting down the gun and talking, or maybe something about me being happy to turn around, walk back to my car, and drive away. I forget exactly. Shotguns have that effect on me.

"I don't want any more Maricopa County, Phoenix, bullshit!"

And who wouldn't agree with that? Maricopa County, Phoenix, bullshit had led me to the doorstep of a crazy woman with a shotgun. She didn't know the half of it.

"Don't you know there's been a break in the Pilgrim case?" I said hurriedly.

The shotgun came down. She stared at me. Then she turned and walked into the little adobe house. I heard her say, "I don't care about that."

"I'm surprised you didn't see it on the TV." I walked slowly toward the house.

Her small face crinkled. "I gave up TV, especially the Phoenix stations. Too depressing. Every night it's three fatal wrecks, a child molestation, and a shooting. Every night."

"Lorie Pope at the *Republic* says you were interested in the Pilgrim case for years," I called into the doorway. I let my hand rest on the butt of the Python in its holster, just in case the shotgun urge hit again.

She said nothing and I called to her again. Arizona was full of eccentrics. Bikers, mountain men, cowboy wanna-bes. The state with freaks of all flavors. Young misfits without the energy or originality to get to Seattle or New York. Old grudge-holders who rolled West until there was nothing left but California, and the money ran out. Californians who were too weird for the Golden State. Street-corner mumblers. Neighborhood junk collectors.

And, of course, crime buffs. They obsessed about police work. A few of them were professional confessors, who claimed to have committed any high-profile crime of the moment.

"I gave up on that," she said. She reappeared in the doorway without the shotgun. She was a slight old woman wearing jeans and a long-sleeved Madras shirt. Her face had been plowed into a thousand furrows by the sun and the world, but she had naturally high cheekbones and large, pretty eyes. They were green eyes and provided the only color in her face. In fact, there was something oddly girlish about her, beginning with her hair, which was still long and straight, parted in the middle like a 19-year-old's but turned to the color of a winter river.

"Pilgrim killed himself, right?" she said.

"Do you believe that?"

"Why not? That's what the FBI always said."

"We found Pilgrim's badge," I said, watching her eyes take the news in.

After a long pause, she said, "Then I guess you'd better come in."

Chapter Twenty-five

"Nothing personal. I like my privacy out here. I lived in Phoenix for nearly forty years, and I was happy to get away from it. My grandparents were pioneers. They farmed down by Seventh Avenue and Broadway. The pioneer stock is gone now. Down here, I feel safe. Until they pave this over, too. God willing, I'll be dead by then. I know who you are. You're the history guy. I've seen you on TV. Guess it makes sense you'd be the one to find Pilgrim's badge. Makes sense. He floated ten miles in the Grand Canal, then got sucked into a lateral. You know what a lateral is, right? The small ditches that flow out of the big canals, take the water to the fields. Water does strange things to a body."

The small woman sat across from me in a room with Navajo rugs on the floor, faded 1960s space age furniture covered with colorful drapings, and an aggressive clutter of newspapers, magazines, and clothing. A fat white cat watched me from a nearby chair. The woman's voice tended to squeakiness, and on some vowel sounds her throat constricted as if saying the words hurt. When she laughed, she covered her mouth with her hand. Her shirtsleeves were too short. We both sipped iced tea from old jelly jars. Hardin was a talker now that the shotgun was back in the closet. Unlike Vince Renzetti, Hardin had no family photos displayed. Instead, the room was dominated by unframed paintings that crowded against each other on walls. Most of the canvases were watercolors, landscapes from familiar places in

Arizona, the kind of sunsets and mountain views that sold well with the tourists in Tubac. I am no art critic—the work seemed competent enough illustration, but only slightly above what you might find on the walls of a motel in the Southwest.

"The canals looked like that." She pointed to a large canvas showing a reedy, tree-shaded waterway, with a blurred dark cluster of picnickers on a bank in the distance ahead of a stormy sky.

"You know, children used to swim in the canals in the Valley. The laterals were all open, not covered with streets and concrete like now. They had trees and grass along the banks. It was very beautiful. People had boats. When I was in high school, my buddies would drive their cars along the banks and pull us on water skis. I read that Pilgrim's hat floated all the way with the body. Isn't that strange…"

"Do you collect art?" I asked.

"I paint it," she said. "It's not much. It calms me. I sell a few. Anyway, you remember 1948, the year he was killed? Of course you can't. You're too young. They were having UFO scares then. I saw a girl in a bikini for the first time. It looked very scandalous. The FBI must not like you. Looking into their precious closed case." She made this segue without any change of expression. "How'd you pull that off, Mapstone? They fought me for every scrap of paper. I bet they didn't give a damn about John Pilgrim when he was alive. But dead, he was their property. His murder was egg on their faces…"

"Ms. Hardin…" I tried to break in.

"Have you ever shot anyone, Mapstone?" she asked.

"Let's talk about the Pilgrim case," I said.

"Oh, I get it," she said. "You're asking the questions here." Laugh. Cover her mouth. She folded her small hands under her arms. "You sound like them."

"Them?"

"The FBI."

I asked her why she used the word murder. "The FBI says that Pilgrim killed himself."

"I thought you'd seen the files, Mapstone," she said. "The cops didn't find any evidence of suicide. No note. No powder burns or flash debris on the face. Who shoots himself and then falls into a canal? And then drives his car back to downtown Phoenix. Did you know the FBI sent two hundred agents to Phoenix after John Pilgrim was murdered? And they stayed for three months?" She didn't wait for an answer. "That's a lot of manpower for a suicide. It was murder. And they always knew it was murder. That's why they covered it up for fifty years."

"I don't understand."

The small old face seemed all expressive eyes. "The Outfit killed John Pilgrim. The Chicago mob. It's obvious."

"Why would the FBI cover that up?"

"Hoover never wanted to go after the Mafia. What kind of historian are you? Hoover denied there was a Mafia. And no wonder, they knew he was a homosexual. They knew his lover was the deputy director. This was a different time. Nobody called them 'gay.' He was queer, and if the public had found out, Hoover would have been ruined. So they made an accommodation, Hoover and the mobsters. He went after communists, and left the Mafioso alone. They even paid for Hoover and his boyfriend to go gambling at Del Mar. It was a cozy little setup."

"Until Pilgrim upset the balance…"

"Something like that. He didn't have clean hands, either. But Pilgrim didn't play the game. The Outfit was moving in, taking over the rackets from the old boys who ran Phoenix. Maybe Pilgrim allied himself with the old boys, the city commissioner Duke Simms. Duke ran the prostitution racket on the south side. Do you know a cop killed another one, right in the police station? It was all about money from the rackets."

That police station had been in my courthouse.

Hardin continued, "Pilgrim was a long way from Washington, making his own rules. It was a corrupt little town. Maybe he wanted a cut of the action. Maybe he was doing his duty. You know he was warned—that's the way the mob operates. Anyway, somehow Pilgrim got crosswise with the Outfit, and they killed him. I can imagine how it happened. They lured him somewhere, out in the farmland by the canal. They probably made him think he was going to meet a witness who could help him. Then when he shows up, he gets a carload of goons instead. They shoot him and toss him into the canal. End of problem."

"And Hoover wanted it covered up, because they were black-mailing him?"

My face must have held a skeptical expression. She said, "You probably think Kennedy was assassinated by a lone gunman."

I looked around the small room. It didn't look like the home of a conspiracy nut. I'm not sure what I would have expected: black curtains on the windows, autopsy photos on the walls? Instead, benign paintings for the tourists, if anyone bought one. What was I buying? Everybody had a theory about John Pilgrim. For the feds, and for Harrison Wolfe, it was a suicide. Richard Pilgrim suspected that his father's vices did him in. Renzetti was convinced that the Soviet agent Dimitri killed Pilgrim. Why was A.C. Hardin's theory any worse than the others? Lack of sleep was catching up with me, and my back hurt from the mushy old sofa I was sitting in. Hardin's cat watched me mistrustfully. I let Hardin talk, squeaking out her vowels.

She said the case had always interested her because her family had known the Pilgrim family, back in the 1940s. She grew up hearing about the death. After Lorie Pope wrote her first Pilgrim retrospective, in the late 1970s, Hardin began researching the mystery on her own. The county archives and newspaper accounts provided some information. She filed for the FBI report under the Freedom of Information Act, and was refused. That only stoked her interest, and caused her to study the Bureau, as well. She tracked down some of the original detectives who had investigated the case and none of them believed the suicide theory, either. These were the deputies and city officers whose names I recognized from the old reports. They convinced her of the Outfit theory. Unfortunately for me, those detectives had passed on long before. She became obsessed with the case, she said, and was a pest about it with Lorie Pope. "I had a lot of time on my hands, I guess," she said. "The Pilgrim mystery became my hobby. I guess if I had been twenty years younger, I would have become a cop."

"So why would Pilgrim's badge end up on a homeless man?"

"Is that where you found it?" she asked.

I told her about George Weed, about the badge found sewn in the old jacket. I showed her a photo of Weed, and she slipped on a pair of gnarled wire-frame reading glasses to examine it. Oddly, the glasses brought out the girlishness of her face. If it were true that the Outfit murdered Pilgrim, would they have taken his credentials and badge? Did they fall into the canal? Did Pilgrim leave them in his car, to begin their decades-long journey to a swimming pool in Maryvale?

"Maybe the man just found it," she said. "Sometimes things are that simple. I don't know."

Chapter Twenty-six

I drove back to Phoenix that afternoon, playing Debbie Davies' Round Every Corner over and over, determined to write my report and move on. The girl-woman in the Madras shirt—after I left I realized she had it inside-out—was no help. Crime buffs rarely are. Some mysteries have no answers. Nobody knows why Napoleon lingered in Moscow until the Russian winter came to destroy the Grande Armée. It was completely out of character from his previous campaigns. But those were the facts. Nobody knew why. America was discovered by sailors looking for someplace else, and at first the New World seemed to have no value. History is chancy. So said Samuel Eliot Morrison, who knew a thing or two about history.

In my puny corner of history, no answer seemed to present itself as to why John Pilgrim's badge had traveled five decades and landed in the jacket of a man named George Weed. All I could do was write what I knew and deliver it to Peralta. I borrowed A.C. Hardin's file of Pilgrim clippings and police reports, which she surrendered reluctantly. She said she had to come to Phoenix next week anyway and would retrieve it then. So, feeling a lift of liberation, I stopped at Mi Nidito in Tucson for a President's Plate. Passing Picacho Peak, site of Arizona's only Civil War battle, the dust devils lulled me into history daydreams. A Union army from California and a Confederate Army from Texas clashed lethargically, then both retreated, no doubt wondering why the hell anybody would want to own what they saw as a godforsaken place of rattlesnakes and dry mountains.

An hour later the city had swallowed me up, its concrete tentacles seeming to have expanded outward just in the day I was away. This valley had lain empty for centuries, forgotten and sleeping, until the aftermath of the same Civil War loosed adventurers and land-hungry farmers on the West. The founding of Phoenix was in the living memory of old-timers in 1948. Now most Phoenicians didn't even know where the water came from. The old pioneer stock was indeed nearly gone. I held on to my pioneer amulets in my mind, memories of Grandfather and Grandmother. Somehow the death of John Pilgrim was linked in the official archives to another name, Dr. Philip Mapstone. His signature on the coroner's jury report. That knowledge focused the inchoate unease that I carried around like a layer of Sonoran Desert dust. What was Peralta keeping from me?

I wouldn't find out soon. For the next week, I avoided the Sheriff's Administration Building and Peralta. For whatever reason, he reciprocated. Not a nagging call or sarcastic e-mail. Instead, I haunted the Arizona Room at the Phoenix Public Library. It holds microfiche of Phoenix newspapers, as well as city directories, maps, and obscure history books. I even wrote one of them. The room had once been my sanctuary, before the teen room opened next door with a constant din of hip-hop music and chatter. "A new dark age," I heard Dan Milton say in my ear. At the Hayden Library at Arizona State, I took too much of the staff's time, gathering everything from National Security Agency Venona documents on Soviet espionage in the 1940s to student projects interviewing the homeless in Phoenix. An archivist with auburn hair named Amy was friendly and helpful. I was a good boy. I missed Lindsey. I was working to prove or disprove at least three different theories. I also spent hours at the state archives, the Phoenix Museum of History, and on the Internet from my courthouse office. Some mornings I brought my files to Susan's Diner and worked while I ate breakfast. If I couldn't solve the mystery, at least I would try to give the taxpayers their money's worth. At night, in an empty bed, I dreamed about 1948, about men in hats and travel by train. But I awoke afraid.

Some days, needing human contact or fresh data, I came up from my quarry of records. Being a native had its advantages, even in a place where nine out of every ten people seemed to come from the Midwest. I knew people. An old high school buddy was a public relations official at the Salt River Project, the nation's oldest and largest reclamation effort. He spent an afternoon teaching me about the 1,300 miles of canals and five reservoirs that allowed Phoenix to exist. I learned about flow rates of various canals, and the impediments that would cause a body to flow this way, not that. The reeds, trees, and swimming children were long gone. But the canals regularly were a dump for trash, evidence, a surprising number of shopping carts, and dead people.

Using 1948 maps, I tried to trace the route Pilgrim's body might have taken. It wasn't easy. Even when I was a boy, the city had been relatively compact. We could drive ten minutes and be in the citrus groves or cotton fields. Back then, streets quickly gave way to roads bracketed by irrigation ditches—laterals—and shaded by giant cottonwood trees. The land had been even more pastoral in 1948. But now, subdivisions, shopping strips, car dealerships, malls, and golf courses covered what was once one of the great farming valleys on the planet. The laterals were mostly underground now, as congested seven-lane streets conquered the charming farm roads. But I did what I could. I walked along the bank of the Arizona Canal, by Seventh Street, where the farmers heard the loud voices and the gunshot the night Pilgrim disappeared. I drove along Fifty-first Avenue, where the lateral once flowed that carried Pilgrim's body until it could travel no more. What was once a lettuce field had become a decaying commercial strip in a transitional suburb. It was no more than two blocks from where George Weed's body was found on April Fool's Day.

Another friend had charge of the historical photo collection at Bank One, a little-known cache of downtown history. Through her, I found pictures of the Pla-Mor Tap Room, Pilgrim's hangout on Central Avenue downtown. It looked suitably dark and seedy, and had been replaced by an office building in the 1950s.

One morning, before the heat became unbearable, I slipped on walking shoes and went downtown. Finally, the police reports, newspaper clippings, and black-and-white photos were not enough. I needed to walk where John Pilgrim had walked. For the moment, this was my Civil War battlefield, my Johnsonian London. I added my imagination to the reports, the stories conjured by Grandmother and Grandfather when I was a child, my own memories. In 1948, downtown held a handful of Art Deco towers, twelve movie houses, eleven hotels, five department stores, countless bars. The rooftops were festooned with radio towers and neon signs—Hotel Westward Ho, Hotel Adams, Valley National Bank. By comparison, downtown Fort Wayne or Akron would have seemed like Manhattan. But they were not surrounded by miles of orange groves, flower gardens, and green fields, all guarded by the ancient mountains and the vast Sonoran Desert.

I walked along deserted sidewalks on Central, my ears assaulted by passing cars playing rap. Cities all over America had enjoyed a downtown renaissance. Not my hometown. But in my mind the sidewalk was busy with people, alive with storefronts, as it had been even in my youth. That was before the real estate boys ran to the edges of the city and paved over the orange groves, the flower gardens, and the green fields.

The Pla-Mor Tap Room was just a block from the old federal building, where Pilgrim would have worked. It was easy to see why it was a hangout. Why did the place fascinate me? This old city would have heard the constant sound of train whistles. Union Station was the center of activity, of comings and goings. It now sat empty, fenced and always in danger of thoughtless demolition. But in 1948, it was a Soviet agent's portal to mischief. What had Dimitri and Pilgrim talked about, the last time they met? Who was armed, and what happened next? I watched the dates stamped in the sidewalks: 1928...1936...1947.

It was May now, and every day broiled above a hundred degrees. I surrendered to casual clothes—even then the fabric stuck to my sweat-soaked skin. Palo verde blossoms covered the sidewalks in a yellow-green dust. Overhead misters spewed their smoky-looking balm at restaurant patios. The glare off the cars made it appear that they were firing futuristic pulse weapons at each other. The newspaper and TV broadcasts settled into their summer staples of forest fires, children drowned in swimming pools, and migrants suffocated in the locked tractor-trailer rigs of smugglers. In the *Republic*, Lorie Pope wrote a story about a subdivision of 80,000 houses planned for west of the White Tank Mountains. "Master planned community" they called it. I wondered if their master plan included water. A brush fire closed Interstate 17 to the north, trapping well-off Phoenicians from their weekend escape to cabins in the High Country. The fire made its contribution to the soup that obscured the mountains.

I was in danger of spending too much time between my ears, as a friend once put it. But every day I was reminded of George Weed's world, whether by the transient sweeping through Starbucks trying to grab somebody else's coffee from the bar, or by the sight of trash-filled shopping carts lined up outside the central library like cars at a drive-in. Homeless children wandered Van Buren. Some homeless adults burned a Victorian house awaiting restoration. A woman attending a convention was attacked—a homeless man was blamed. Bedraggled men with skin corrugated by the sun huddled in little shade spots. Everybody had a theory. Nobody knew what to do. It's a shame. It's an alternative lifestyle, and who are we to judge? One day I went to the carwash on Van Buren and Grand, where a tall young guy was bumming change. He wore a filthy do-rag and looked as if he hadn't bathed in a month. When he came to me, I just shook my head. Then he approached a dark-skinned Latino man who wore a sweat-stained shirt emblazoned with a landscaping company logo. The Latino rebuffed the transient, too. As the guy walked away, the landscaper looked at me and shrugged. It was a look that said, there will always be two kinds of people, those who work and those who don't.

I found no comfort in my usual hangouts. They seemed to conjure strange signs and premonitions, if even in absurdities. Drinking in a dark corner of Durant's, I overheard a conversation. It was typical guy talk. But the phrases gradually drew my attention: "You know that's got to be so damned sweet," "Yeah, my son had the hots for her," and "cheerleader legs," a familiar name, and "What a waste she married that professor guy. Maybe she's repressed…" I eased my head around to see who was talking, and it was a couple of old career guys from the sheriff's office. Talking about Lindsey. They couldn't see me, and I resisted any Frank Sinatra-like impulses to walk over and defend my wife's honor.

I felt more of a melancholy detachment than a jealous zeal. My only contact from Lindsey that week came one day when I was on the Internet. A console suddenly popped up on the screen of my Mac, and there in the console was a high-resolution color photo of Lindsey smiling, blowing me a kiss. Then the console disappeared, with no trail left on the history directory of my browser. The horny old deputies would never know how beautiful Lindsey looked when she was hot and sweaty, working in her garden, her brown-black hair pulled back in a ponytail. Or her native kindness, whether in caring for the old tomcat or in reading every article I wrote in my history professor days and pronouncing them brilliant. And as for their observation about being repressed, Lindsey would say, "Repressed is the word people use when they mean 'not like me.'" I would say the reality of Lindsey is beyond any old man's fantasy. Ah, I was spending too much time in my own head, not a good thing.

On a Thursday, I came back to my office to find the door open and Kate Vare sitting primly at my desk. I was hot, sweating, feet aching, and shouting at her as I crossed the threshold into the room.

"What the hell are you doing in here? Who the hell do you think you are?"

She came up out of my chair as if she was launching herself as a missile with overdone shoulder pads.

"Mapstone, you son of a bitch! You arrogant, lying bastard!"

"You ought to know about lying, Kate. Breaking into somebody's office."

"Break in, you asshole, you're lucky I'm not here with an arrest warrant!"

"What the fuck are you screaming about?" I demanded. We were nose to nose across the desk, both armed. She opened her black leather City of Phoenix portfolio, pulled out a jail mugshot, and slammed it on the desktop.

"This is what I'm screaming about, bastard! As if you didn't know!"

The photo was of the homeless woman from the parking lot, what seemed like months gone by. Her name was Karen, or so she said. She claimed she knew George Weed. She said she wanted help with visitation rights to her daughter.

Kate studied my face. "Don't you play dumb, you bastard. You know who this is."

"Of course I do. She came up to me one night, and asked about George Weed."

"What are you talking about? Who is George Weed?"

"The guy in the pool, the guy with John Pilgrim's FBI badge sewn into his coat."

"Lying bastard!" she shouted, exhaling so exuberantly I could feel her breath tousling my hair.

I started to say something but she grabbed the photo and waved it in my face.

"Heather Heffelberg!"

"That's her name? She said it was Karen."

"You stupid bastard, that's the fourteen-year-old girl who was kidnapped out of her own bedroom in Paradise Valley six weeks ago. It's only been the biggest case to hit this city in years. The media are on it. The brass are on our asses every day about it. The FBI has entered the case. This woman, whose name is Karen Barshevsky, was seen in that neighborhood the night before Heather disappeared. Karen is the common-law wife of Jake Roberts, aka Jake English, aka Randy English. Five years ago they kidnapped a teenage girl and raped her and held her captive for a month. Both of them walked on a technicality. Tell me this is really all news to you, bastard!"

I sat in one of the straight-backed wooden courtroom chairs that faced my desk. I said, "It is news. And my name is not 'bastard.'"

Kate's tense body looked as if it was ready to leap over the desk. She sputtered, "I can't fucking believe this! This...You... The fucking sheriff's office is more incompetent than I ever believed. You...you're not even a real police officer!"

"Kate, I've had nothing to do with your disappeared girl case."

She started to speak. But she just glared and fell into my desk chair with a heaviness that belied her slender frame.

"So you were in here rummaging around with Peralta last week because you thought I was holding out on you?"

"I'm still not sure you're not holding out," she said, although in a calmer voice. "You're always trying to claim credit. You write a book report, and Peralta goes 'ooh, ahhh' and you're on TV as this big crime buster."

"I never sought that out—"

"Oh, spare me," she said. "If you are telling the truth, and you've really been wasting your time with this dead vagrant." She shook her head as if she were trying to dispense with a bad dream. "I just can't believe it. Karen just walks up to you?"

"In a parking lot, one night about a month ago."

"Every cop in town has been trying to find this woman."

"She found me," I said.

Kate's usually tan pallor was now the color of a cranberry. "I can't believe you," she said. "Look at you. Look around you." She swept her arm to take in my bookshelves and historic photos. She stood, walked over, and rapped her knuckles on the bulletin board that held photos from the Pilgrim case. "You live in this dream world. In the real world, I have to go on calls. I can't just work one case because my friend is the sheriff. So earlier today, I went on a call. A woman had been dumped by her lover. So she went home and drowned her son and daughter, and then tried to kill herself. That's the real world, Mapstone! Tell me what your history says about that."

"Oh, Kate," I said, trying to be the calm one.

She leaned over my desk and shouted, "Tell me! You can't even see what's in front of your face!"

"I live in the same world." I shrugged. "It sucks. But human nature is unchanging. I was reading a newspaper clipping from 1948 about a woman, right here in Phoenix, who tried to murder her children. It sounded like what you're—"

But she was gone. I was surprised that the glass in the door didn't shatter when she slammed it.

Chapter Twenty-seven

The big Oldsmobile took me home through the streets of the historic neighborhoods north of downtown. I avoided the seven-lane speedways of Central or Seventh Avenue. Up comfortably narrow Third Avenue, where the Roosevelt district had been lovingly restored. Stately bungalows and new city condos and apartments sat on streets lined by eighty-year-old Mexican fan palm trees. Margaret Hance Park had a few picnickers and walkers, even on a hot afternoon. You'd never know a freeway pulsed beneath the park. I took in the familiar mountains and skyscrapers that ornamented the park's vista, and closer, old Kenilworth School with its classic columned entrance to the west and the new postmodern Burton Barr Library to the east. The Mission Revival Mormon Church had been saved from the freeway and now housed a puppet theater. A little farther north, Third crossed McDowell and entered Willo, with its trees and front porches baking sweetly in the 105-degree sun. This was my Phoenix, a lovely sanctuary that also held my personal history, even if the millions in their cookie-cutter subdivision pods never saw it and complained that Phoenix had no soul.

I noticed the car in the rearview mirror, so close I couldn't even see his front bumper. Then he switched lanes and roared next to me. My stomach tightened. Down came the passenger window, and I could see the face of a thirtyish man in a polo short.

"Get out of the way, you asshole!" he screamed with a bucket-shaped mouth, his face suddenly crimson. Then he sped north on

Third and soon disappeared. His back bumper held an American flag sticker with the words, POWER OF PRIDE.

I used to like this town. Phoenix was a sunny, dull place with no culture or ambition, but it had a sweetness and a good heart. Now we've got malls stuffed with people from Iowa and Wisconsin, low-wage workers in the call centers and landscape outfits and service joints, Indian casinos, mass-produced subdivisions, bigger money than you could imagine in Paradise Valley and North Scottsdale, 250 golf courses. But it's a big hardboiled place where ordinary guys carry around their rage like an over-stuffed wallet and everybody calls someplace else home.

I made it home with the horizon turning white and the wind picking up. A FedEx envelope was leaned up against the stucco wall. Lock the door behind me, feel the blessed air-conditioning, make a sweep of the house...back door locked, courtyard doors secure, closets clear, nobody hiding under Grandfather's mahogany desk in the study. Out the picture window, the wind began slapping the palm trees insistently. I coughed instinctively, sat on the staircase with its floor-to-ceiling bookshelves, and stared out at the familiar old neighborhood. The envelope showed a return address from the University of California at Berkeley.

My old friend from grad school days had come through. The envelope contained five sheets of a typed report, from the Senate Select Committee on Intelligence from 1975. The pages were black with the now familiar war paint of redacted information. But the report was clear enough. In 1944, a Soviet agent named Georgi Antonov came to Phoenix and set up a cover life as a refugee from Poland. He took a job as a waiter in a local restaurant. His real work was to pass along secrets from the American atomic weapons program at Los Alamos, New Mexico. By 1947, Antonov, who used the code name "Dimitri," was spying on the nuclear test site in Nevada, always returning to his haven in the small city of Phoenix. A year later, Dimitri was ordered to return to Moscow. He remained in the United States—defecting to an FBI agent in Phoenix. The agent's name was lost in a horizontal black slash. Dimitri died in 1972, having run a hat shop in Cincinnati for many years.

Dimitri didn't kill Pilgrim. Dimitri defected to Pilgrim.

I said out loud, "Fuck!"

The wind responded with a loud moan, as if it were sweeping my theories down Cypress Street.

Soon I was caressing the spines of the books, recalling forgotten volumes. Lindsey and I had been reading McCullough's *John Adams* before our private civilization had been invaded by the Russians. I could pick a hundred flaws in the book, but I had no grudge against popular history, as my colleagues in the professoriat did. McCullough got rich while the rest of us published obscure, unreadable papers—or went to work for the sheriff's office. My finger lingered on the spine of *Middlemarch*, one of Lindsey's favorites. I found one of Dan Milton's books misshelved—with the novels rather than history. It was his insightful look at social change in the 1920s, *Coolidge Jazz*, a book that made me realize how much everything is connected, how nothing happens in isolation. Soon this reverie propelled me into the kitchen, where I made a martini—using Lindsey's favorite Plymouth gin instead of my Bombay Sapphire—and then I settled in the big leather chair before the picture window. The closest firearm was in another room. I let it be.

The men came in with amazing ease. They were in the room before I could even move out of the chair. Somebody gave a command in Russian, and a tall man with a goatee and sad eyes aimed a clunky yellow plastic gun at me. Panic locked my legs in place. I tried to turn and roll out of the chair but it was too late. The Taser darts hit me straight on. My legs, starting to stand, collapsed as if the bones were suddenly liquefied. My abdomen was consumed in a great spasm. Men's faces studied me with curiosity. The tall man held a straight razor, the blade rusty and chipped. I felt a wave of bile coming up my throat, then the room closed around me, black.

I usually know when I'm dreaming. Not this time. My eyes opened when the sweat from my forehead dropped into my lashes. The house was silent except for my panting and the soft whoosh of the air-conditioning.

Suddenly three cars materialized on the street. Two sheriff's cruisers and a shiny black Crown Victoria. It was no dream. I bolted up from the chair, even as a pounding came on the front door.

"Let's go," Peralta ordered, looking cool in a cream-colored suit, the coat cut roomy to accommodate his Glock semiautomatic pistol. I stared at him for a long moment to make sure he was real. I started out the door but his meaty hand struck my chest.

"Bring your gun, Mapstone. You're on the job."

So I retreated back into the house, retrieved my Python and Speedloaders, locked up, and then followed him. He walked to the Oldsmobile.

"You drive," he said. "I want to make sure you're taking good care of county property."

We sped over to the Piestewa Freeway and turned north, following the two sheriff's cruisers. The speedometer needle was pushing against ninety, me driving and Peralta saying nothing. A quarter of a century ago, when we were partners, it was no problem to play the silent guy game and barely speak for an entire shift. But this time I was cranky after a few miles.

"If we're on the job, where are we going?"

"DC Ranch." One of the silver spoon developments in the McDowell Mountains. We sped on, climbing through Dreamy Draw and the North Phoenix Mountains and quickly reaching the 101 beltway. The big Olds engine seemed barely challenged; my foot had plenty of room between the accelerator pedal and the floor. I tried again.

"And what's at DC Ranch?"

"Yuri."

I felt an involuntary shiver. I glanced at Peralta, who stared ahead.

"If our intelligence is correct, we'll find Yuri in the Page-Frellick House. Ever been there?"

"Nope."

"It's a custom job that backs up to Thompson Peak. When they built it in '98, it was priced for $3.7 million, and a retired executive from Canton, Ohio, bought it. I went there once for a Christmas party, bunch of Republican bigwigs. The fireplace was bigger than my first apartment. Anyway, it's been vacant for a year or so. The economy, you know. So they rented it out…"

"How did we find this out?"

"Your wife, Mapstone. She gets results."

We got no closer than a command post just off Scottsdale Road. The parkway was blocked, and deputies and city cops were turning away homeowners in their Ferraris and Rolls Royces.

Peralta walked over to a redone bus that held the sheriff's mobile command center. Beside a large golden badge, lettering proclaimed MARICOPA COUNTY SHERIEF'S OFFICE, and in smaller letters below, MIKE PERALTA, SHERIFF. My old friend had done OK. I slid my badge onto my belt, borrowed a pair of binoculars, and wandered around. This had been empty desert even when I was an undergraduate. As a kid, I would come out here with Grandfather to hike and target shoot. I remembered the preternatural silence, where even a buzzing fly sounded loud. Now it was the province of the superrich, retired CEOs looking for anonymity and Lasik surgeons from Minneapolis looking for a winter home. The houses dotted the rocky hillsides and perched above dry washes and arroyos. Walls and gates reminded anyone who forgot that this was private property.

For the moment, at least, the sheriff had suspended property rights. The air was full of screeching tires and revving engines as angry residents were turned away. It mixed in with the traffic sounds from Scottsdale Road and the occasional scream of Lear jets taking off from Scottsdale airport. My eye went to a group of men in black uniforms, Kevlar helmets, and vests. They were saddling up on all-terrain vehicles, with exotic-looking weapons slung over their shoulders. Emblems on their backs said FBI. In a moment, they drove single-file across an expanse of sand and rock, then disappeared down a bank into a wash. The ATVs were amazingly silent.

"An FBI team," Peralta said, reappearing behind me, with his suit coat gone and his shoulder holster prominent. "It's their operation."

Eric Pham walked up behind us and nodded. He had covered his starched white shirt with a Kevlar vest bearing the letters FBI.

"I think we've got them, David," he said.

"All we have to do is hope the dust storm doesn't hit," I said. So far, the wind was up, whipping us with occasional sand, but the sun was still out and we had at least an hour's daylight.

"All we have to do," Peralta said, "is sit here and enjoy the show."

Chapter Twenty-eight

Even the binoculars didn't provide a very good view of the house. I saw native stone, a wall of tinted glass, and a roof set at a rakish angle. Then I didn't see much. The storm came on, cloaking the mountains and then the scattered houses in dusty haze. At this time of day it almost looked like the fog in San Francisco, except for my persistent coughing. Back to the west, Camelback and Mummy mountains were barely visible. I heard some deputies cursing. I made my way quietly into the command post, where two rows of consoles were being monitored by deputies and FBI agents wearing slender headsets. TV screens showed a view of the desert, then the house—apparently the assault team carried cameras so the brass could watch the fun. An agent turned to Pham, Peralta, and a Scottsdale police deputy chief: "Team Blue is in place." In another minute: "Team Red is in place."

Barely audibly, Pham said, "Begin operation."

Peralta turned and walked outside. It didn't take much to bore him, especially if it was a multi-jurisdictional operation like this one. I decided to follow him. Just as I stepped onto the ground, I heard a muffled "whump." Turning toward the house, I saw a flash and heard another concussion. From the command center I heard someone call, "Showtime."

Peralta faced toward the action, his hands behind his back, his powerful shoulders tensed.

"You think they'll screw it up, don't you?" I said, trying to ease my own anxiety, tamp down my hope that Lindsey and I might be reunited soon.

"What I think doesn't matter, Mapstone."

"What about what you know?"

He faced me, one black eyebrow barely raised.

"The Pilgrim case," I said. "You know more than you're telling me."

He studied me with a slow orbit of his eyes. "The Kate Vare thing? Don't be paranoid, Mapstone. She was convinced you were holding out on her about some vagrant chick you interviewed. She was raising a stink with Chief Wilson and the county supervisors, so it seemed easy enough to let her check the files in your office. Don't worry, we didn't disturb your precious library of history books."

"That's not what I'm talking about."

"What then?" he asked, his voice suddenly impatient.

I was about to launch into it when we heard an unmistakable crackle from the direction of the house, then expletives from the command center. Peralta hurried back in, and I followed him enough to stand in the doorway.

"...taking fire...one suspect is down. He's down in the kitchen. An officer is down. Officer down..."

"How many do we think are in there?" I asked, and was ignored. Over my shoulder, the sound of automatic weapons fire had become steady. But these were short bursts, apparently from both sides. We were dealing with trained, disciplined scumbags inside that three-million-dollar pile of rocks.

Then the only sounds were wind and traffic.

"Building is secure. Building is secure. We have one officer down and four suspects down. Send in medics."

Two ambulances were flagged through the roadblock, escorted by a Scottsdale PD unit. The tightness in my gut started to let up a little.

Someone shouted, "One of 'em's unaccounted for. Hang on..."

Then, after a few centuries: "Yuri. Yuri's not among the suspects."

I stepped back outside, as if propelled by the Russian's dark magic. My hand clutched the butt of the Colt Python, as if Yuri would suddenly appear from around the corner of the bus and kill us all. It didn't seem impossible. The dust storm was full upon us now, the wind coming in hard horizontal bursts. The timeless logic of the desert trying to reclaim its own. The mountains were no more than a quarter mile away, but I could only see murky oblivion in that direction. I closed my eyes against the flying particles and prepared to step inside the command center. But a bulk came the other way, nearly knocking me down. Peralta.

"Let's go," he said, a rare wild look in his eyes.

"What?"

He spun me and pushed me like I weighed ninety pounds. Behind me, "Goddamn it, David, let's go!"

I ran to the car. Peralta was right behind me, but he had retrieved a shotgun from one of the cruisers.

"Go!" he ordered. I assumed he meant to the house, so I blew past a befuddled deputy and aimed the Oldsmobile up Thompson Peak Parkway, then into a side road and quickly climbed into the foothills. Getting closer, I saw the ambulances and sheriff's cruisers pull around to a wide driveway where a gazillion-car garage was built into the rocky face of the hillside. Medics were talking to one of the ninja tactical guys.

Then everything changed.

One of the tasteful desert-toned garage doors disintegrated. Pieces were still midair when the grillwork of a Hummer exploded out of the garage.

"Get off the road," Peralta said, almost to himself.

But I was already ahead of him. Old cop intuition, which was hardwired in me by training and by four years on the street, had come alive like some forgotten tribal knowledge. I braked hard and slammed the gearshift to "R." The Olds responded with a primal "clunk" deep in the rear end—no digital pulses from twenty-first-century auto technology here—but the car moved backwards at once. I quickly slid into the hard desert ground, uprooting a stand of prickly pear and brittle-bush.

"Oh, hell," Peralta said. I looked toward the house and an FBI ATV and its rider were crashing to the ground on a trajectory from the Hummer. Next it slammed across the top of the sheriff's cruiser, whose hood gave way under the Hummer's jacked-up tires. The cruiser's windshield shattered and the tires blew out. By then the Hummer was on the road and flying past us. It was the same black Hummer from that day in Roosevelt.

"Follow him," Peralta commanded.

"What?"

"Goddamn it, David, go!"

I eased the Olds out of the scrub and onto the asphalt. Then I punched the accelerator into the floor.

Chapter Twenty-nine

If the Russian had taken off across the desert, we never would have caught him. Instead, he wheeled out onto Scottsdale Road and turned south, toward the city. This was the racetrack for the rich and famous, but the black Hummer quickly passed a clot of SUVs and pricey sedans doing a mere sixty and commandeered a clear stretch of the slow lane. Within a mile, the speedometer on the Olds, with its long thin numbers and circular dial from the industrial designers of the 1960s, was pushing one hundred.

"How the hell can he go this fast?" I panted, feeling barely in control of the car. "I thought SUVs were lead sleds."

"Maybe not," Peralta said. "Don't let him get on the freeway!"

"And I'm going to stop him how?" I yelled.

The clear stretch didn't last long. As we neared Bell Road, I could see a parking lot of commuters, looking forward to happy weekends or fights with the spouse, spread out in four directions. Dust careened across the road in swirls and wild patterns. Headlights were lost to the gusts. Traffic was stuck at the entrances of the 101 beltway, whose concrete mass swooped over our heads. The Hummer barely slowed. I'd kept him off the freeway.

"Holy shit," I whispered, braking down to eighty, taking the left-turn lane and honking the big Detroit claxon to clear cars away. The Russian jerked to the right, through a forest of red cones cordoning off some street-widening. Across the aircraft-carrier deck of Oldsmobile hood, I watched as cones, dust, wood, unidentifiable debris, and finally steel reinforcing rods flew off in the Hummer's wake. He cut back into the slow lane, sending a panicked Lexus into a 360-degree spin—I could make out a plume of blond hair inside the driver's window—and ending up glancing off the door of a shiny Lincoln Navigator. I heard horns and crashes but didn't have time to watch. The Hummer blew through the chaos, crossed Bell against the light, and sped south. Somehow, after jagging into oncoming traffic and nearly taking out a light post, I was right behind him.

Now the needle was insistently pushing against 120. I still had an inch or so under my foot. The former owner, the drug dealer, had helpfully added new shoulder harnesses and seat belts. I steered with one hand and buckled up with the other.

"Where's the cavalry?" I wondered aloud. The dust storm made it impossible to get choppers in the air, but I looked in vain for police emergency lights coming behind us. I could hear Peralta on his cell phone.

"They're setting out stop sticks at Doubletree," he said above the din of canvas roof and wind. "Just keep going straight, you son of a bitch."

I couldn't tell if he was directing that at me or at Yuri, but as if the Russian could hear us, he veered off to the left on a side street. The Hummer strained against simple physics, and for a moment it was on two wheels. This is it, I thought. But somehow he made the turn. I pumped the brake and took the turn at fifty, hearing the wheels scream and—I swear—something like rivets popping somewhere in the chassis. But the Olds felt steady once we were going straight again. I pushed it, and we came within a car length of the black Hummer.

In an instant, the Russian made a right and tore across a lawn. I hesitated only a second. He crashed through a stucco wall, which didn't hold him. I followed. My peripheral vision caught a large patio, expensively outfitted with one of those outdoor grills that was bigger than our kitchen. A poolside flashed by. Then we were enveloped in green.

"I played here just last week," Peralta said. "Dammit, he's going to ruin the grass."

The Hummer sped out onto the Gainey Ranch golf course. Only the dust storm prevented the potential carnage of a foursome in his path. He plowed through a rough and went due south, cutting tracks into the fairway. I avoided the rough and followed.

"Put the top down!" Peralta commanded. He had already pulled the hand release on his side and I popped the lever above my head. Then I depressed the button on the dash and the roof went away, propelled by forty-year-old mechanics and a stiff wind. I coughed from the dust. Then I saw Peralta's white shirt and slacks levitating, and he was standing. His tie was blown back over his shoulder and he had the shotgun in his hands.

"Hang on!" I yelled and punched the accelerator. The Olds advanced to within maybe ten feet of the Hummer's rear end and Peralta let loose a shot. The rear window became a spider's web. The second round shattered the glass entirely. But the Russian cut sharply, and when I moved to keep up with him, Peralta fell back into his seat. The Hummer went through a low hedge, over a curb, and into a parking lot. In the rearview mirror I could see a forlorn groundskeeper chasing us, cursing us.

The Olds' tires hit the asphalt with a yelp and we were moving again. I followed the Hummer back to the west through pricey residential streets, tasting dust and particles in my mouth. Then we turned on Scottsdale Road again, neatly avoiding the stop sticks, which sat useless several blocks to the north. I glanced at Peralta, who was cradling the shotgun.

"Are you still using those hot loads that are against department regulations?" he demanded. Hot loads were custom bullets made for maximum stopping power. The downside: sometimes they could go completely through the suspect and take out three civilians and two walls. My gunsmith assured me that wouldn't happen with the ones I carried.

"Are you?"

I said, "Yes. I need an edge. I'm just a bookworm, remember."

"Good," he said. "Get me close again."

I glanced at him, and there was a look in his eyes I had only seen two or three times in our twenty-five years of friendship. Something primal, bloody-minded, and irrational, as if his riff about the Aztec blood coursing through his veins was not entirely hyperbole. He was close to a cop killer, even if the cop had been a female computer nerd. He was operating on something not well understood in university lecture halls.

Getting close again wasn't easy. We flew south into denser parts of Scottsdale, past Lincoln, McDonald, and Chaparral. But traffic was heavy, the visibility was worse, and the Russian kept changing lanes every few seconds. I could see red and blue lights behind us, but they kept falling back. The Olds didn't handle with the precision of a sports car. Instead, it surged. But it was ultimately fast, inevitable. I understood why the drug dealer liked it, besides his passion for preserving a little history of the automotive age. But it was a crazy fast thought, one I would only remember later. We were going so fast.

At Camelback, the Hummer struck a glancing blow at a Scottsdale Police cruiser; the big rig barely slowed while the front of the car was trashed. We swerved through the intersection, debris snapping against the floor of the Olds. The Russian took the oncoming fast lane across the Arizona Canal bridge, then came back into the southbound lanes. I followed. Fifth Avenue flashed by, obscured by dust. Particles tried to get under my eyelids, clung to my lashes. Lines of SUVs, minivans, BMWs, and old heaps were left behind.

"Goddamn it, David," Peralta shouted. "We're going to lose this cocksucker again!"

Indian School Road and Old Scottsdale were coming up fast. There were no police units in sight.

"No, we're not!" I shouted back. "Buckle up, goddamn it!"

It was a millisecond of opportunity, and only a fool would have tried it. I would never have done it. But I did. The Russian had to brake suddenly to avoid a gargantuan Escalade that was stuck in the middle of the intersection. He jerked right, slowing again to keep from flipping into the Starbucks. I put on the power and slid left around the Escalade. I forced the wheel hard to the right, catching the rear end just before it fishtailed. A truck was coming west on Indian School. I beat him through the rat hole that had opened in traffic. Suddenly I was just ahead of the Russian. I said good-bye to the Olds and rammed into the Hummer's left fender. The car jerked. The eerie sound of sheet steel being crushed and bent filled the air. The steering wheel bit back at my hands as the Hummer threatened to push us aside or over. I saw Peralta gripping the dashboard. But I was not unarmed: the 442-cubic-inch engine of the Oldsmobile was under my control. I fought to keep the wheel to the right and slammed my foot into the gas.

Brick and glass came up fast. Then a sound like an explosion.

⟨⟩⟨⟩⟨⟩

We were suddenly in a stationary world. I stared at the ruined front of an art gallery. My collarbone ached against the trusty shoulder strap. Give me a couple minutes and I might have thrown up.

"David!"

I focused on the big man next to me. It was Sheriff Peralta.

"Shit!" He fell backwards against me before the first burst of fire raked across what was left of the Oldsmobile. Then he rose quickly and fired three rounds from the shotgun. I unfastened the belt and pulled on the door handle. Miracle: the door survived, and opened like its first day in the showroom. I rolled out onto the pavement, feeling glass puncture my knees. Peralta scuttled out behind me. And for a long thirty-second count we huddled against the side of the car. Then Peralta mouthed "Go," and I came around the backside, toward the carcass of the Hummer. My arm rebelled against the weight of the Colt, which at first shook in my hand. I moved fast behind the Olds' rear bumper, knowing Peralta was going around the front. But nothing was left in the Hummer but the remains of the airbags. We sprinted through the debris of the gallery toward the back door, which lay open. I tried to remember everything from the academy, two and a half decades ago. But my legs were rubbery and holding the gun in a combat stance seemed to take superhuman effort.

We came into the alley. Somewhere over my shoulder sirens were coming. The alley was empty. But it wasn't. The wind yielded the briefest moment of clarity, and a man was running, maybe two blocks away. There was no time. Peralta was too slow. I holstered the Python and ran like hell. I kept close to the buildings, as if I could dive to safety if the man ahead of me decided to send a magazine of bullets my way. In another life, in a seaside city, before Lindsey, I had been a runner. Ran every night. Now I felt the damage in my right knee. But I remembered a few tricks. After my initial burst, I settled into a stride I could sustain. I closed the gap. The man didn't see me.

A monstrous wind came down the alley, but it was at my back. I crossed Seventieth Street, saw the oleanders sway as if a small hurricane was coming through. Palm tree husks flew crazily through the air. Dust clouds swirled in orange and purple phantoms high above. Ahead of me, the man jogged west, toward Goldwater Boulevard. Then I put on another burst. My shoes pounded on the asphalt, but the wind absorbed all sound. Back walls and dumpsters became my markers in the race. Deeper spaces opened in my lungs, and my heart settled into its long forgotten runner's rhythm.

There was no time. He got to Goldwater and started to look back. I closed to maybe fifteen feet. There was no cover. Not too damned smart. But maybe this wasn't the Russian at all. Maybe it was just a citizen. I drew the Python and dropped into a combat stance.

"Stop!" I yelled through a mouth thick with dust and suppressed panic.

The man stood on the sidewalk, his back to me. He was a big man, about my size. Even in the oppressive heat he wore a dark sweatshirt. He didn't move.

I swallowed and called up a tiny bit of saliva. "Deputy sheriff! Drop your weapon!"

I danced a little to the side, keeping his torso in the aligned twin sights of the Python. The gun's stainless steel body glittered weirdly in the dusty light. Everything around us was brown. Streetlights came on in the murk, even though beyond the storm the sun was up. I tried to see what he had in his hands. He wouldn't face me.

"Drop it now!" I yelled, starting to put pressure on the trigger.

Something black and metallic clattered to the ground. He was not just a citizen.

"Get on the ground, hands out from your body!" *Where the fuck is the cavalry?!*

He slowly lowered himself to his knees. He was still facing away. But I moved to the curb and could see the side of his face. No sensitive eyes or goatee from my dreams. He was clean-shaven. I couldn't make out much more. I eased up closer.

"On your belly!" I commanded. "Lie down! Face down, hands out!"

The thought seeped in: What if he can't understand enough English to know what I want? My heart was hammering now, the worry point just below my sternum turned into a hot poker.

I only realized I had come too close when he lunged at me. It was a stupid rookie mistake. Somebody his size shouldn't have been able to spring up and close the distance between us so fast. But he did. Somebody on his knees should have been vulnerable to the standing officer pushing him to the pavement. But he wasn't.

We crashed together to the ground. He was momentarily on top, but I clubbed him in the forehead with the Python. He fell backwards and we faced each other, both sitting on the ground. But I had the gun.

"You're her husband," he said, his eyes widening. There was barely an accent. Blood trickled out of his forehead like a stigmata. He was handsome in a hard-featured way.

"Husband." He said the word like "open sewer." He shook his head. "Her husband, David."

He smiled at me predatorily. His teeth were yellow. "This Lindsey." He said her name again, stretching it out obscenely. "*Lindsey*. She is what I want. Her little helper, Rachel, was just the start. But when I get this Lindsey, I will do things to her that will cut you up inside. You'll never be safe. This will never be over…"

Just then the wind died, and something dark and fast cracked against his temple. His eyes went back in his head and he collapsed.

Peralta stood over us, cradling the shotgun. He kicked Yuri over and handcuffed him. He held his head up by the hair and the Russian came to, gurgling in pain. Peralta spoke in his ear in a low voice.

"It's over, scumbag."

Chapter Thirty

A summer afternoon in Phoenix. Outside, the temperature is 114, and if I walk over to the large windows of my office I can check the horizon beyond the mountains, to see if the billowing monsoon clouds have arrived from the Sea of Cortez. But I sit in my old wooden swivel chair. Lindsey sits facing me, on the desk, wearing a short black skirt. Lindsey is blessed with fine knees. I am blessed with Lindsey's fine knees. I am thinking about this but I am stroking her long, slender wrist. Wrists can be such sensual places, given the right circumstances. As I run a light finger along her skin, Lindsey smiles and sighs. Up on the wall, Sheriff Hayden's expression doesn't change. Or do I catch just a twinkle in his eyes? I am sleeping without nightmares now.

Back when I was a patrol deputy—now I sound like a geezer—crime scenes were fairly simple affairs. Nowadays, they were major productions. So for hours after Yuri Sergiovich Popov had been shackled, stuffed into an armored FBI van, and whisked away to the terrorist resort at Guantanamo, I idled inside a corral of yellow tape in Old Scottsdale. Entire blocks were cordoned off, for reasons I didn't understand. It must have killed a few struggling businesses, of which Arizona always has an abundance. Peralta did most of the talking to cops and agents, about our wild ride down Scottsdale Road.

I was left to sit on the curb and contemplate the sunset. With the dust storm gone, sundown was a big-sky show of lurid pinks, crimsons, oranges, colors with no names. A coppery borealis emerged for five minutes directly overhead. Even the cops paused to look up and marvel. And just as the color retreated into the deep blue of twilight, a sheriff's cruiser pulled up and a door opened. Lindsey stepped out, waved to the driver, and came my way. After everything of the past few weeks, she still walked with that subtle strut that only I appreciated. Her skin was pale fire. She is the kind of woman who doesn't know how beautiful she is, which, of course, only adds to her appeal.

Repressed, hell.

In seconds, we fell into each other's arms—lightly at first, as if our hands wanted to make sure it was real, and then a tight, life-affirming embrace. Then we both were talking at once, stopping at once, laughing, starting again, and each still hearing every word from the other. I wasn't doing a lot of thinking right then. But I felt another presence, crazy as it sounds in the telling. For just a moment, bathed in the Arizona twilight and sheltered by my lover's arms, I sensed a lost friend. But the cycle of life seemed benign.

Dan Milton had lived a full life of good fights and passionate loves. He embodied Oscar Wilde's tenet that anybody can make history, but only a great man can write it. He was and he did. Dan Milton knew that the losses and dangers of mortality were burrowing tunnels under each of us, silently, year by year, and someday the ground would give way. He lived deep and wide, to have no regrets. I think he found grace that was joyous and not just awful. He was never afraid. Rest in peace, my friend. Twilight was gone. Lindsey took my hand, and I took her home.

Now, in the courthouse, my contemplation had gone from her wrist back to her knees. My darling had been born in the Summer of Love. She had been blessed with fine knees. Something against county regulations would undoubtedly have transpired on that blotter—it had before—if the door hadn't swung open to reveal Peralta.

"Hear those hammers, Mapstone?"

Actually, I had been distracted.

"They're rehabbing the floor below. They'll be up here by the fall. We'll have to find you a new place."

"You can't kick Dave out of his office," Lindsey said. She slid around the desk and sat demurely in one of the straight-backed wooden chairs.

"Blame the county supervisors," Peralta said. "I'm sure we can find you something over on Madison Street."

"Like a cell." I said.

"You're dreaming," Peralta said. "We're so overcrowded that you'd have to kill somebody to get that kind of office space." He didn't smile. "Anyway." He crossed in his long stride to the other chair and fell into it. The wood moaned. "Anyway, that commie SOB Yuri is out of the way. You two lovebirds are reunited…"

"It's nice," I said.

"Well, don't be too damned self-satisfied," he said. "All you did was prove to be an adequate pursuit driver and a fair arresting officer. Otherwise…"

Lindsey smiled slyly at me, her blue eyes keeping me calm.

"We'll just never know about that FBI badge," Peralta continued.

"I turned in my report."

"Oh, right," Peralta said. "The Chicago Outfit murdered Pilgrim. Even though there's no evidence."

"It's what the best evidence shows."

"How much did the taxpayers of Maricopa County pay to send you to the Bay Area?" He folded his arms across his big chest and glowered at me. With Peralta you never knew where the theater ended and the real-life asskicking would begin.

"Admit it, Mapstone. You couldn't solve this case."

"I did my best."

"You failed. I bet a rookie in patrol could have gotten further than you. All that book learning and you still failed."

"He didn't fail," Lindsey said.

There was a slight tapping on the door.

"Come!" Peralta said. Every office was Peralta's office.

A gaunt lined face appeared around the doorjamb. A.C. Hardin. Wearing a sun dress and bangles on her wrists.

"I said I'd come by for my file. Is this a good time?"

I motioned her in and made introductions. She sensed the plume of anger hanging in the room and was eager to leave. But Peralta held her with his presence, although his bulk remained folded in thirds in his seat like a deck chair.

"So you studied this case?"

She nodded, then said, "Yes," as if more reinforcement was needed.

"What do you think happened to Pilgrim?" Peralta asked.

Hardin looked uneasily at me. I just raised my eyebrows and smiled. I was daydreaming about Lindsey. My fingers were still happy from stroking her hand, her wrist…How could something as ordinary as a wrist tell so much?

Hardin was saying, "Like I told your deputy here, it was the mob out of Chicago, and the FBI covered it up." Peralta gave a noncommittal, "Umm." Then he stood and started out. Hardin came closer to my desk, her hand out for the folder. It was like guests leaving the party. I pulled out the papers she had lent me—none too helpful, frankly—and reached across the desk. She reached her slim, young-girl arm, to take it. And her bangles slid up on her forearm.

And I noticed.

It made me sit back in my chair. Hardin swiveled and walked toward the door. She was wearing high-heeled sandals that clacked against the dark wood of the floor. Peralta held the door for her. Lindsey was standing, too, closer to the bulletin board. She was watching me.

I said, too loudly, "Amelia!"

Hardin stopped in the doorway, turned, and looked at me curiously.

"Stay just a sec," I said, rising and quickly crossing to the bookshelves. "I just want to ask one last question."

My finger raced across frayed book spines. There: a 1948 Phoenix city directory. I thumbed it. Found the page. And damned if the name wasn't there.

Hardin had stepped back in the door. The hundred lines in her face seemed to deepen. I closed the book, with my finger keeping the place. I was afraid to move.

"Didn't you tell me that you grew up here?"

"That's right," she said. "That's a lot of what I paint. What I remember about this place, before they ruined it."

"On Verde Lane, right? 2320 West Verde Lane?"

She nodded. "Before it was even in the city limits." Then she gave a little drunken lean against the doorjamb, looked at me, and started out. But Peralta was there. The top of her head came up to the midpoint of his necktie.

"I need to go," she said, trying to push past him. "I have to…" He gently herded her into the room.

"It's funny you say that because the city directory lists an Aimee Weed at that address. And that's the mother of the man we found carrying Pilgrim's badge."

Hardin's mouth tightened, but she said nothing, refusing to look at me. Peralta said, "Let's sit down for a minute," and he guided her to a chair.

"Am I under arrest?" she asked quietly.

"We're just talking," Lindsey said, sitting on the edge of the desk. "You can go if you like."

Hardin folded her arms tightly across her chest.

"Amelia," I said. "I can get your birth certificate."

"I always hated that name," she said.

Big rooms hold quiet strangely. Sometimes it's as if the quiet of decades ago still lives in the highest pockets of the high ceilings.

"I had a brother named George," she said at last.

"Why did he have the badge?" Lindsey asked, her voice diamond-cutter gentle.

"My mother was a very stupid woman," Hardin said. "After dad died, she had to go to work. She became a secretary in the federal building. That would have been 1947? I can't believe how long I've lived."

Then silence. Finally Lindsey said, "That doesn't sound stupid. She did what she could, I'm sure."

"She was stupid to fall for John Pilgrim."

"They were lovers?" Lindsey asked.

"He promised her he'd leave his wife and marry her," Hardin said in a louder voice. "And Georgie and I would have a new daddy."

"So," I said, "Pilgrim gave George the badge, maybe to hang on to for a few days?"

"No."

"What then?"

"I didn't know Georgie took it," she said. "He was such a sweet little boy. The perfect little brother. I hate the world, the way it wads up people and throws them away... " She glanced at the photo of the dead homeless man on the bulletin board and quickly looked away.

Peralta said, "So let me get this straight: the homeless man was your brother? And you and he were children when your mother was dating this FBI agent?"

"That's about right," Hardin said, still facing Lindsey. Then, softer, "It doesn't really matter now, does it? All these years? I still remember it like it just happened. It was a warm November, and Mom and Mr. P.—that's what we were told to call him—took us for a picnic. He drove us in his Buick. We drove out of town, and spread a blanket under the cottonwoods."

Peralta locked eyes with me, but I had no information to telegraph.

"We ate these little sandwiches with thousand island dressing," she continued. "And we played by the canal. Mom made me watch Georgie while they walked a ways down the bank. I don't know when they started arguing. They argued a lot. That was nothing new. But I hated it. The voices. The things they said. I knew it upset Georgie, too."

"What happened next?" Lindsey asked.

"Mr. P. hit her. He hit her so hard that she fell on the ground, and she cried. He was such a son of a bitch. Later, I realized that was the moment when he told her he wasn't going to leave his wife. And that was it."

"You never saw Pilgrim again?"

Her voice changed. "He had left his gun in the car's glove compartment. His badge, too, I guess. After he was shot, he staggered a little, and fell into the canal. Mom got us back in the car and we drove back to town. Then we left the car and walked back home. And she cried a lot. I never knew what happened to his gun or badge."

"Your mother shot him," Lindsey said.

Hardin shook her head, her small mouth in something like a smile. "I was eight years old, and my daddy had taught me how to fire a gun. And that man never hurt my mother again."

Epilogue

"*Salud!*" Peralta said. "Or *vashe zdorovie!* In honor of our Russian."

"I taught you that," Lindsey said.

Peralta bought celebratory drinks across the street, at Tom's Tavern. It was the oldest political hangout in the state. But unlike mere mayors and governors, who might merit one photo on the wall, Peralta was the subject of three photos and a lush portrait. Lindsey called it "the shrine." If he was self-conscious, he hid it well.

"So how the hell did you know?" Peralta demanded, a quarter of an inch into his gibson. He nodded to Lindsey. "Did you know?"

"History Shamus rocks!" Lindsey beamed, squeezing my hand. "But I don't know how he did it."

"It was her wrist," I said. "She had old scars on her wrists just like George Weed did."

"That was a hell of a roll of the dice," Peralta said.

"Not really. I just had to understand what I was seeing. I saw the scars when I went to her house in Tubac. I saw, but I didn't pay attention. Has that ever happened to you?"

Lindsey nodded. Peralta said, "No."

"But then I remembered a *Phoenix Gazette* newspaper clipping from Christmas 1948. It was about a mother who tried to kill her two children, and succeeded in killing herself. She slit their wrists." Lindsey gasped and gulped her martini. I went on, "We think of these things as happening only today, and they probably do with more frequency. But this was 1948. The article didn't name them. But it said the mother was despondent over a failed romance. I didn't put it all together until she reached down for the report and I saw her wrist again."

"Not bad, Mapstone," Peralta said.

"Kate Vare taught me something after all," I said.

"What? Well, I knew you two could work together."

"What will happen to Amelia?" Lindsey asked.

"I don't know." Peralta started tearing his napkin into tiny strips. "I'll turn it over to the county attorney, and see what she wants to do. But Hardin was eight years old when the crime happened. She gave us a confession without being Mirandized. What a mess. Sounds like something for my wife to fix."

"You ought to visit her," I said." She misses you."

"No, she doesn't."

"Yes, she does. You don't know everything, as much as that might surprise you."

We drank two rounds each and then Peralta put down his credit card.

"Well, you did OK. I'm proud of both of you. I think you should take a long weekend and get reacquainted."

But now it was my turn to ask a question.

"You still know more about this case than you've told me. You knew more about it than I did the day we found the body in the pool."

"I knew everything because of you." He smiled.

"Now I know you're lying." I didn't smile.

"What does it matter, Mapstone? We got the bad guys, and the bad girl, and everybody gets to go home safe tonight. It's been a good day for law enforcement."

"Except that my grandfather's name is on that coroner's jury report, on John Pilgrim. What the hell is really going on?"

Peralta looked longingly at his empty glass.

"There's a guy I knew," he said, his deep voice nearly a whisper. "He served in the Marines in World War II. But when he came home, he was still a young guy, hot-blooded. And Phoenix wanted to make sure Mexican-Americans were in their place. If they had won a Silver Star, then that was doubly true. So this guy liked to go out on the town. He could mix it up, and he didn't take shit from the Anglos, either. So that's the story, OK? I just wanted to make sure he wasn't involved..."

Now it was my turn to slap the table. "Come on, Mike! What kind of story are you telling me? Some guy you knew?" I had never seen him look so surprised.

"All right," he said. "This guy, who came back from the war, had a sister. One day she was walking by a bar downtown. Not far from here. It was a sleazy dive called the Pla-Mor Tap Room. She's a pretty Latina, seventeen years old. One of the Anglos comes out and follows her. He's trying to put moves on her, but he's so drunk he can barely function. But she was scared to death. And when her brother finds out, he goes to the Pla-Mor Tap Room. When the Anglo walks out, he takes him into the alley and beats the crap out of him. He didn't know the Anglo was an FBI agent. And a couple days later, the FBI agent disappears. I'll never know why this guy wasn't a suspect. So anyway, I knew the guy, and I knew the story. He turned out OK, really OK, in fact. But..."

Lindsey said, "You're talking about your father, aren't you?"

Peralta was very still. Finally he said, "You both did good."

<>◇<>

Sometime around midnight, with Lindsey sleeping beside me, I lay in our bed and listened to the old house around us, and beyond that, the sounds of the misbegotten big city. On the bedside table, my badge gleamed in the ambient light. Peralta refused to believe I would even consider the job in Portland. He said he knew me too well. Lindsey, who knew me best of all, reached her hand across me and sighed happily.

To receive a free catalog of Poisoned Pen Press titles, please contact us in one of the following ways:

Phone: 1-800-421-3976
Facsimile: 1-480-949-1707
Email: info@poisonedpenpress.com
Website: www.poisonedpenpress.com

Poisoned Pen Press
6962 E. First Ave. Ste. 103
Scottsdale, AZ 85251